SEX IN THE CITY
LONDON

EDITED BY

MAXIM JAKUBOWSKI

Published by Accent Press Ltd – 2010

ISBN 9781907016226

Copyright © individual stories: Individual authors 2010

Copyright © compilation: Maxim Jakubowski 2010

The right of individual authors(as shown on stories' title pages)
to be identified as the authors of this work has been asserted by
them in accordance with the Copyright, Designs and Patents
Act 1988.

The stories contained within this book are works of fiction.
Names and characters are the product of the authors'
imagination and any resemblance to actual persons, living or
dead, is entirely coincidental.

All rights reserved. No part of this book may be reproduced,
stored in a retrieval system, or transmitted in any form or by
any means, electronic, electrostatic, magnetic tape, mechanical,
photocopying, recording or otherwise, without the written
permission of the publishers: Xcite Books, Suite 11769, 2nd
Floor, 145-157 St John Street, London EC1V 4PY

Printed and bound in the UK

Cover design by
Zipline Creative

Contents

Introduction

I AM RELIABLY INFORMED that the art and practice of sex is well-known outside of major cities too, but that's another book altogether!

Our new SEX IN THE CITY series is devoted to the unique attraction that major cities worldwide provide to lovers of all things erotic. Famous places and monuments, legendary streets and avenues, unforgettable landmarks all conjugate with our memories of loves past and present, requited and unrequited, to form a map of the heart like no other. Brief encounters, long-lasting affairs and relationships, the glimpse of a face, of hidden flesh, eyes in a crowd, everything about cities can be sexy, naughty, provocative, dangerous and exciting.

Cities are not just about monuments and museums and iconic places, they are also about people at love and play in unique surroundings. With this in mind, these anthologies of erotica will imaginatively explore the secret stories of famous cities and bring them to life, by unveiling passion and love, lust and sadness, glittering flesh and sexual temptation, the art of love and a unique sense of place.

And we thought it would be a good idea to invite some of the best writers not only of erotica, but also from the mainstream and even the crime and mystery field, to offer us specially written new stories about the hidden side of some of our favourite cities, to reveal what happens behind closed doors (and sometimes even in public). And they have delivered in trumps.

The stories you are about to read cover the whole spectrum from young love to forbidden love and every sexual variation in between. Funny, harrowing, touching, sad, joyful, every human emotion is present and how could it not be when sex and the delights of love are evoked so skilfully?

Our initial batch of four volumes takes us to London, New York, Paris and Dublin, all cities with a fascinating attraction to matters of the flesh and the heart. We hope you read them all and begin to collect them, and that we shall soon be offering you further excursions to the wild shores of erotic Los Angeles, Venice, Edinburgh, New Orleans, Sydney, Tokyo, Berlin, Rio, Moscow, Barcelona and beyond. Our authors are all raring to go and have already packed their imagination so they can offer you more sexy thrills ...

And it's cheaper than a plane ticket!

So, come and enjoy sex in the city.

Maxim Jakubowski

What Are You Wearing?
by Matt Thorne

WE'VE GONE OUT FOUR times when he asks me.

I've already decided I'll have sex with him, if he wants me, but I'm wrong-footed by his suggestion. He claims it's research for a screenplay but I know he's lying.

The name of the auction house -- Greasby's – seems fitting. They hold the viewings on Mondays between two-thirty and six. If you don't go you have no idea what you're buying because the details are so vague. It might say something like 'Green Case containing 25 x New Knickers', but nothing about whether the panties are La Perla's finest or polyamide horrors from Littlewoods; for Damian's purposes it's too risky to take a gamble.

It used to be only the most dedicated scavengers who showed up at auctions but the downturn has removed all the embarrassment from the process, especially with all the new booty arriving from Terminal 5. There's good money in suitcases if you're prepared to itemise and have the patience for eBay. Not a fortune, though: most times they take out the valuables and sell them separately. Damien isn't interested in the laptops and iPods, but he does get upset when they remove the shoes. Shoes, he believes, should be part of the deal.

'I'm no retifist,' he tells me at the end of this fourth date, after he's explained what he wanted us to do, 'but when I'm checking people out on the tube it's always the footwear that clinches it. That's not just a male thing, right? Women feel that way too.'

'Nothing worse than a sexy man in cheap shoes.'

'Exactly, right? And when you see a woman in fucking Crocs it's like she's given up on ever wanting to get fucked again.'

'Well, maybe not ever again, but certainly not that day.'

'You agree. Now I'm not saying women should totter round in high heels the whole time, but there are plenty of other comfortable yet attractive options. What's wrong with gladiator sandals?' He strokes the inside of my arm, our first physical contact aside from kisses of greeting and farewell. '*You* never wear ugly shoes.'

I stick my feet out from underneath the tablecloth and examine my shoes – white patent Escada sandals I should've retired by now but wore tonight because I knew Damian would appreciate them. 'Yeah, but that's different, I get sent mine for free. Maybe you shouldn't be spending so much time on the tube.'

He doesn't like it when I criticise him, especially when I point out that his life is less glamorous than he wishes. His mouth gets anxious, amplified by his thick black moustache. He looks at his watch and changes the subject. 'Can I tell you about something I watched on YouPorn today?'

This is his attempt at regaining the upper hand so I just smile and say sweetly, 'Isn't that why you like me?'

He returns my grin. 'Cum-shots. A goth couple. Well, the girl was a goth, I'm assuming the man was too although you never saw him, just his helmet occasionally and most times not even that. You heard the fucker though. Every time he ejaculated on her, he started

4

sniggering. At least I assume it was him. It would be just too perverse if he invited a giggly mate round to film him every time he jizzed on his girly. I mean, can you imagine that?'

We both take a moment to consider this.

'Anyway, there were about fifty splurges edited together into a five or ten minute film. He came on her face, between her toes, up her back, in her shaven armpit, in her hairy armpit, in her ears, on her shaved cunt, on her hairy cunt, on her tits, on her bum, up her bum, in her anus, in her hair, in her mouth, on her teeth, down her legs … and every time he bust a nut that infernal sniggering. It was an amateur film but I felt more sorry for this woman than any professional porn actress I've ever seen. Aside from Sabrina Deep and anyone who's ended up at the wrong end of Max Hardcore.' He looks up and makes one of his mental leaps. 'Did you have sex on your wedding night?'

I don't know why, but this question startles and embarrasses me much more than the porno talk. 'No. I was too full.'

'So when was the first time? The next morning?'

'No, we slept late and nearly missed the flight.'

'On the plane?'

'Don't be ridiculous.'

The waiter delivers our coffees, smiles and backs away.

'When you arrived?'

'No. We were jet-lagged and the complimentary champagne sent us to sleep.'

'So when you woke up?'

'No, we were hungry and we went for dinner and then we were tired again.'

'When then?'

'The next morning.'

'Wasn't your husband anxious?'

'No. He knew we'd get round to it.'

Damien takes a moment to consider this. Then he says, 'I had some friends. The first time they made love after they were married, he kept saying, "I'm fucking my wife, I'm fucking my wife," every time he thrust inside her.'

I find this less profound than he does. 'Shall we discuss your proposition now?'

He smiles. 'You're up for it then?'

'It's not what I expected, but yes, Mr. Joy, I believe I am.'

'Good. There's something else. It's a story, OK? We're characters. I want you to go to the Jury's Inn in Islington and check in under the name Victoria Coles. When you go to your room you will find a suitcase waiting for you. I want you to choose some clothes from the suitcase and then go to The Castle, which is a pub more or less opposite the hotel. I'm not going to give you any back-story aside from this … you've come to The Castle because you are horny and you need to get fucked as a matter of supreme urgency. Do you understand?'

'I understand. But …'

'What?'

'I know this probably isn't what you want but I'd appreciate it if we could have a safe word.'

'Why? Don't you trust me?'

'I'd trust you more with a safe word.'

He seems reluctant. 'Like what?'

'November shovel.'

When I arrive at Jury's Inn, I'm expecting the front desk to request a credit card for extras and wondering how I'll explain why I'm checking in under a different name to the one on my Marbles card, but instead they simply say, 'Enjoy your stay, Ms. Coles,' and hand me the keycard.

There are three suitcases in the corner of the room and a note from Damien:

AS THIS IS OUR FIRST TIME, I THOUGHT I'D EASE YOU INTO THIS GRADUALLY. HERE ARE THREE CASES FILLED WITH WOMEN'S CLOTHES. I HAVEN'T LOOKED INSIDE THEM AND YOU ARE FREE TO CHOOSE WHICHEVER YOU WISH. AS THE SHOES HAVE BEEN REMOVED I HAVE PURCHASED A SELECTION OF FOOTWEAR IN YOUR SIZE THAT YOU WILL FIND ALONGSIDE THE CASES. WEAR WHICHEVER PAIR BEST SUITS YOUR CHARACTER BUT YOU MUST NOT WEAR YOUR OWN SHOES! THIS IS VERY IMPORTANT. ALSO, BECAUSE I THOUGHT YOU MIGHT BE SQUEAMISH ABOUT WEARING A STRANGE WOMAN'S DIRTY UNDERWEAR, I HAVE FILLED THE DRAWER NEAREST THE TV WITH A SELECTION OF BRAS AND KNICKERS. PLEASE DO NOT MAKE A CHOICE TO PLEASE ME BUT SELECT THE UNDERWEAR THAT BEST SUITS YOUR CHARACTER. IF YOU DO FEEL COMFORTABLE WEARING A BRA AND KNICKERS FROM THE SUITCASE SO MUCH THE BETTER.

SEE YOU VERY SOON
DAMIEN

I read the note twice, wondering whether I'm going to get

annoyed. I decide against it and lift the first suitcase onto the bed. Whoever originally owned this suitcase was clearly a stylish woman – it's full of expensive designer gear. But she's also a slob: the clothes smell bad and the first two dresses I pulled out were marked with off-white stains. I find myself wondering whether I believe Damien's claim that he hasn't looked inside the cases – what if all the clothes belonged to fat women, or old ladies? I brought some safety pins with me and I am, it's true, an average size 12, but it still occurs to me that maybe this would force my decision and I'll have to wear these designer duds after all. I consider this a moment, then open suitcase two.

The clothes in this case clearly belong to a poorer, and somewhat conservative, woman. I'm relieved to discover that, once again, she is my size, which means I do at least now have a choice of outfits. While the other case had been cleared of anything that might identify the owner, in this one there's a plastic wallet containing a temporary paper I.D. – no photo – to get her into a Greek hotel nightclub (The club's logo, bizarrely, is a lime-green iguana performing fellatio on an electric-pink dildo). The name has been filled in with a pink pen and I'm amazed to see it was the alias Damien has given me – Victoria Coles. Is he deliberately toying with me? Or did he purchase this case first and decide to widen the choice later? I'm not sure how I feel about being given an identity along with the clothes and wonder whether there was anything else in this case that might fill out this woman's character.

I dump the contents onto the bed. Among the clothes are three spectacles cases, an asthma inhaler, a toiletries bag, a make-up bag and an alarm clock. I open the spectacles cases first. Ms Coles has taken three pairs of

8

glasses on holiday: one pair of sunglasses and two pairs of glasses: one stylish and modern with Prada frames, and a far more dowdy pair she presumably only wears indoors. I'm short-sighted myself so I go to the bathroom, pop out my contacts, and try them on. Her prescription is much weaker than mine but not so much that I can't wear them, at least not for the few hours it'll presumably take Damien to get me into bed.

It's started to rain heavily. I unbutton the blouse I wore to the hotel and let it fall onto the bathroom floor. I study my body through her glasses, imagining I'm observing myself through her eyes. I still have another case to sort through, but I want, just for a minute, to imagine myself as Victoria Coles. I look at my bra and wonder whether Victoria would wear something like this. It's not particularly stylish or elegant, just a purple and nude bra from the Elle Macpherson range, but somehow it doesn't seem right for Ms Coles. I go back to the clothes heaped on the bed and discover my intuition is spot on – all her bras are either black or white. I take off my bra and drop it onto the bathroom floor.

I suddenly find myself with an overwhelming desire to know whether Victoria ever wears G-strings. And as this curiosity sweeps over me I remember how quickly I confessed my voyeuristic tendencies to Damien. Even before we'd gone on our first date I'd told him how I'd persuaded my brothers that the only way to secure their diaries was to entrust them to me, and about the time my first female flatmate kicked me out of our shared accommodation when she found my fingerprints on her secret snapshots of her boyfriend's stumpy cock. Maybe it was reverse psychology; by telling me I didn't have to investigate these ladies' underwear he guaranteed I would.

And yes, there is a G-string in the suitcase. I knew it! Out of character, but that's why it's here – the contradictory detail that makes a person real. Plain girls are always kinkiest. Not that G-strings are necessarily kinky – I know lots of women find them practical – but I can't help associating them with rappers and encouraging men to put their fingers up your anus once they've stripped you down. I have to acknowledge that Victoria's solitary G-string is tasteful, a rather pretty blue Cosabella brief with pink flowers and a matching lace trim that makes me think of the icing on birthday cakes. I gingerly open it up and look inside, expecting the prettiness to hide dried secretions and crap tracks, but it's the freshest item in the suitcase, so I take off my jeans and knickers and slip it on. Then I go back into the bathroom and as I'm looking at myself in the mirror something extraordinary happens.

I metamorphose.

At first I assume it's the glasses I'm still wearing, but when I put my hands down to my thighs I feel the muscles lengthening beneath my fingers. My whole body is tingling and stretching, the most immediately diverting development being the way my inverted nipples right themselves and pop out like the teat on a baby's bottle. My fingers go up to touch them and I remove Victoria's glasses. Unable to see without them, I have to move forward and squint in the mirror. When I'm that close I see my face has changed completely. My formerly blue eyes are now hazel, my cute button nose has become long and straight, my eyebrows have thickened considerably and my pretty, angular face has filled out.

I am someone else.

But I am not unattractive. I misjudged poor Ms Coles. My hair is my best new feature. My own hair looked great backcombed when I was a teenage goth – not something I copped to as an adult, one of the reasons I felt embarrassed when Damien told his story about the sniggering ejaculator and his girlfriend – but since then it's always been thick and hard to manage with too much grey I can't be bothered to hide.

All of these thoughts come quickly, of course, soon swamped by fear. But before I can panic I hear a voice – not my own – inside my head telling me, *Relax, you can stop this at any time. Do you remember your safe word? Don't say it. Just nod if you remember what it is.*

I nod.

When you say your safe word aloud you will return to normal. Would you like to practice now?

I nod again and put my glasses back on, wanting to witness the transformation. 'November shovel.'

For a moment I am transfixed by the sight of my pubes shrinking and vanishing back down my thighs and inside the G-string as Ms Cole's untended thatch turns back into my neatly maintained muff, but as I stare at my knickers I feel transformations in my fanny that I didn't notice when I was changing before. I stick my hand down the front of my G-string and clutch myself.

Ready to change back? the voice asks. I nod and feel my labia changing shape beneath my fingers. My clitoris swells beneath my fingers in an entirely new way as it becomes *her* clitoris. I have a very small clit, the glans, shaft and prepuce mostly hidden inside my labia, but Victoria's is much bigger, protruding above the majora. It's full and thick – not one of those freaky ones you sometimes see in weirdo porn films that look like a miniature penis, but big enough that I doubt any of Victoria's boyfriends ever struggled finding it. I pull down my knickers and shuffle closer to the mirror, wanting to get a better view. *Are you sure you want to go see Damien tonight?* the voice asks me. *We could enjoy ourselves alone.* And I have to admit she has a point. But I'm too curious. I want to know if Damien has changed too. And if he is somehow responsible for what's happened to me. I can't believe this is possible, but I need to find out.

It's a different receptionist when I go back down and she doesn't comment when I hand her the keycard and head out. The rain's got much heavier while I've been in the hotel and I find myself wishing that Victoria had packed a raincoat. I cross the road to The Castle, still absorbing the changes in my body. *Her body.* I can't stop myself from fingering the extra weight at my hips and wondering whether Damien will find the transformation sexy. I walk up to the bar and order a Southern Comfort without thinking, even though it's a drink I've never had before in my life.

I sit at a table in the corner by the window and look around the other people in the pub, wondering whether Damien's already here in disguise. There are two men drinking alone, one of whom is sitting at the bar chatting with the barmaid and another at a table at the back drinking a pint of Guinness and reading. I don't think either are my secret lover.

There wasn't a watch in Victoria's suitcase so I'm not wearing one, but he must already be at least ten minutes late. Damien's always arrived early before so I wonder if this is also part of his new character.

The door opens and a tall man in a black suit and white shirt enters. He looks round the room, sees me and grins. It's definitely Damien, albeit in someone else's body.

The person he's inhabiting is nearly a foot taller, and

has a sharper edge to his physical appearance, especially his face. Inside this stranger, Damien looks smug and excited, like a man test-driving a Porsche. He walks towards me. 'This is going to sound cheesy, but I'm sure we've met before.'

'Really? I don't think so.'

'Are you sure? Sometimes you see someone and you recognise them and you don't immediately know why but you definitely know them. Are you here alone?'

I nod.

'Would you mind if I joined you? We could work out whether we do know each other. If that isn't going to annoy you ...'

'Are you confident? I'm only interested if you're confident.'

I can see he's surprised by this – doesn't fully understand the new me yet – but hides it well, taking a seat opposite me and saying, 'I think you'll find I'm very confident.'

Fifty-seven minutes later we're back in the Jury Inn, standing outside my hotel room door. He kisses me for the first time and as exciting and bizarre and unique as this all is, I can't help feeling wistful that our first kiss should be through other people's mouths. The kiss becomes a passionate snog and Damien – who tonight is a man named James – dips down and scoops up the material of my long skirt as he strokes my thighs and brings his fingers up to my crotch. Victoria's fanny feels much more active than mine – I've been feeling new internal wobbles and twinges all night and she's already much wetter than I normally get until at least ten minutes of full-on foreplay. I turn away from Damien and push my keycard into the slot.

13

The door opens and James backs me towards the bed. I turn away from him and crawl across the duvet towards the banked pillows and cushions, pretending I'm trying to escape. He lifts up my skirt and throws it up over my hips as if uncovering an artwork. He stares at my butt for a moment, then reaches out and stretches the damp G-string back from my ass-crack. 'Oh,' he says, 'I like this.'

I assume he's referring to Victoria's underwear rather than her anus and I smile, about to reply, *I thought you would*, when I catch myself and manage to avoid blowing the game. I gently move away from his attentions and take off his jacket. Then I unbutton his shirt and unzip his fly. When I pull out his cock it's one of those *agaric* mushroom kinds, with a thin stalk and a large helmet that is so shiny beneath the hotel room lights that it looks like it's been polished. He whispers, 'I'm bigger than him. Wider. Uncut.'

I laugh. 'Was it worth breaking character to tell me that?'

'I am, I promise. Take me in your mouth and I'll prove it.'

Since it seems to mean so much to him, I kneel down on the floor in front of James and put his cock in my mouth.

'Now, be careful,' he tells me, 'I don't want to choke you.'

'Stop boasting.'

'November shovel,' he says, and it turns out he's telling the truth. The cock in my mouth swells in an entirely different way to a penis growing harder from oral attention. But his body changes shape too and I have to suck hard to stop the cock getting away from me as his body shrinks. I give it a couple of licks, trying to judge how he's feeling, then put my hand around it and gently slip it out of my mouth. 'You know what I'm thinking? I'm thinking this opens up lots of possibilities …'

He grins. 'And I want to explore them.'

'Damien,' I say, feeling able to talk about this now he's paused the fantasy, 'I have to confess something … as fun as this is, I am a bit disappointed that you didn't want to see me naked first. I mean, as myself …'

'Oh, I do want that, more than anything. But I needed to test you first …'

'Test me?'

'I needed to know whether this would freak you out. I probably shouldn't admit this and I can promise you that you're the first woman I've done this suitcase thing with, but this isn't the first time that I've had one of these weird experiences and in the past, well, it's been hard to find a partner-in-crime. I knew you were open-minded, that's what all the porno talk was about, testing your barriers, but there's a difference between being sexually adventurous and being able to cope when the usual rules of the universe no longer hold …'

'Damien, wait up, you're going too fast. Do you mean that you're the one who's making us change? That you can control this?'

'No, not that. It's hard to explain. Ever since I was a child I've occasionally had these incredibly lucid dreams where I see myself able to do extraordinary things. And I've found that if I follow what happens in these dreams … if I go to the places I see when I'm sleeping and re-enact what I do in the dreams, then I gain the ability to do these things in real life.

'Three months ago I had a dream where I went to an auction house, purchased a suitcase … I didn't even know such a thing was possible … took this case home, dressed in the clothes and then … you can see how hard this

15

would be to explain if you hadn't experienced it … turned into the person whose clothes I'd bought.

'Now a normal person probably wouldn't think anything of such a dream. But because I've had these sort of weird experiences before, I went on the internet and looked up where these auctions take place, went and bought a suitcase, took it home, and *transformed*.

'The experience was fun, and trippy, but there's only so much you can do in someone else's body. I went to a club, picked up a woman, took her home and fucked her. And it was interesting, but creepy, because I knew I couldn't tell her what was really going on without freaking her out.

'So I decided that the best way to enjoy this would be to find someone I could share it with. Of course, I had no idea whether it would work for you, but then I had another dream where I was inside someone else's body fucking someone who looked like you do now.'

'That's not fair,' I say petulantly, 'you've had this experience already.'

He smiles. 'Not exactly, but, I must admit, I didn't realise you'd be quite so chilled out about this.'

'I was scared when I changed,' I tell him, 'but now that I know that the transformation's not permanent …'

'But aren't you frightened that such things are possible? Doesn't it challenge your belief system?'

'I don't have a belief system. And I've always been open to having my consciousness expanded. Maybe this'll seem weirder to me once it's all over, but right now all I want is your cock up my cunt.'

He's gone a bit limp while he's been talking so he wanks himself as he advances on me once more. 'November shovel,' he says again, becoming James. I go to pull off

16

my G-string but his fingers halt mine. 'Take off your skirt but leave your knickers on for a moment. I do want to fuck, more than anything, but what you said before, about wanting me to see you as yourself. I wonder if we could try something. Take off your skirt.'

I unzip it and kick it to the floor. 'Shoes too?'

'No, there's something about those shoes that is just so fucking sexy.'

I laugh, pleased that I made the right choice. They're just a pair of ordinary flat brown shoes, but somehow they perfectly complement Victoria's G-string and cunt.

'Get up on your knees,' he tells me. I do so. 'Now,' he says, 'show me your holes.' I do as I'm asked, slipping my finger under the material of the G-string and pulling it back, allowing him a full rear view of my cunt and ass.

'Spread it a bit,' he instructs. I do so. 'Now change back.'

'November shovel,' I say, and there's something wonderfully exposing about returning to my normal self.

He groans. 'I don't think I could ever explain how erotic this sight is.'

I make the transformation back and forth a few more times, letting him enjoy himself as he watches the movements of my asshole and pussy. Then he gets up on the bed, holding the G-string to one side as he enters me. I let him take me as Victoria – she's bigger and wetter – then once he's inside, I turn back.

'Oh God,' he moans, as the transmogrification of her cunt into mine provides his penis with a squeeze more intense than any amount of Kegel exercises would allow me to furnish. 'Now you do it,' I say, while he's inside me as me, and the swell of his cock inside me is not painful at all but more divine and intense than anything I've experienced before. I let him fuck me for a while and

17

then ask, 'Are you thinking what I'm thinking?'

He withdraws his penis from my vagina and I have an anxious moment wondering whether this is going to work or if it will do some terrible trauma to my insides.

But it has to be tried, so I let him finally remove my sopping G-string and lick my asshole for a while and then grease me up with some lubricant he's brought before sliding inside my butt as James.

'Are you ready?' he asks.

'I am a little scared.'

'I won't do it if you don't want me to.'

'No,' I tell him, thinking about how James's cock swelled in my mouth as it turned into Damien's and deciding my rectum can take it.

'November shovel,' he says.

It does burn badly to begin with, especially as I think he's up to full size but then he swells again, but then his fingers find my clitoris and the pain turns to pleasure. I stuff my hand into my mouth and bite down.

'Is it too much?' he asks.

'No,' I say, 'but don't move for a moment. November shovel.' I transform into Victoria and her rectum must be wider than mine or more used to getting it this way as the pain from before immediately lessens. He continues to finger my clit as he sodomises me without mercy.

When it starts to ache just a little too much, I ask him to turn back and he does so. After feeling the full force of Damien's wide cock in my arse, James's smaller penis feels much more manageable and I relax enough to let him fuck me until he comes.

He's feeling bad because I haven't orgasmed yet. 'Is it the situation?' he asks. 'Is it too weird?' It amuses me that even in this situation his ego remains healthy. 'No,' I tell him, 'I just find it hard to come when I'm being ass-fucked. It's too intense or something. Besides, our clits need more attention.'

I roll over and just for an instant I'm not even sure who I am any more. Then it comes back to me. I'm still Victoria. He crawls up on me and puts his hands on her thighs and begins to kiss and lick me. I have this strange sensation in my head where my brain keeps trying to force me to acknowledge that it's not my clitoris he's expertly stimulating, a distinction that our body is finding it increasing hard to make. I transform back to myself and he takes a moment to locate my now much smaller clitoris with the tip of his tongue. But when he does find it, it's suddenly so much more intense, and I stay as myself until he brings me to the greatest, most oddly guilt-free climax I have ever experienced.

'You want to come on us, don't you?' I ask him afterwards, remembering his talk about cum-shots on our date.

'Do you have to keep saying "us"?' he asks. 'It creeps me out.'

'Really?' I reply. 'It turns me on.'

'I definitely chose the right person for this, didn't I? And yes, I do.'

He arranges himself on top of me and starts masturbating. I change back and forth as he's doing it. He may not like me talking about it, but he certainly likes the reality of it, my face turning into Victoria's and back again, and with every transformation he grips his penis and wanks faster.

It's a game for both of us, the suspense being whether he'll come on my face or hers. As he's doing this I remember reading an online confession by an American teenager who said that something similar to this was all the rage at high school and college parties – ten girls would kneel in a circle while ten men would wank and rotate around them, so that you never knew whose face would get whose load. The game seemed delightfully inclusive, in a twenty-first-century way, as the teen had written that the game wasn't any fun unless there was a mix of attractive and ugly women and men.

The whole point was that the girl geek might get a face full from the quarterback, or that the boy nerd might get to shoot his sperm over the homecoming queen's perfect features, and afterwards these people would feel closer to each other than anyone from my generation ever did. Call it sexual networking.

He didn't transform as he wanked, staying as James the whole time. It was Victoria's face he shot over, a relatively small payload but still impressive for his second time of the night. 'I wonder if his spunk tastes different to mine,' he says, and then to my surprise, licks some from my cheek. 'Turn back,' he tells me, 'I want to see what you look like with my jizz on your face.'

I do so, and he kisses me, the sperm sticky between our lips.

Later that night, before leaving the hotel room and returning to my husband, I ask Damien, 'So how long do you think this is going to last? Is it a one-time thing? If you get more suitcases will it happen again?'

'I can only go on the past,' he says, 'and when this sort of thing has happened before it's generally lasted for two or three months. And when it stops it's usually about a year or so before I have another dream.'

'OK,' I tell him, 'I will carry on doing this for as long as it still works. When we stop changing, it's over …

20

agreed?'

He doesn't say anything for a moment. He seems to appreciate that I'm offering him a 'Get Out of Jail Free' card, but at the same time is unable to quite accept it. 'But if this hadn't happened ... how long would you have continued seeing me then? Would you have left your husband for me?'

'Never. Maybe our affair would've lasted longer, but who knows? Maybe this time will be different to your past experiences. Maybe we can keep transforming for years.'

'Maybe,' he says, 'but I doubt it.'

'Agreed then?' I ask.

'Agreed. But just in case, in the meantime, I think we should make the most of it. How soon can you get back here?'

'Next week,' I say, looking at my watch, 'but I still have another couple of hours tonight. He's used to me coming back very late.'

'So what are you saying, the other suitcases?' he asks, and we both look at them.

'Well, I've already looked in one of them, the designer one, and I don't want to turn into her, but the third one ... I haven't looked in there yet ...'

He smiles. 'Oh,' he says, 'I think we're both going to find what's in there very exciting.'

'Really?' I ask, getting out of bed and walking, naked and achy, to the third suitcase and unlocking it, 'let's see.'

About the Story

I'VE ALWAYS BEEN INTERESTED in the process of going to a luggage carousel at the end of a journey. For a while I'd thought about writing a novella about a couple of thrill-seekers who steal people's luggage from airports. Then when I did a bit of research into this, I discovered that there's a perfectly legal way of doing this: buying other people's lost luggage from auction houses. Most writers, I think, are fascinated by other people's secrets, and, for me, the whole fun of writing is imagining yourself into somebody else's life. It occurred to me that a couple going to buy other people's suitcases and dressing up in their clothes could be a good starting point for an erotic story. Some people don't like descriptions of clothes or dressing up in fiction, but for me there's nothing more exciting or memorable, whether it's Belle de Jour's 'butterfly-printed knickers' or Abby's 'silk tap pants' (in Nicholson Baker's *Vox*) or darling sodomite Albertine's 'black satin dress' (Marcel Proust's *Remembrance of Things Past*.) The exciting thing about writing this story for me was that it was a good justification for writing about dressing and undressing, of focusing on knickers and bras and shoes.

It wasn't until I started writing the story that a further possibility occurred to me – what if, in dressing up in these other people's clothes, my characters became these other people. I liked the idea because it seemed a good way of dramatising the fantasy of making love to someone and thinking of someone else, only in this instance the characters were both making love to their partner *and* someone else at the same time. I set the majority of the story in and around Islington, as that area's always struck me as a strangely sexy part of the city, filled with hidden nooks and crannies that occasionally hide an illicit couple or two. And because it was where a stunning woman I sat next to at a dinner party made me a present of her underwear at the end of a dinner, stuffing it inside my jacket pocket as I stopped by the door to kiss her goodnight.

Thames Link
by Justine Elyot

I SING THE PRAISE of the sleazy man.

The man with the shifty eyes, the man with the floppy fringe, the man with the sensual lips, the man who drinks a little too much red wine and eats a little too much cake. You might see him on the train; his eyes follow you over the top of his paper and you try not to recross your legs too often. He might be standing at the bar so you have to feign enormous levels of animation with your companions. Perhaps he works with you and there is a rota in place among your colleagues so nobody has to go into the photocopier cupboard at the same time as him.

He's a creep, he's a sleaze, he's a perve. He's my kind of guy.

I know, I sound insane. Who on earth likes men like this? I suppose it's his honesty that appeals to me. No 'I really like you as a person'. No discussion of mutually admired bands and comedians. No number swaps or long waits for the phone to beep. Better than the man who moves in with you before revealing his wardrobe of skintight latex. Better than the man that waits until you have his ring on your finger before asking you if you fancy a pint down the swingers' club. This is a man who wears his cock on his sleeve, and quite rightly so.

He'll speak fluent innuendo. He'll sit too close to you

on the bus. He'll walk behind you in the park, watching the sway of your backside. In the ultraviolet light of the disco, he'll try to get a hand up your skirt.

No, he isn't a rapist, it's not about power. It *is* about sex. He wants it. Not you. It.

And there's something about that I find refreshing.

I have a sleazy man of my own, tucked away in my address book for days when I don't feel pristine or perfumed. On days – and they come all too often now – when I feel rumpled and seedy, when my tights are clinging damply to the crack of my arse and my skin is grimy with the London summer, I call him.

I'm going to call him now, actually.

'Morning, foxy. What can I do for you today?'

'When are you free?'

'Hmm … it's looking like a late one. Could take a two-hour lunch break, though.'

'Lunch sounds perfect. Midday?'

'Blackfriars tube. Wear the green dress. Hold-ups. No knickers. Got that?'

'No knickers,' I repeat, my clit puffing up, my silky scanties already wet. Who cares? I will have to take them off before I leave.

'Don't forget your perfume, Jane,' he says softly before hanging up.

How could I forget that? The application of scent is the precious first step in the ritual, setting the tone for all that is to follow.

These are his rules: I must draw back the bedroom curtains and open the window, so that the block across the green is visible to me, and I to it. I must strip naked and lie down on my unmade bed. I must take my vibrator and masturbate to orgasm, plunging it deep inside, juicing it up until it gleams. While I am doing this, I must think of some of the filthy, slutty things I have done for him in the past – easy enough, for there are plenty to choose from. Once I am red-faced and spent, I must take the vibrator and rub it across my pulse points, making sure I am generously anointed before smearing any remainder on to my nipples, breasts, belly, thighs. I must dip the vibrator back in and repeat the process until there is nothing left to apply. Only when my skin is stiff and heavy with the smell of my sex am I allowed to dress.

Today, a sheer white peephole bra, some nude laced-topped hold-ups and the green dress. The dress I was wearing when we met – though that sounds grandiose, as if we have a story or a future. The day we picked each other up, perhaps.

The dress is made of very light cotton in *eau-de-nil*. It buttons all the way up and has a short, flippy skirt whose hem is only just beneath the lacy bit of my hold-up. The merest breath of breeze is enough to give my thighs a tickle, and on some of the windier tube platforms I have to clamp it down with my palms flat on my legs, shuffling bent double like an ancient babushka.

Then it is time to slap industrial quantities of gloss on my lips and mascara on my lashes before slipping into strappy sandals and running for my train.

Once again, it is a hot day, humid and dirty, the way it was the first time we met. The station platform is crowded – several previous trains have been delayed – so I know I will stand no chance of being able to hide my sex-drenched self in a corner seat away from the masses. I will have to force it on my carriage-mates, mingling it in with their smells of onions and cigarettes and engine oil and boiled aftershave, all with a sweaty top note.

When the train arrives and its doors slide open, I look for the least respectable grouping I can find. I light on a bearded bikerish type and his heavily pierced moll, wondering idly who on earth would wear leather trousers in this weather as I push myself towards them. The smell is heady, though, and powerful, almost cancelling out my pussy perfume. Almost, but not quite. I catch them looking at each other, half-winking, guessing at what I might have been up to. If Shaun were here, he might nod at me, indicating that I was to try and get myself felt up by one or both of them. We've done that before. But he is not here, so I hold myself away from them, strap-hanging and concentrating on the trickle of sweat travelling downwards from the nape of my neck, breathing myself in, not daring to catch any eyes.

The train was less busy when we met. We both had seats, opposite each other. About halfway through the journey, I looked up from my book for the eighth time to find him staring at me. He made no attempt to be furtive about it. He simply watched me with a face like stone and narrowed eyes, from Herne Hill to Blackfriars.

What does one say? 'Do you mind?' 'Can I help you?' 'Is there a smudge on my nose?' I could not decide, so I returned to my book, though I did not read another word. I squirmed inside all the way to Blackfriars, where he alighted.

I watched him walking down the platform. Despite the July heat, he was wearing a coat – a light grey ankle-length raincoat. Every few paces he would stop and turn to look at me and my eyes would dive guiltily back to the page. It was strange, that such a simple gesture could be so very sinister. He wanted me to know that he was watching me, and I had no idea why.

For the rest of that week and a few days beyond, the same thing happened every day. The seating opposite, the staring, the turning and looking. I tried to stand as far away from him on the platform as I could, yet he always hunted me down to my carriage. I had no idea how I should deal with it. Should it be dealt with? I could not even work out how I felt. I thought I should probably be intimidated or something. It was a bit like having a stalker, although he never stayed on the train to my station, or followed me home. I wasn't intimidated, though – I was rather *excited* by the whole thing. It was like a mysterious game of hunter and prey and I was intrigued, speculating on how the situation might develop. Besides, I could handle myself. You had to, when you were a woman living alone in London. Despite the fact that he was not my type at all – too short, too fleshy, not enough cheekbones – I began to think about him while masturbating. He pushed me into a darkened railway arch and ripped my skirt in his haste to fuck me. He tied me to a bed and told me that from now on I belonged to him. He plunged his hand into my knickers and fingered me on the train, right in front of all the other passengers, telling me that he had known this was what I needed all along. When I imagined his voice, it was not deep and manly, but a little bit nasal and whiny. For some reason, this made him seem all the hotter – the idea that I could be taken like that by somebody so ordinary. Only a slut would fantasise about an ugly man who stares at her on the train. Only a slut, whore, bitch … yes, yes, yes.

On the tenth day he was reading a newspaper. Except he wasn't reading it – he was staring at me from over the masthead. And the newspaper was the one I worked for.

Even though it was popular enough with the commuters, I began to feel a little freaked out. Did he know I worked there? Had he followed me to the office? Had he followed me home? Was he ever going to talk to me? Was he waiting for me to crack and talk first? Did he fancy me and this was his bizarre courtship ritual? Or what?

On the eleventh day, after an evening of peering through my curtains to check for dark shapes in the bushes, I determined to say something.

He was reading that paper again. I looked briefly around the carriage to make sure nobody was listening in and said, as quietly as I could, 'You're making me feel uncomfortable.'

He said nothing, just continued staring. Was he hard of hearing? I tried again.

'You're making me feel uncomfortable. Could you stop staring?'

He put the paper down on his lap. 'I could,' he said, and the sound of his voice made me gush between my thighs – not nasal or whiny, but creepily soft. 'But I don't want to.'

'Why not?'

'I think you're the most gorgeous thing I've ever seen. I can't take my eyes off you.'

'Oh.' I was stymied. 'Right. You could have just asked me out instead of …'

'Come out with me then.'

'I … OK.' Somehow my sex brain had overtaken my rational one. Surely this was a bad idea.

'When do you finish work?'

'Six.'

'Half six, then. Three Kings on Clerkenwell Green.'

'That's …' I was about to say *very handy for work*, but something told me he already knew. 'Right,' I substituted lamely.

We engaged in a mutual stare while the sun-dazzling brown Thames glided by in my peripheral vision. Next stop Blackfriars.

'Don't be late,' he said, standing and gathering up his belongings. There was more than a hint of 'or else' in his tone.

'What if I … can't make it?'

'You can. I'll see you there.' He smiled, though it was more like a smirk. 'I know you'll come,' he said.

He knew more than I did, then. All day at work, I contemplated the foolishness of my actions, deciding to stand him up, then wondering what I would say on the train the next day if I did. Maybe I would have to start getting the bus to work. Or rather, buses. No, that was going too far. It was just a drink after work. No obligations on either side. The pub was popular and would be busy. He would not be able to abduct or rape me. What about going home though? We would be travelling in the same direction … I decided to tell a friend what I was doing.

'Hi, Mags,' I said cheerily. 'Just wanted to let you know, I'm meeting someone for a drink after work at the Three Kings. So if he turns out to be an axe murderer …'

'Aha. Got it. What's his name?'

What was his name?

'I … Oh God. I'm not sure. I've forgotten.' Somehow this seemed more acceptable than telling her I didn't know.

'He's made a big impression then. So if you aren't at work tomorrow, I'll tell the police to look for a nameless man.'

Crestfallen, I mumbled, 'Yeah. Oh look, maybe I won't go after all …'

'Oh, stop it, woman! Go! You only live once. It's been two months since Paul did the disappearing act – I bet he isn't waiting around for Ms Person with a Name.'

'No. You're right. You're bloody right. Thanks, Mags.'

He chose his venue well.

The Three Kings is situated exactly where the lane curves round towards the Green, so there is no question of having a quick spy before you approach – as soon as you can see the building, you are visible from it.

The steps of St James' Church opposite were thronged with post-work drinkers and foreign students and their pint glasses. I squinted at the bare chests and acres of sunglasses, but saw nobody who looked like my mysterious date. They all looked healthy and sun-kissed and wholesome, not pale and full-lipped and surging with perverse lust.

My throat was dry and tight; I hadn't eaten all day and I needed a shower. Perhaps, I thought, I should go home. I turned back, looking unseeingly into the window of the junk shop over the road from the pub. A reflection loomed behind me, quicker than I could respond to, and then there were hands over my bare elbows, clammy hands, and hot breath in my ear.

'Where do you think you're going? I hope you weren't thinking of standing me up.'

His voice, thick and greedy, pretending to be jokey but with a deadly serious undertow.

'I'm … not sure,' I confessed weakly. Now I was in his clutches. *In his clutches*. I liked the phrase. I liked the idea. But would I like the reality?

'I am,' he said, dripping his poisoned honey into my ear. 'I'm sure. I knew you'd come.'

'You couldn't know that.'

'I could. Come on, I've bought you a drink.'

There was nowhere to sit, so we leaned against the wall. He picked up a glass for me from the pavement –

white wine, though I'd have preferred mineral water under the circumstances. All the same, I took a gulp, grateful for anything wet. He watched me over the rim of his pint glass, just as he had done that morning over the newspaper.

'I like your dress,' he said, and he leered. A true and unmistakable leer. Behind his eyes, his mind was stripping it off me and pushing me down on the church steps before pounding into me, right here, right now, in front of everyone.

It seemed wrong, somehow, to say 'Thanks,' in response, but I did it anyway.

'Thank *you* for wearing it,' he said, with a catch of something in the back of his throat. For a split second, he sounded self-conscious and it was such a relief. Oh, was he human after all? But then I realised it was laughter. He turned quickly to face me, his eyes vivid, skittering from side to side. 'And thanks for coming.'

'You knew I would come,' I pointed out, somewhat sulkily.

'Oh yes. But thanks anyway.'

'So come on. How did you know? You worked it out by the power of your stare? Are you some kind of Sherlock Holmes character, and you're going to tell me what I had for breakfast and the name of my childhood pet?'

He snuffled a bit and moved the toe of his boot closer to my strappy sandal, so that they touched. 'No, nothing like that. Just applied a bit of psychology.'

'What? Explain?'

'Very curious, aren't you?' He smiled slyly.

'What ... do you mean?'

'I've given you your answer. And that's all I'm saying.'

'You ...' I was beginning to feel seriously out-manoeuvred. Even more so when he took the glass from my hand and put it on the wall next to him.

'But I'm very glad you came.' He took my hand and grazed my knuckles with his lips and whiskery chin. 'Like I said, you're gorgeous. My favourite kind of gorgeous. Filthy gorgeous.' He flicked out his tongue and licked a knuckle. I tried to draw my hand back, but he was too quick, pulling me closer to him and whipping an arm around my waist. His hand patted my hip while he continued to say weird and creepy things to me. I could have disengaged, I could have looked around for help from the crowds of evening drinkers, I could have told him to fuck off.

I didn't.

'You like the attention, don't you?' he said. 'You like men and you like sex. Is that true? Would that be fair?'

'Yeah.' It was true. It was fair. 'But ...'

'It's OK, sweetheart. It doesn't make you a bad person. A "bad girl", maybe, but not a bad person.' He grinned at me, then his hand shifted down until it rested on the curve of my arse. I looked up sharply, appalled at how arousing I was finding all this, feeling I should put up a fight, but having absolutely no desire to stop him. He gave my bum a proprietary little smack, drawing a few giggles and whispers from some of the people nearby. 'I think you're a dirty girl. I'm certainly no Mr Clean. What do you think?' His hand was bunching at the back of my skirt, drawing it up so the lace of my hold-up would have been visible to anyone watching from the right angle.

'Of what?' I asked, feeling drugged and stupid with need now. My knees felt as if they might buckle and my cunt had sucked all the humidity from the air into it.

'Of me taking down your knickers.' His fingers crept

33

under the dress and slipped between my burning thighs. 'And giving you what you want and need.' They pressed lightly against my gusset, finding it soaked. 'And deserve,' he whispered, rubbing the wet cotton between my swollen lips and over my clit.

'People … looking,' I said, my tongue too big for my mouth.

'I can hardly blame them, can I?'

'Might be people from work,' I urged, but I did nothing to stop his lazy fingering of me all the same.

'You work near here?'

'Yes.' It came out like a shiver; I was so sticky and damp all over I could barely think. 'I thought you knew that.'

'No. I guessed you might, judging by the train route. I guessed you'd have to be no more than a stop or two beyond me, to make it to the office for ten.' A fingertip slid under the elastic. 'Christ, you're wet. I knew you would be.'

I could see a group of men in suits, ties off, collars open, watching us curiously, making inaudible comments.

'They know what you're doing,' I moaned. 'We'll get thrown out.'

'Let's go somewhere more private then.' I could hear the sucking sounds of his finger in my slick heat; in my confusion, I perceived them as deafeningly loud. 'Unless you want them to watch. Do you like being watched? I bet you do. I bet they're wishing they had their fingers where I have. Not just the fingers either. Shall I invite them along?'

'Oh, don't,' I wailed, having to work at remembering that this was not a good place to start rotating my hips and pushing down, begging for more, harder, deeper.

'Don't invite them? Or don't find somewhere more

private?'

'No … let's go somewhere they can't see us.'

'That's a very good idea. They'll know, all the same. They'll know I'm taking you away to be fucked. You do want to be fucked, don't you?'

'Mmm.' My lips were pressed tight, my voice strained and high-pitched. I nodded sharply to emphasise the importance of the point. Two fingers speared my cunt, holding me in place, owning me.

'Good. I think I know a place.'

The fingers sloshed out, he pulled down my skirt and patted my bottom again.

'Come on,' he said, taking my hand and entwining fingers so my own wetness was transferred to me. We walked in front of all the people lolling on the church steps and through an arched gateway leading into the churchyard.

Behind us I could hear some whistling and laughter.

'Oh God, you can't be serious! In a churchyard! All those people out there saw us come in! What if we get caught?'

'My erection doesn't travel well,' he said grimly. 'This place is shady and dark. And if we get caught, we get caught. I'm having you now, no matter what.'

'I don't want to be arrested!'

'You won't be.'

We walked along the side of the church, through a dense grove of trees. We were only halfway down the path before the illusion of distance from the London crowds descended. The chatter and clink of glasses was muffled by the foliage, even as dry as it was, and the endless traffic drone receded to a mild buzz.

He saw the place before I did – a tree trunk bent backwards at an angle that made it comfortable for leaning against.

'Right, that'll do,' he decided. 'Knickers off and leaning back on that tree trunk with your legs either side, please.'

I was breathing heavily now, desperate for him to use me, but faintly aware that this was my very last chance to back out. Did I want to use it? Should I get out of here and run like fury to Farringdon tube?

'You've brought a …?'

'Of course. Don't know where you've been, do I?' He flashed a smile, then unexpectedly jerked me towards him and kissed me. 'But I know where you're going. Straight on the end of my cock. Go on, then.' He nipped at my earlobe, then spun me around and gave me a gentle push towards the tree.

In a dream now, I stepped out of my knickers and left them on the scrubby crackly ground, then I slowly, carefully aligned my spine with the bark of the tree and parted my thighs either side of the trunk, which was slightly thicker than my body. My legs were well spread now, the bottom button of my skirt straining a little so that I had to pull it up to my waist, exposing my overripe pussy and sweaty thighs.

'Mmm, let me look at you like that for a minute,' said my sleazy seducer, folding his arms over his brown and orange striped shirt and standing with feet wide apart to accommodate the obvious bulge in his suit trousers. 'God, that's exactly how I've imagined you this past fortnight. That's how I've got myself off every night, thinking of you, spread and ready for me, just like that. Fuck, you're perfect. No, don't shut your eyes. Look at me, sweetheart. Take a really good look around. Because by the time I've finished with you, you won't be seeing straight for a long, long time.'

He unfolded his arms and strode towards me with a demonically purposeful air.

'Look at her,' he said, running hands up my soaked hold-ups to my even more soaked splayed sex lips. 'Lying there with it all on show, just ready and waiting. You really need this, don't you?'

'Please … just … hurry up.'

'Can't wait? Been sitting on the train every day wanting to pull up your skirt like this and show me your hungry pussy? Hey?'

'Yes,' I yelped. He lowered his mouth to my hot core and gave it a long, luscious slurp.

'I can tell. You're streaming with juice. You want it badly, don't you?'

'Mmm, oh yes, I really do. Do it, please.' By now I was rubbing my spine up and down the tree trunk, feeling everything clinging to me, ready to just grab at him and shove him inside.

'Oh, I'm going to.' He stood straight and started unbuckling his belt ruthlessly. 'I should have brought some rope. I'd love to tie you up here, keep you like this.'

'Oooh.' No more words. Beyond that now. Just bucking my hips up, flexing my calves, holding my thighs apart with kneading fingers.

His hands shook as he skinned on the rubber; he had to brace one palm on the tree trunk to keep from falling over. 'I can't believe this is happening,' he muttered, to himself more than me, before slapping his body up against mine and swarming up inside me to the hilt in one sweet, sharp thrust. 'Ah yes,' he mouthed blissfully. 'Ah yes. You. I've got you.' I brought my legs around and tucked them under his bottom, feeling the muscles tauten, preparing for action. 'All the way up you,' he whispered, wanting to hold on to the moment a while longer. 'You're going nowhere, babe.'

'No, no, I'm not.' His body was heavy and hot on mine; it would not take much for us to start melting into each other, becoming one on the tree trunk. He pushed himself upwards without letting me off his hook and began unbuttoning my dress until it flapped either side of me. He pulled the cups of my bra over my nipples and gave each one a hearty suck. 'Salty,' he said. He traced patterns in the grimy sweat of my abdomen with a fingertip. 'You're hot. I'm going to make you hotter.'

He held my arms at my sides and began to slide his cock in and out, slowly at first, excruciatingly slowly – I could tell that he was having to make an effort to keep from coming then and there.

'You don't know my name, do you?' he said conversationally, presumably as part of this endeavour.

'No,' I shuddered, digging my heels into his soft pale buttocks to spur him on.

'I know yours. You're called Jane.'

'How do you know?'

His pace began to pick up; his chest crushed down on my breasts, one of his shirt buttons chafing a nipple with each stroke.

'Your security pass. You wear it on the train. You aren't wearing it now.'

'Oh. Shit. Yeah. I suppose I do. Oh, please, more.'

He wedged a hand between our pelvises, reaching for my clit and strumming it. 'More? I can give you more. So, you don't know my name. But you're lying here in the open air taking my cock and begging for more. What does that make you?'

'Oh, fuck, a slut, a slut, a dirty whore!'

'Well … put,' he ground out, ramming me into the tree's trunk now, holding me down by one shoulder while his other hand worked over my clit. I was so hot, surely I was steaming, surely I would be a puddle of sweat and pussy juice by the time he was finished with me. The canopy of dry leaves overhead blurred; I even had sweat in my eyes, stinging them shut, so I had nothing more to concentrate on than the burning hot hammering taking place between my thighs and the bunching fingers on my clit and what a whore slut bitch I was to let a total stranger do all this to me without even asking his name and … oh … when I came, I cried out all kinds of things, things that made no sense at all, things that brought him smashing into his own dark climax, and he fell down on me and sank his tongue into my mouth, ending it all with the most violent kiss I could remember.

'Fuck. Oh fuck,' he said when he let my mouth free. 'You beautiful fucking whore.'

My throat was so dry I could do no more than rasp. 'Wow.'

'Even if I never see you again, I can die happy,' he said, nuzzling my neck, careless of its city grit.

'But you could,' I whispered. 'If you wanted.'

His lifted his head, staring at me again with those shifty blue-green eyes.

'I mean,' I stammered, not quite sure where I was going with this, 'not like in a heavy sort of way.'

'In a friendly fuck sort of way?' he enquired dryly.

'Well, yeah. If you want.'

'I want,' he said. 'I'll make you do things you never imagined you'd do.'

'You already have.'

'Good. And it's Shaun, by the way.'

Perverse bastard that he is, he made me go back to the Three Kings with him for a drink. I had to sit on the steps in my rumpled, sweat-patched, dirty dress. There was a dead leaf in my hair, my make-up was melted to fuck and my legs bore definite tree-bark patterns. This time, though, I enjoyed the attention. I enjoyed the thought that anyone looking at me could see I'd just been firmly and thoroughly shagged by the ordinary-almost-even-ugly bloke sitting with his arm around me, fingers playing idly with the hem of my skirt. We kissed like swooning lovers until dark fell and we took the last train home together, parting at the station.

No spending the night. No acting like boyfriend and girlfriend. Strictly hot, sweaty, horny, kinky, casual sex.

Which is what I'm looking forward to right now. I'm crossing the Thames, my knickerless bottom pressed into the biker's leathery thigh, wondering if he can *tell*, wondering what Shaun has in store for me today. It is difficult not to let my fingers stray crotchwards. Shaun has proved to have the very best kind of dirty mind – an endlessly inventive one – and he has led me down some very peculiar paths indeed since that tree-lined one at the side of the church. Without exception they have been worth the detour; I have discovered tastes and predilections I never knew I had.

At last the train draws in at Blackfriars and I look forward to the prospect of breathing in some slightly less stale air, fighting my way through the crush to get through the door and on to the platform.

At the ticket barrier I spot him, slouching against the wall in an open-necked white shirt, his floppy hair smoothed back against the heat. As usual, he waits until I almost pass him before putting out an arm and dragging me over to him by the wrist. He puts his nose in the crease of my neck and takes a deep draught of my dried-on scent.

'Mmm. Have a good wank, did we?'

'Not bad, thanks.'

'What did you think about?'

'I thought about the time you lifted my skirt in St James Park and spanked my arse in time to the marching band.'

He chuckles. 'That was a good one. Got another good one lined up for you now. Come on.' He kisses me, very quickly but still managing to get a sliver of tongue in there, and leads me around to the station entrance. In a small alcove, away from the main drag, he shields me from view with his body and lifts my skirt.

'Time for a quick check,' he says, making sure I am not wearing knickers, and that I am wet, as I am expected to be. Not a difficult rule to obey; I am always wet when we meet, whether I want to be or not.

I shut my eyes and rest my head against the sooty brickwork, breathing in tarry heat, hearing the pneumatic drills that are like the pulse of the City, always there. The thing about London is that, whatever you are doing, you can always bet that somebody has done it here before. Somebody has stood here, maybe before the river Walbrook was built over, being felt up by a nasty man who had nothing but dishonourable intentions towards her. Maybe then he was wearing a tunic or maybe he was wearing a top hat and a fob watch. But I bet he was here, and I bet there was a girl here with him, giving herself up to her dark side.

Once he has slicked up his fingers and given them a sniff, he leans over to kiss me. I used to find his kisses sloppy, but I have grown to love them, love their indiscipline and barrier-breaching, love their careless, breathless adolescent quality.

He takes me by the hand and leads me towards the bridge, but we do not cross it. Instead we take the steps

41

down to the Embankment. At this section of the Thames, it is little more than a concrete pathway, the river rushing busily in front while the Blackfriars underpass road roars behind a wall. With the railway lines thundering overhead, it is not exactly a spot people choose to linger in, but, all the same, there is a brief hinterland of scrubby greenery between the path and the road with some stone benches set at intervals for lovers of ear-bleeding urban racket.

He waits until we pass under the railway lines we travel together most mornings, then he pulls me down into the yellow-brown grass and hisses, 'Here!'

'Here?' I wrinkle my nose. 'People walk past here.'

'They don't stop though. People walking down here are usually in a hurry to get somewhere else. They won't look either side. They look ahead.'

Already he is pushing me on to my knees, lifting my skirt. The grass is prickly and I am conscious of the midday sun scorching down. If Shaun is an Englishman, does that make me a mad dog? A mad something, at any rate, to let him do this to me in our most public place yet. He has unbuckled and freed himself; he sits down on the grass and pulls me into his lap, making me gasp as I find myself swiftly and inescapably impaled on his hot, hard cock. I am facing forwards, kneeling with my knees on either side of his thighs; his arms are wrapped around my ribcage, holding me in place. I am not sure how this would look to a passer-by – I think it might not be completely obvious that I am shafted by a prick beneath my flimsy skirt, but I cannot say for certain.

We sit there like that for a while, getting used to the position, trying to plan how it will work. I gaze across to the Tate Modern and the Millennium Bridge, wondering if our dotty shapes look lewd or innocent from that distance. Trains curve incessantly around the railway bridge, in and out of the station, cutting sparks on the tracks and making that strange piping and shushing noise that they do. Their rumble makes the ground we are sitting on vibrate; their fumes surround us on all sides. And then Shaun lifts me slightly and then slams me back down, and the main event has begun. I have to lean forward, to find my angle. I put my palms on the baked earth and give him the leeway to thrust while I jiggle back and forth, already too hot, already too wet, but knowing I cannot stop this until I have shown my slutty core to the towering London skyline.

'Do you think they can see us from the trains?' asks Shaun, his vigorous thrusting making it clear that he does not care either way. 'Do you think they are looking out of the window watching you get fucked in the open air at lunchtime on a workday? They know that this is your idea of a lunch break. You don't get a lunch break. You get a fuck break. That's what you need. A daily fuck break. That's what you're going to get. I might pencil you in for tomorrow as well. You should see my diary, Jane. Meetings, meetings, social, meetings, fucking my slut, meetings, more meetings. Uh!'

He pulls me back up to his chest abruptly and for a second I wonder if he has come already, but then I see that two suited men are wandering up the path, speaking loudly into mobile phones in competition with each other. Shaun buries his lips in my neck, making us look as much as possible like normal lovers catching a quick lunchtime rendezvous. The men barely give us a second glance, though one double-takes briefly and smirks in Shaun's direction before moving on under the railway lines and away.

Then Shaun bends me back over and commences a

43

savage onslaught, hard and fast, until I am dripping and scratched and raw and burning. 'They knew I was fucking you, Jane. They knew it,' he whispers, and I come, and he comes, and the Oxo Tower shimmers in a heat haze that blankets all of us while we fall forwards, wailing and sighing, on to the hard ground.

Half an hour later we are sitting outside a riverside pub, drinking lager (him) and vodka and orange (me). It is beginning to occur to me that, in the space of six weeks, this sordid arrangement has become an addiction – something that will damage me if I cannot learn to control it. The combination of heat and sex and alcohol makes me light-headed and bold and I say things I would not normally dare to.

'The men can't take their eyes off you,' he is saying, relishing the words. 'They can probably smell you. One day I might invite them over.'

I raise my damp eyebrows at him. 'One day, Shaun. This can't go on for ever though, can it?'

His face falls a little. I want to touch his hand, but it seems against the rules somehow. Too intimate.

'I've met someone at work,' I tell him. 'It's nothing much at the moment. Coffee, chat. We're going to the cinema this weekend. Might come to nothing, or it might get serious. And if it does, I can't do this any more.'

Shaun looks away, over the river, for a moment, then looks into the dregs of his pint.

'You want to be a nice girl,' he says flatly. He looks up at me squinting against the sun, waiting.

'No. Not necessarily. I don't know. I want to be … Jane. Jane who's a slut sometimes, but a person as well.'

'There aren't enough sluts in the world,' says Shaun wistfully. 'Not perfect ones like you, at least. I might have known …'

'Shaun,' I say, a little distressed. 'I'm not saying …' I don't know what I'm saying.

He drains the last drops of his drink and bangs his glass down on the table.

'Well, you don't have time to say it now, anyway. I have to get back to work. To the offices of the London Merchant Bank. On Threadneedle Street.'

I catch my breath. He has never told me anything about himself before. He is standing up, taking something from a pocket. Paper and pen.

'That's where I work,' he says, 'and this is where I live. Not far from you, I think.' He scribbles down an address, three streets away from my flat and puts the paper in my hand. 'If you want to call round. Tonight. Tomorrow night …' He shrugs. 'I'll leave it up to you.' He dithers, as if unsure how to end our encounter, looking around to the exit and then back at me.

Time to seize the day. Time to also seize his hand.

'Promise you won't ever stop being sleazy?'

He smiles, toothy and broad. 'No question of that.'

'I'll see you tonight then.'

We snog for ages, by the river, ignoring the sniggering remarks of the boozy bankers, then I have to run for my train, all the way back to where it began.

About the Story

ONE OF MY MOST vivid childhood memories is of looking up at the Houses of Parliament while Big Ben chimed the hour during a dramatic summer thunderstorm. I was seven years old, soaking wet, and filled with an exhilarating sense of being at the living heart of all things. My obsession with London was born then, on my first visit to the city, so I was fascinated and excited to hear about this anthology.

I made it an ambition to live and work in London, and managed to fulfil this earlier than I expected – at the age of ten – when my father's job stationed him on the north-western fringes of the metropolis. I moved away, came back, moved away, but was always drawn back by the magnetic attraction London has for me.

My story in this collection, *Thames Link*, has its basis in truth. For a time, I was that girl in the eau-de-nil cotton dress (from Marks and Spencer, if you're interested) on the station platform, and there was indeed an odd stalkerish character, wearing a lightweight raincoat at the height of summer, who possessed a paranormal ability to find the seat nearest to me on the train. Everything thereafter is fiction but, for a long time, I have wondered how that scenario might have eventually played out, had I not moved from that particular suburb and abandoned my Thameslink commute.

I will never know, which is almost certainly for the best. The likelihood of it ending badly, or dully, or frighteningly is pretty high. In my mind, though, I can pretend it ended erotically, which is always the best way.

The part of the story where Jane imagines the ghosts of a former London trysting at Blackfriars reminds me of the endless stories that ran through my head when I lived there. I could not walk from shop to pub to tube station without thinking of all the things that had happened on that soil before – violent things, romantic things, tragic things, epoch-making things. In the end it was rather overwhelming and I fled to the country. Away from London, my head is less crowded, but I love to return when the cranium starts to rattle and fill it up all over again.

Monster
by Francis Ann Kerr

SHE HADN'T THOUGHT ABOUT what she'll do there. Or with whom. At night Old Street turned into a long meandering road that led nowhere. Although the scattered nouveau pubs were open, no one was about. She followed the ring road. This was the awful bit. Was it the left or the right? Her nipples were frozen big and shiny in their rubber sheaf under her jacket. She'd almost passed for normal on the tube, although one or two of the passengers had stared at her with bright, alert eyes. A cover-all coat down to her boots, military grey, fastened securely over her ensemble, but her spiky shoes gave it all away. It was cold, people were covered in winter layers, but it wouldn't be like that in the club.

It was that Thursday in the month: the Torture Garden – London's most brazen fetish club. They switched it frequently to different venues – all of them in the innards of rotting back streets that seemed to have fallen off the A-Z. It was always a bitch to get there. Especially in this October chill. It was never quite so difficult on the way back though; afterwards.

She'd only been there a few times, always with friends. One of her mates was a writer; he did whole books for a couple of thousand quid and scraped a living. The other worked in a swank film office in Soho, tracking down obscure films. And she was a physiotherapist; the clinic where she worked specialised in sporting injuries. The only thing they all did together that was the same was to snort coke off a light monitor. It was their little joke. Tom and Jake were like her older brothers, they helped and encouraged her, but wanted her to be turned on by the scene without actually getting sucked in. In the same way, they introduced her to coke, but didn't expect her to actually wade out and buy grams herself.

They'd probably be surprised to know where she was now. She could see a mysterious line of punters in the distance. They seemed to be carrying bags filled with something, costumes and accessories probably. There was always a strict dress code at these things to stop the riff raff getting in. Closer now, she could see some had defied convention and had come as they were, PVC or latex'd up, standing insolently in the street. She was the only woman standing alone and hoped she looked impassive. Already waves of energy were circulating, pre-tension. Suddenly she was in front; without saying anything, she opened her coat and flashed her white rubber nurse's outfit. They waved her in.

Her eyes adjusted to the instant gloom. The venue seemed to be a rambling enclave of womb-shaped rooms. In the distance she could hear the sound of a whip smacking something. She stumbled around, ignoring the loners that stuck around the edges. Not yet. She found the ladies and joined a dozen or so other people getting ready for show-time. Some trannies were hanging out there; it irked her that they could do the make-up and everything ten times better than real women. Off came her coat and underneath was the itsy-bitsy rubber playsuit that skimmed her nipples and covered her tail-bone, leaving the rest to the imagination. A nurse's clock and fake Red

Cross sticker completed the fantasy. For anyone in the know it was an ironic take on her regular white work-wear, but she hoped tonight that no one would recognise her.

In the neon-lit mirror, she applied last minute make-up. Another veneer of gloss, just a sprinkling of powder. Her green eyes leered huge back at her; the more nervous she was the larger they got. She stared back at herself, she looked hot, almost frenzied. Her pupils had dilated to pinholes. She'd had a little snort in the loo, and tentacles of sensations were beginning to kick in. Her outfit was the *de rigueur* of skinny chic, although she looked too thin in regular stuff, the beauty of rubber was that it accentuated every curve. She knew plump girls had a terrible time with it because it showed up every ounce of flab, but it did wonders for her. Ignoring the others, she massaged her breasts until the nipples pushed out pertly through the rubber. Instantly she looked sexier. Turning around, she bent over and inspected her freshly exfoliated behind. A big powder brush added a dusting of glitter. Her neighbours were beginning to sit up and take notice.

She'd removed her panties so everyone could get a better view, her ass cheeks looked sleek with just a suggestion of firmness. She'd hennaed her blonde pubic hair to make a pleasing contrast between her skin and small V of fur. She preferred a bald vagina mons so that she could see and cup her vaginal lips herself. It was a pity that men, the boring straight men that daily invaded her clinic, had no imagination. Even if she dallied with them and all that was missionary, they could barely keep up with her. Mr I'm-not-looking-I'm-putting-on-false-eyelashes, honest, was all eyes. Now she'd really got his attention, she slipped a mischievous finger right in there. Her juices were as warm as bath water, she prodded herself a little bit, then turned round and looked right at him, licking her sticky finger. No one said anything as she exited. This was why they all came to a fetish club; you could do these things and no one gave a shit.

In her four-inch heels, she cut an attractive figure striding confidently around the club. She felt Amazon-like just doing it. In one section people were dancing wildly, and she paused a moment to look. There were one or two handsome men, jiving bare-chested, one blonde obviously semi-professional dancer that made the club night actually look like its own promotional posters, but the rest were odd and dumpy, although she admired some of the older people who still had the gall to get it on. A tall man with a shaved head glanced at her. She wasn't in the mood for dancing just yet though. She bought a beer and sucked it appreciatively. No one got glasses with a bottle these days.

It was suddenly harder than she thought going it alone. There were lots of people all divided into little groups that she didn't understand the dynamics of. Best to observe. She felt more at home in a smaller room painted blood-red. A number of fake regency thrones, with thick velvety cushions, were lined up, as if waiting for the queen to arrive. She grinned, her feet were panicking already in her elegant but inflexible PVC shoes. She could sit a while and check out who came by. Before she'd even downed the last sip of beer, two young men appeared out of nowhere. They looked trim and youthful, but instead of acknowledging her, they dropped to the floor and began to negotiate the area around her feet. With inquisitive fingers, they caressed her shoes with their bare hands. There was no other form of contact, just undulating movement. It was easy to get caught up in the moment. Suddenly her feet were blissfully free, her shoes had been removed; two handsome men were worshipping literally at her feet. The caresses turned moist as they used their tongues as well as their hands. In a stray thought she wondered if her feet really tasted that good, but now the slave tongues were licking fervently in between her toes, and it felt exactly as if they were salivating over her pussy.

Damn, that felt good! She'd never tried this before; Tom and Jake had had to drag her in at first just to take a look at the scene. Now she was experimenting freely. Surprisingly, their sucking activity was turning her on. She expected their next move to be a hot-whispering up her legs to savage her clit. But they didn't. True fetishists, obviously, they just steadfastly licked her toes until aroused to boiling point, when she nudged them away. Instantly they disappeared, and she put her shoes back on and went in search of more pleasure.

Now she felt a bit more into it, she didn't avoid the throngs of people. She stood around the bar and this time ordered a rum and coke and fell into conversation with two good-looking guys.

'What's your name? You've got nice breasts,' the dark one said, actually cupping them as he said it. The other, Steve, went further, 'I prefer a bit of nice ass,' his hand actually glancing against her bare bottom. Evidently they were into threesomes, but they were a bit too pushy and impatient to take advantage of her already excited state.

She carried on drinking. So this was the difference when you came to these things on your own: rather than just looking and smiling and being there with your mates, you noticed that people actually did things. She walked past a man kneeling and masturbating openly at the sight of an older man in a Nazi outfit whipping a young girl with dark hair. She seemed to genuinely enjoy each stroke, although it left a mark on her skin. The voyeur masturbated into his fist and abruptly left. She drank it all in; tried to make sense of it all. So many taboos: a man dressed up as a toilet with mini-urinals in which you could relieve yourself, a woman with a wedding dress and veil slashed to reveal her nubile sex organs. Her mind boggled.

A transvestite with a long wig drifted over.

'Do you mind if I speak to you? I'm Dave.' His smile was pretty. He looked gentle. Bare-chested, his nipples were pierced and he'd tied red ribbons through the rings. They made perfunctory conversation, like the two girls they weren't, before, hesitatingly, David got to the point.

'Could you play with my nipples for me?' It was an unexpected request, but tonight was about discovery, so she indulged him. Within a few minutes they'd grown long and firmly erect, like a playmate vixen with super nipples she'd seen once in a magazine. It still didn't feel like a sexual act, and they chatted idly while she stroked and pulled at his nipples.

Her prowling sexual urges had mostly been contained, but out of nowhere the tallest man she'd ever seen suddenly stepped out of the shadows. His frame was big too, and his shaved head and clumsy boots made him look like something out of a horror film. Clad in slippery PVC black, he looked ominous. 'Monster', as in Frankenstein's monster, the word slipped instantly into her mind. His eyes were a blurred blue and had an hypnotic effect on her. Instead of dismissing Dave, who was still enjoying having his nipples teased, he directed them to a discreet corner of the room where they could play in fuller darkness.

Monster told her his name and asked her where she was from. Surprisingly, his voice was high and soothing, he seemed surprised that she was there all by herself. She assumed he was a regular. She continued to administer to Dave's nipples and ribbons. It was as easy as breathing.

'Do you mind if I play with myself?' asked Dave, his voice breathless with anticipation.

'Sure, go ahead.'

Dave pulled out his cock, which was a medium size, and began earnestly massaging it. The swishing sound of a bobbing foreskin filled the air, along with the smell of pure sex.

'You like your cock then?' she asked Dave.

'Yes, I do. I'm not gay you know. I just like dressing up and having my nipples played with.'

Meanwhile, Monster was the man with the magic hands. His every touch was light and deft, sending tingles throughout her whole body. Before she'd even realised what was happening, one of his fingers had slipped from her upper thigh and had eased itself into her excited vagina. She jumped. His other hand patted her. She relaxed. The feeling was awesome; all the start/stop excitement she'd endured was pent up and longing for release. His fingers were all over her clit and slipping and bumping their way inside her. She didn't even notice that now Dave was playing with both her tits and her clitoris too; she was too excited, sitting there with her boobs hanging out and her pussy being expertly manipulated. A small crowd had gathered.

'Are you enjoyin' yourself darlin'?' whispered Monster in a thick London accent.

'Yes!' she said, her voice almost coming out as a scream. A couple of men started playing with her now, feeling her breasts and licking at her legs. She tensed up, and Monster responded straight away.

'You want them here?'

'No.'

Just a hand, and they melted away. Monster took over her clitoris now. Dave was close to coming and his moans were getting louder. The sheer naughtiness of the whole scene – her body clamped tight in rubber, the feel of the nipples with their absurd ribbon, Monster's teasing fingers – it was all too much. She was jerking and rubbing herself on his fingers now, someone – she didn't know who – cupped her breasts.

'Agh!' she came loudly, louder than she would dare in her shared house in Angel. But it was a fetish club, so she could.

She turned to Monster. Something large bulged beneath his PVC suit, but he didn't open it. Dave was off after shoving his telephone number in her hand. He was offering to give her a lift home, but Monster waved him away. There was something hard to define about Monster; she couldn't say whether he was good-looking or not. He attracted and repulsed her at the same time. He kissed her and enjoyed shocking her with his pierced tongue.

'Oh, I'm bad, shoving my tongue down your mouth like that.'

'What about you, don't you want to come too?' her eyes looked downwards. Monster looked at her and knew he had her whole attention.

'Do you want me?' he said. 'I need something special. Come and take a look.'

He took her hand and pulled her in the direction of the dungeons, the very heart of the club. A knot of black-leather and rubber fetishists were huddled together watching a mistress casually whipping her eager slave. Monster stood behind her and shielded her body from stray hands.

The slave was a little man in his forties. There was

something exceptional about his willingness to bare all in public and submit to his mistress, who was a sexy twenty-something. They watched intently. Monster casually rested his hands on her breasts. She'd come already just with his finger, but now he was preparing her for a greater thrill. His hands were all over her as he whispered in her ear, 'I'd like to spank you.'

She shivered. The slave seemed to be enjoying it, but would she? Those eyes burned into hers. Instinctively, he understood her dilemma, as she hovered between her thirst for experience and first-time nerves. She pressed her back to him and he continued to prepare her, his hand thinking nothing of casually gliding up her short dress to play with her vagina. Around them the swishes intensified.

She turned and faced him. 'Not here.'

'I've got just the thing for you.'

He obviously had the run of the place and led her off up a couple of flights of stairs. In her heels and growing excitement, she could barely walk straight. Monster picked up some straight tequilas to go with them and what he called his 'bag of tricks'.

Finally he opened a door to the 'Red Room' which contained little private booths discreetly tucked away. More than one couple were enjoying themselves and the hum of pleasure came at them from every direction. It was charming and decadent, like something out of the Hellfire club. She went to sit down onto the plush sofa, but Monster intervened.

'No, I want you to sit on this chair. No, not on your bum, turn round, that's it – lie on your tummy. Put your hands out.'

All the time his hands were on her, kneading and soothing. He opened his bag and took out a long length of rope. It was purple, soft, and he let her feel its silkiness with her hands. 'Special bondage rope that. See baby, now you'll have to trust me. Completely.'

He looked even more menacing in the red haze; although his eyes remained soft, their meaning was indiscernible. The feel of his caresses was like a familiar lover; he instinctively knew when to touch her and how, but was this going too far?

'I just want to tie your legs, darlin'. Your arms will be free. Won't you play for me?'

He was doing things with the rope now, she tried to turn her head, but he pushed it back.

'Be patient, it's a surprise.'

Her knees were fixed together, the ankles raised high. She tried to pull her feet apart, but couldn't. The rope felt luxurious on her skin but held her firmly. She pushed her breasts up so that her back arched. Her position was a lewd one, but she didn't care. Now he was standing in front of her with his bag open.

'What toys do you want to play with?'

She looked into the bag – there was something that looked like a horse whip. The wooden things were probably paddles. There was lubricant, hand-cuffs, a range of jelly, dildos too, and other things she didn't want to think about too much.

'You've been a naughty girl, haven't you?'

His voice was thick and commanding.

'I don't think you deserve to play with these toys yet. No, I have to punish you first.' One hand pulled under her hips and tugged up her little dress. His hand massaged her pert little bottom, and it was not afraid to play along the outline of her ass and stimulate the vagina lips. Her face nestled in cushions; she luxuriated in the feeling. This was something she had never experienced before. It felt warm

57

and good, even the new feeling of the ropes anchored her into her pleasure. Her body felt weightless. Anything seemed possible in the subtly darkened chamber. She was a world away from just looking, now she was doing. And Jake and Tom would be astounded.

Now he was easing her onto her knees with her bottom stuck high in the air.

'If anyone could see you, little slut, do you know what they'd do?'

His hands were now getting rougher, the pace more brisk.

'Would they get turned on? Maybe?'

'I think they'd want to give you a good hiding!' He growled the last bit, and a little knot of fear began to form in her mind. His strokes got faster, more direct, but the tingling feeling seemed to be everywhere. Slowly, his hands began to increase their pressure. There was no sense of pain, just the physical feeling of solidity, of muscles being manoeuvred – not unlike the work she did in her day job. Her skin smarted, but not unpleasantly. The tempo increased and the sound of his spanking administrations rang out, until she was sure the other couples could hear them too. Faster, faster! She squirmed deliciously – it was better than she'd expected. All the blood was rushing to the area and her clit was now throbbing. She started to moan and rock herself on the sofa.

'Good girl. You like that don't you?' Now the spanks were getting faster, drops of sweat from his shaved head fell down and rolled over her bare back.

'That's better bad girl, do you want me to make you come now?'

One hand continued slapping, now the other was burrowing into the incredible slickness of her vagina. The restrictive rope only heightened the sense of frenzied action.

'Mmm. Somebody's excited. You want this don't you?'

'Yes. Yes. Yes!' Her cries jumped out of her mouth in little barks. His fingers now were reaching in, pushing her in the same rhythm as his hand on her ass. Frantically, she arched her back even further, forcing him to ream her harder. Perhaps the spanks got harder too, but she could no longer even detect their force as the room spun. Her buttocks were white-hot with energy and desire. She was beyond caring, this was it.

'Agh! Yes! Yes!' Still her pelvis was jerking against the sofa. Monster was now massaging her where his hands had just spanked and reamed her. They were both soaked in perspiration; the smell of sex and burning rubber screeched at her.

Now he was untying her, stroking her, petting her. The outline of his cock stood out in a rigid hard-on under his PVC.

'Kiss it,' he said, and stroked her face when he accepted a pretty kiss on the outside of his trousers.

'I think it's time for you to go home now.' The voice was soothing again.

'What about you?'

'I've got to save myself darlin'. I'm only going to give it to you when you really want it. Do you want to experience more?'

She looked at the profile of his all-knowing face and smiled. 'Yes, Monster.'

He must have thought it sounded like 'master'.

'Give me a hug then for now, just a sweet hug.'

They embraced and she felt dwarfed by his huge, massive bulk. But it was reassuring, and she could feel the girth of his hard-on.

'Ah, that makes me feel better, to get a nice hug.' He looked into her eyes and smiled. 'I guess we'll be doing that again. And I've got a lot tricks to show you. If you want to that is.' His expression was comical, part nervous, but with a hint of lust. He wanted to show his interest, but not too much. This was a fetish club, there were rules.

After the hardness of the pleasure play, now he was the soft one; underneath the PVC he was tender, raw. No doubt, he'd tell her that other girls didn't understand him. She patted him. Monster, she said to herself. She wasn't normally into spanking, but he was so interesting she felt she couldn't resist him. This looked like the start of some interesting times.

Yes, they'd meet again. She smiled into his eyes and planted a kiss on his cheek. Around her the room was reeling with the smell of sweat and excitement and spilled beer. It was different every time at the club; never dull. When her friends asked her why she went she always smiled. She didn't have to give her reasons. She knew why she came here. Because she wanted to.

About the Story

IT TOOK ME AGES to get the courage to go to the fetish club The Torture Garden. And then after I'd been there once, I realised that every time they changed the venue so it was always a struggle to find the next location. London is full of side streets that seem to meander into nothing in the A-Z and the venue in Old Street was one of those where I got lost. That's the amazing thing about the city, in the middle of a perfectly ordinary street there's an amazing club or weird shop. That there's all these possible worlds, but you need the know-how and the confidence to access it.

It's hard having the right dress code for the fetish scene to get in, as well as being able to travel by public transport without causing a riot. As a newbie, I was amazed at the diversity of what turned people on. It wasn't actually wall-to-wall sex, but an incredible display of erotic desire, and not all of it turned me on. *Monster* is a story where there is no honest-to-god penetrative sex, but plenty of focus on spanking, transvestites and foot worship. The main character isn't particularly into any of these themes, but nonetheless, tries them out 'because she can'. The empowerment of going there for the first time alone, and experimenting is a liberating one. The story focuses very much on the politics of the various group dynamics inside and the etiquette of casual sexual touch. The alcohol and orgasm are just the flames that momentarily light the dimly lit interior of this London location.

Shame Game
by Valerie Grey

HERE YOU ARE: NERVOUS, waiting for her to arrive, wearing the evening dress, thong and stockings that she has sent; crossing and re-crossing your legs. You have turned off most of the lights in your small flat, preferring darkness.

All you know is that she has told you that the two of you will be going out tonight. You do not know where. She will pick you up at the appropriate time. You are trying not to think too hard about the night ahead; you recall the last time she picked you up and took you out in London at night. That was the time with the blindfold so you didn't see much of where you were in the city or how you got there. But every time you remember a part of that night, your stomach clenches. She shamed you. Humiliated you terribly in front of me, but in the end it was worth it, when you pleased her, and she gave you the love and attention you need.

Still, you also remember how nothing seemed to bother her, no matter how agonized you were. The best thing about that night was that you could not see anything: you could not see the faces of the others, or see their ages, or see their smiles.

Why didn't you just say no before tonight? You could have done, but then you might have lost her. She would have either punished you or abandoned you.

So she called, had the clothes delivered, and told you to be ready by 7 p.m.

You could have said no, but you didn't.

You wonder if there is something wrong with you because you know she is going to severely humiliate you again.

No normal, no *sane* woman would let this happen to her – not after realising what could be done to her. But you know. You have lived through it once already.

So why do it?

Why do you enjoy it?

Unable to be still any more, you begin to pace your small living room. You walk from the armchair to the glass doors facing your small balcony and back.

You touch your hair, making sure it is in place. You tug on the dress, trying to make it longer. It shows too much of your legs.

Your hands won't stay still. You glance at the clock over and over again. You were ready at 6.45, long before she said to be ready. Now it is 7.20.

The waiting is making you uneasy, more nervous. And you imagine things: what will be done to you. Images of shame and lust and …

Finally the intercom buzzes.

You rush to the speaker and click the button. 'Yes?'

That French accent: 'Buzz me in, chérie.'

You push the button that unlocks the front door to the building.

There's a funny and strange feeling in your stomach.

She knocks on the door to your flat.

You open it and step back so she can enter.

Her eyes flick around the flat, taking in the used furniture and worn fixtures. You blush, feeling that you are not good enough for her. She comes from old money, you come from nothing.

She holds a white wrap in one arm. She tells you to face away from her.

You do so, and she slips the wrap over your shoulders. It's like a poncho, but instead of being complete, it is split so that the front is open. She reaches down and takes the chain that is hanging from one side. She clips it to the other side of the wrap, closing it. There is still a gap of maybe two inches down the middle of your body, but you are mostly covered.

She says, 'It isn't cold out, but you may need this later tonight … depending on how you do.'

Hearing those words, you tremble. She knows you well, knows what has just crossed your mind and she smiles. Smiles are usually comforting, but this smile makes you knot up inside.

You have seen this smile before.

You feel moistness between your legs.

Again, you are afraid, not of her, but of what may happen to you. But you don't resist, just as you did not resist the last time. She commands and leads you as no one ever has led you before. She is the true mistress for whom you have yearned, for all of your twenty-three years.

She reaches out and touches your cheek, lightly, caressing, loving.

She is forty. She is beautiful. She is rich.

You are hers to command.

'Come on now.' She walks out of the flat. You stop and lock the door, but she does not wait. She strides away down the hall.

You scurry behind her, the wrap flowing behind you.

You catch up with her.

She glances at you.

She says, 'One step behind me, to my right.'

This command, making you less than she, humiliates you and makes you angry.

Your sudden rage forces you to speak out. 'Why must I be behind you? This is not fair.'

The steel in her eyes makes you shrink inside. You look down, instantly humbled. She does not have to speak to make her displeasure known. A glare, you find, does just as well.

She says, 'Is there anything *else* you wish to complain about?'

'No.' Your voice is soft and stuttering. She has a presence that makes you feel small, like a Lilliputian from *Gulliver's Travels*.

You ask, 'Where are we going?'

She says, 'To dinner. Then, depending on you, perhaps we'll go on and join a small gathering afterwards. And no, it is *not* going to be the same one we visited before. *If* we go, this one will be completely different.'

You suck in a breath, remembering your last humiliation, the last time she took you to 'a small gathering'.

She says, 'I must make sure that you are aware of your role, little one. If you wish to speak, you must first receive my permission. Whether we are alone or with others. Do you understand?'

You nod and say, 'Y-y-yes.'

You hate it when you stutter like that.

She says, 'An appropriate way to ask permission would be "Madam, may I speak?" Would you please say that for me now?'

'M-m-madam, may I s-s-s-speak?'

'Very good. In no time you will not have that silly

stutter. You will become accustomed to me and my ways, little one.'

Little one. She stands five foot nine inches to your five foot one.

Damn her Riviera-bred superiority. Is this the French way of getting back at the English for centuries of God-knows-what?

You are in the parking lot. You hurry to keep up, glancing ahead to see what kind of car she will drive tonight. She always chooses flashy rental cars.

She leads you to a long black limousine. A driver, a tall man with very white skin, waits. The driver opens a rear door. She climbs inside, with grace, as if she is accustomed to limos. You scramble in after her. You have never been in a limo and it shows: you are trash, you come from the poor.

She points to where you are to sit. Without complaint, you settle into the leather seat and look at her timidly. She ignores you because she has the phone to the driver and is telling him that he may leave.

She lowers the phone. 'You want to be a good girl for me, *oui*?'

Your mouth is dry and you can only nod.

'You must speak the word.'

'Y-yes.'

'Good, I am pleased that you wish to be a good girl. Show me one of your breasts now.'

You are shocked at her demand but why should you be? You knew she would ask this, or something similar. You glance at the privacy window dividing the limousine. It is down and the driver is looking in the rear view mirror.

Your hands shake as you lift them to the clasp holding the wrap. Your fingers are clumsy and it takes a while for you to loosen the clasp. The wrap slides off your shoulders when it is released. Your eyes fill with tears and you lift one shaking hand to the strap of your gown. Pushing it off your shoulder, you close your eyes, and then peel the top of the gown away from your left breast.

As the air touches your bare skin, goose bumps appear and your nipple becomes erect. You struggle to contain the sobs that want to burst out of you.

You slowly open your eyes and through your blurred vision you can see that she is smiling. She hands you a dainty handkerchief. You blot your eyes with it and sit with one breast bared. She nods to the front of the limousine and you cannot help but look there also. Your face flares bright red as you see the driver's eyes in the rear-view mirror. He grins at this unexpected show.

The drive from your miserable flat in East Finchley into West London feels like an eternity. You don't want to look at the driver, but your eyes are drawn to him. Each time you look, his eyes are in the mirror and you know that he is enjoying the sight of your bare bosom.

Your hands have lifted and fallen so many times. You want to cover your skin, your nipple, but you know that you cannot. You cannot go against her wishes.

You clasp your hands together in your lap. Your face is still red and your eyes are moist. You are trying to keep your face expressionless: stoic.

You can feel moistness between your legs and wonder how you can be excited by this treatment. It seems so wrong to you, but your body is not responding in the same way as your mind. Your mind can feel humiliation, but your body experiences only sexual excitement.

The limousine slows and you look through the window. It stops in front of one of the nicest restaurants in South Kensington. This is your reward for this evening, for your obedience. And at least as you are in public she might not do anything to you here, or so you hope.

The limousine stops. You both wait until the driver opens the rear door. Your breast is still bare. She slips out of the limo, again with the grace of an aristocrat, and she turns to look at you. She nods her head once and you understand her completely. With her and the driver looking at you, you lift the dress to cover your bare teat and slide the strap up and back on to your shoulder. You lift the wrap and drape it over your shoulders and slowly alight from the limousine. She turns away from you as you step on to the sidewalk and she walks to the entrance. Again, you scurry behind her. Secure in her superiority, she walks through the glass door and goes to the maître d's station. You are behind her. There is a quiet conversation between her and the maître d' and then you both follow him to a secluded table.

She, of course, is seated first, while you stand.

Then you are seated across from her.

A waiter hurries to the table. She orders wine, not asking if you want any wine, or anything else for that matter. She flicks one hand at you and you realise that you still have the wrap on. Self-consciously, you shrug it off and let it drape over the back of your chair.

The wine is served and she raises her glass to you after tasting and approving it. You lift yours, smile shyly, and sip as she does.

Now that you are in the restaurant, in public, you feel more secure and less threatened. She makes small conversation with you. You begin to relax. Others are seated nearby, mostly well-dressed couples. The alcove that you are seated in has room for six tables. She leans toward you and asks, 'Are you a virgin?'

What kind of question is that? Before you can respond

she speaks once more. 'I asked you a question. I expect an answer, a truthful answer.'

'I am not.'

'How many men have you had?'

You lower your face.

'If you do not answer, I will think that you would prefer a penalty.'

You lift your eyes and see hers have that steely quality again that makes you afraid and nervous. Before you can choke out your answer she speaks once more. 'You have earned a penalty, which will be paid after I hear your answer.'

'Two.'

'Now that wasn't so bad, was it?'

'Y-y-you are humiliating me. You know very well my feelings about men. Those two times – I was forced.'

'Such things are not unheard of.'

You sit tensely, waiting. She smiles the smile of a crocodile. You now think of the penalty you will pay. You don't want to know what it is, but you also want to get it over with. You watch her as she looks around the alcove. All the tables are full.

She leans forward again and says, 'What do you think your penalty should be? Name it.'

'D-don't kn-know.'

'Then I must choose for you, yes?'

You nod.

She leans closer. She says, 'Give me your panties.'

A gasp of shock escapes from your mouth and you immediately look at the table when some of the other diners glance towards your table. They heard her command.

You grab your wineglass. You take a large swallow and set the glass down. You look mournfully at her. She cannot mean what she has said, not here, amongst all these strangers. You sense that she will not accept anything less.

You sit like a stump.

She waits, tapping her foot; you know that your refusal to obey will only result in another penalty.

You lower your hands to your hips and begin to pull your dress higher up your legs. You squirm to lift it so you can get at your panties. But as you tug at your dress, you realise the dress needs to actually be raised even higher than you thought. You glance across the room. A man and woman watch you squirm. With a moan you look down and scrabble under your dress. Your fingers touch a piece of underwear fabric and you tug it down. You lift your arse from the chair and feel your panties slipping beneath your buttocks. With a whimper, you tug harder and the panties slide below your ass and on to your thighs.

Now you sit back down and lift one thigh, pulling your panties down on that side, then lift the other leg and do the same. As you squirm back and forth, you glance around and see that the couple watching you are very curious about you.

You get the panties to your knees and move your legs until they fall around your ankles.

You then squirm your feet until your heels are completely free of the underwear. The man and woman are still looking at you. You want to yell at them to stop being bloody looky-loos.

You take a deep breath and bend over and reach for the panties. You sit back up and hold them in your lap, scrunching them into a tight ball.

Throughout this entire ordeal she has been watching you and smiling as she sees the contortions you have gone through to try and keep what you are doing unknown. She leans forward and holds out one hand. Blushing deeply, you lift your clenched fist and very carefully lower the ball of fabric into her palm.

She lets it sit there, in the open.

You blush harder and glance toward the nosey man and woman. *They are still watching.* She opens her palm. Your panties almost fall from her hand, before she catches the waistband on a finger tip. You hear a loud laugh; your head jerks toward the sound. The man and woman are laughing and you turn scarlet. Then he lifts his glass and toasts you.

Softly, you say to her, 'Please put them away. Please.'

She frowns. 'Did you *ask* for permission to speak?'

You groan, as you know she has done this to trap you, to catch you speaking without permission.

'No, Madam, I did not. I am truly sorry. Will you please forgive me?'

'Certainly, little girl. I am *most* forgiving this evening. I will forgive you once you show me your lovely breast again.'

You take a deep breath and slip your shoulder strap down and then lower the front of your dress. You hear a chuckle from the other table.

Defiantly you sit, one teat bared for her. Your anger cannot hide the embarrassment you feel. Your nipples are both hard and poking out.

She sips her wine. 'You may put it away now, little girl. You are angry, no?'

'Yes, Madam, I am angry. You humiliated me again.'

'Did you not enjoy it? Wasn't it thrilling?'

'Others saw me.'

'Ah, but I think you enjoy this very much. And you have such pretty little breasts. You should be proud of them and want to show them to me.'

She is right and you do not want to admit this.

The waiter arrives and you realise that your breast is still exposed. You hunch over and quickly lift your dress to cover it, hoping that he did not see anything.

You sit up as calmly as you can, blushing deeply, and do not look at the waiter.

She orders for the two of you, without asking you what you want. She is very much in control of this evening. You sit quietly. She smiles. She knows this is hard for you. She is proud of your compliance.

You relax as much as you can. Your eyes flick to the man and woman. They continue to watch you. You loathe their eyes.

The waiter comes and serves dinner. You both eat and nothing is said. You appreciate the silence; it gives you time to compose yourself.

Soon the meal is over and she gives her credit card to the waiter. Before long he is back and you are ready to leave.

She stands and then you rise from the table too. You slip the wrap over your shoulders once more and she fastens the chain at the front, closing the garment. Then with a nod to the man and woman that have watched you, she strides out of the alcove and you follow her with as much dignity as you can muster.

The limousine appears as if by magic and she waits for the driver to open the rear door. She enters first, of course, and motions for you to sit across from her. She lifts the phone for the driver and gives him directions to a place in Richmond.

The traffic is heavy, the drive is long. Eventually, the limousine turns into a long driveway. There is a large house at the end. Almost a mansion, you think.

Who lives here?

She says, 'Now, my pet, you will be a good girl while we are here. I do not want any hesitation or whining tonight. Understood?'

Your stomach clenches. '*Oui*, Madam.'

'Be sure you remember that.'

The limousine stops.

The driver opens the rear door.

She is out, waiting for you.

You step out and wait for her to move, your cue.

You both walk to the front door. A servant in black-and-white uniform opens it and you are led inside. She stops you. The servant holds a mask – just a simple black mask. She takes the mask from the servant and fastens it on to your face.

Most of your face is covered, but you can see out of the eye slits.

You shudder; you know for sure that she is going to make you do something that you will not want to do. But you will do it, and you will feel both shame and arousal while you do it.

She leads you through a set of large double doors. There are many people beyond the doors – men and women standing and talking, drinks in their hands, laughter issuing from their elegant, well-bred, wealthy mouths.

She easily moves through the group, stopping and talking with several – English, French, German, even Russian, as she is fluent in all. Spanish too. These are her people: the upper crust of European society. And who are you but some lower-class slave from Liverpool who rents a shoebox flat in East Finchley. A girl who grew up with a sadistic step-mother and a drunken factory worker for a father. So who are you and why are you here?

73

You follow her and find that you are ignored once they have taken in your body, your dress, and your mask. No one talks to you, but they ask her about you. You discover that you are a *find*, a *treasure*. The compliments do not make you feel any better. You are an object of shameful flesh, not a woman. Not a person. You feel uneasy. You only have your dress to cover your body and you remember the last evening with her, and what happened: the complete humiliation, the eyes upon you.

A man separates himself from the crowd and taps a glass for silence.

The talking ceases.

All eyes are on him.

He speaks. 'Tonight we have the pleasure of a young woman who will be a significant participant in our *game*. She is here of her own free will and she will not be paid for this evening's entertainment. Thus, she is neither whore nor captive.'

He looks at you.

You look down. What is this *game*, this *entertainment*? What the hell have you gotten yourself into?

She leads you across the room. Now people are looking at you more closely. You are trembling as you follow her to another room. There are chairs and couches spread around this room, but the main piece of furniture is something that looks like parallel bars, with the bars positioned much lower. She leads you to this thing, this object. You find that the closest bar is level with your waist. She moves you forward until your belly is pressed against it, and you are facing away from her. She strokes your arms, your back. You cannot stop trembling.

'Be still and be good. You will not be hurt. Trust me. I will not allow for you to be hurt.'

Her hands reach up to your shoulders and slip the

straps of your dress down your upper arms. Your breasts are the only things holding the dress up now. You whimper softly. She gently presses your back and you have to bend over the bar pressing into your stomach. Each of your arms is taken and fastened to the second bar.

You are restrained.

You are vulnerable.

She leaves you.

You are alone.

It is quiet in here now. Too quiet.

You strain your ears. Where are all the people?

Minutes feel like hours. Then you hear heels clacking and the buzz of conversation. You sense many people are standing behind you.

A man speaks: 'Ladies and gentlemen, our friend has brought this *treasure* to us. To be a part of our game. So we will play with her. She has an aversion to having her bottom used, so we will be using that. Each man and woman will pair up and draw numbers. Then, starting with number one, the female half of the couple will insert one of the devices provided inside our little guest's bottom. As long as she allows this to be done to her, each couple will then pass to the other side of the room. But, if she wishes for the insertions to stop, she need only ask and we will stop. The remaining men, however, who are partnered with a woman who has not had the chance to test her anus, will then be allowed to fuck her. Let me get the devices and we will proceed.'

Your head is spinning – you cannot believe what you have just heard.

She slips up beside you. You are quietly sobbing.

She leans down to your ear. 'Pet, the devices are dildos. They are small at the start but get bigger each time. I will prepare you, but once the game starts I cannot interfere. I promise you that no harm will come to you. You only have to endure.'

You see two men carrying in a table. On it is a tube of lubricant and a row of dildos – some are very small, thin as fingers, but as your head turns to the other end of the table, they become grotesque, huge, frightening, rigid, inhuman: the sex of aliens and demons.

You glance down to the floor and bite your lip. She steps to the table and lifts the lubricant. She moves behind you and you feel the hem of your dress rise. Cool air tingles about your thighs and arse.

You feel her pulling your cheeks open and rubbing lubricant on to and around your anus. You begin to whimper. And you jerk hard when you feel her finger slip through the ring of muscle. She spreads lube inside you too.

She bends over to whisper. 'All you have to say is stop, no more. Then it will stop.'

You begin to cry. You cannot help yourself. Through teary eyes you see the first woman pick up the smallest dildo. She disappears behind you and you feel it at your tight anus. There is pressure and the dildo slips in.

You groan.

You turn your face to your mistress. You say, 'Madam, may I speak?'

'Of course.'

'How many are there?'

'Oh, darling, about twenty. I think.'

You grunt as the first dildo is pulled out of you. Another woman comes and picks up the next dildo. In no time your cheeks are pulled open and the second dildo is inserted inside your arse. It's removed and the third, fourth and fifth quickly follow.

You are breathing in shallow gasps by then.

You hear a voice announce a break and you take several deep breaths.

You could always ask for this to stop? But what then? You will be fucked by a large number of strange men. Even worse, you will earn her anger, and she will either punish you or abandon you. And then what will you have? What will you be without her attention and love?

Soon another woman is in front of you, selecting the sixth dildo. She disappears behind you and once again your cheeks are pulled apart and the dildo is thrust inside your ass. When you are filled with the seventh device, the penetration hurts and you start to pant. Sweat beads on your forehead and runs down your back. Each insertion and removal that follows causes you to grunt audibly.

When the tenth device is in use, you actually gasp; it feels so huge inside you. But this one is left protruding from your ass as another break is taken by the guests.

You can only imagine how you must look and you flush deep red.

Your arse squirms and you can hear chuckles.

She stands next to you, holds your hand.

'M-m-madam?'

'*Oui*, my sweet?'

"M-may I-I s-speak?'

'Yes, *ma chérie*.'

'H-h-how many are left?'

'Eight. Just eight to go.'

'Oh God, oh my God.'

'You can do it.'

'Oh Madam …'

'I have faith in you, darling.'

You feel the tenth removed and feel air whoosh up inside your gaping hole. You clutch her hand tight and close your eyes. The eleventh, the twelfth, the thirteenth, the fourteenth and the fifteenth, all force a desperate cry from you, both on entry and removal.

You feel lubricant running down your leg ... or something else ... from your arse to your leg, dripping ...

Your ass feels as though it will never close again. It feels so wide open. Another break is taken but you cannot stop panting. Your bottom hurts so much.

Didn't she say you would not be hurt? Perhaps she meant permanently.

'M-m-madam?'

'Yes, my pet?'

'M-may I s-s-s-s-speak?'

'Go on.'

'W-will you be dis-disappointed if I-I cannot d-do more?'

'No, pet, you have done much more than anyone believed you could. I am impressed.'

'B-but if I stop, they will ... they will fuck me. The men ...'

'It is all right. I will not think any less of you.'

'Not men, n-never m-men, Madam.'

'I know, sweet.'

'Oh madam, I hurt – I h-hurt.'

'It will go away. Be as strong as you can. I am very proud of you, pet.'

The break is over and the fifteenth device is removed, forcing another gasp from you. You whimper softly. You feel the pressure and groan out loud as the sixteenth dildo slides into your ass. It feels impossibly huge and your ring is burning. Panting hard, you feel it slide back out, pulling your ring with it. You grit your teeth and grunt as it pops out. Through tear-stained eyes you see the next woman pick up an enormous, grotesque dildo.

You strain to be still and quiet, but when the tip

touches your anus you cannot bear it.

'S-stop, p-please s-stop.'

The dildo is removed. You hear excited murmurs.

She holds your hand tight and you stand on shaking legs.

You know what is coming next.

You feel hands on your dress and it is pulled down from your chest, over your ass and down your legs, leaving you naked save your stockings.

Your feet are pushed apart and you wait.

Before long you feel the prodding of a cock behind you and your vagina opens to take it. He thrusts into you and you moan softly. Your hips are grabbed and he fucks you, fucks you hard. His belly slaps against your rear. All you can do, all the energy you have only allows you to brace yourself for his thrusts. Mercifully, he is soon at his crisis and you feel the jets of life splashing inside the walls of your sex.

With his last jerk he pulls out and you immediately feel another cock poking at you and then pressing inside. He is no better than the first, fucking you hard and coming quickly. He pulls out and you must stand, bent, and let them all look at you.

At your abused flesh.

Sperm trickles out, running down your thigh. Naked, humiliated. You feel disgust at yourself.

You hear the excited voices leave the room. Only she remains with you. She releases you from the bar and puts the wrap around you. Your fancy evening dress has disappeared. The chain is clasped and she takes your hand. The two of you walk out together.

You hobble because your bottom hurts.

She leads you through the front door and to the limousine.

This time when the driver opens the door, she helps you inside and sits next to you.

You are taken in her arms, she holds you a long time.

She does not say anything.

Until the limo stops and the door opens.

'Out,' she says.

She pushes you; the driver pulls your arm.

They handle you so roughly that you fall to the ground.

People stop and stare.

You lie on a narrow hard pavement, wearing nothing but the wrap.

The limo drives away.

There are at least a dozen men and women looking at you, some laughing.

You know the area. Soho. The lights, the music from the clubs.

Someone lifts you. Strong arms. Two men, in suits.

One says, 'We been expecting you.'

The other says, 'A dainty little birdie right on our doorstep.'

They drag you into some kind of club. A dark club. Loud, pounding music, a song from the 1980s: 'Candy-O' by The Cars ...

Inside, a woman with enormous breasts dances naked on the stage and men watch her.

'What are you going to do with me?' you ask softly.

'You are to be punished,' one of the men says. 'You are to dance and fuck here. For six weeks.'

You start to cry.

'At the end of six weeks,' the man says, '*she* may come and take you back. If you are lucky.'

You turn to me and say, 'Bloody hell.'

And you are right.

About the Story

I LIVED IN LONDON for three years (1996-1999) as both a student and a bum. London is where I had my first affair with an older man (I was 20 and he was 45) and my first serious lesbian relationship that lasted 13 months. My heart was broken in London. London can do that to you: excite and hurt you at the same time. My favourite bookstore was Murder One and my favourite band was Love and Rockets, and Bauhaus, of course.

The inspiration for this story comes from the older man rather than the girl I loved. Sometimes lust and love is about control and surrender – but how far can each party go? I was curious about D/s but ultimately I could not submit myself 100% to anyone, man or woman.

I went to some seedy strip clubs in Soho and I'd look at the dancers and wonder how they got there, what happened in their lives that found them wiggling and jiggling on the stage. I had fantasies that they were prisoners, made to dance, and was surprised that the notion turned me on.

The Girl on the Egyptian Escalator
by NJ Streitberger

SPENCER COULD HEAR HER from the top of the escalator. Having spent a frustrating hour trawling the china and glass department for a glass bowl to replace the one that had recently been sent to punchbowl heaven, he was irritated, tired and somewhat in need of a drink.

It was his own fault. Sale season at Harrods was rarely conducive to effective decision-making and he regretted entering the building almost as much as smashing Laura's bowl.

It had been a genuine accident. Unavoidable. Well, as unavoidable as domestic accidents involving excitable collies and their indulgent co-owners can be. He had simply been tossing a stuffed squirrel into the air for Jolyon to catch, making sure it did not get caught in Laura's mother's chandelier when the wretched dog, having secured the battered and much-chewed soft toy with a flying leap had swept his considerable tail across a low table, taking with it a small cigarette box (empty of cigarettes for many years) and the aforementioned fruit bowl, similarly devoid of contents.

Why anyone should wish to keep empty receptacles in places of extreme vulnerability was a mystery to Spencer but, due to the somewhat terrifying nature of his putative mother-in-law and the unassailable psychological grip she exerted on his bride-to-be, he kept his thoughts to himself.

He was marrying into genteel, patrician, vaguely aristocratic and very rich Knightsbridge old money. He had encountered Laura at a charity ball held at the Natural History Museum a year earlier. She had been accompanied by an American hedge-fund manager whose swarthy appearance and pitbull aggression had seemed entirely out of keeping with the pale, willowy blonde draped languidly on his arm. Spencer had been in a party of colleagues from the bank who were one of the charity's biggest patrons and had found himself sitting next to her during the lavish dinner. Her companion, whom Spencer had immediately dubbed 'The Neanderthal', had eaten little, perspired a lot and absented himself from the table more times than was strictly necessary, leaving Laura alone with a wobbly apologetic smile and an unspoken but evident entreaty to be rescued.

Spencer had done the honourable thing and seduced her. When she had taken him home to meet 'Mummy' and 'Daddy' he detected less a sense of approval than relief at the fact that he was Anglo-Saxon, British-born and had decent prospects in a more respectable branch of the much-maligned world of high finance.

Even so, he never felt quite at ease among the faded chintz and porcelain of the family home in Egerton Crescent and the feeling that he was a barely tolerated outsider was never far from his mind. Consequently, he had felt himself evolving into the kind of man that his relentlessly middle-class mother had always rather wanted him to be: polite to the point of obsequiousness, burying his natural masculine vulgarity beneath shovelfuls of politeness. He had even adopted their way of referring to Harrods, in effect the family's local store, as the 'corner shop' run by that 'loathsome little rug merchant'.

Much as he tried to deny it, he was having second thoughts about his future with Laura. Not that there was anything intrinsically wrong with her – she was beautiful in that deceptively wan, fragile way that covered a will of steel inherited, no doubt, from her imperious mother. As such she was perfectly suited to her position as head of valuations in the photography department at Bonhams which was situated, usefully, just around the corner in Montpelier Street. But he was beginning to wonder if the prospect of marriage to Laura was worth the aggravation of embracing her family for the rest of his life. It was a tough call.

Lately, his old self had started to cry out for exercise. Nights at Boujis with the boys, racing his mountain bike through red lights and along every pathway in Kensington Gardens except the one designated for bicycles. He was starting to rebel.

Now this. A frustrating, panic-induced trip to the 'rug-merchant's' corner shop. He had just managed to narrowly escape castration on one of the poles placed strategically for that very purpose at the head of the descending escalator, after a double-wide American woman had tailgated him through the store like a Mack truck, when the sound of a distant but arresting female voice rose to his ears from somewhere below on the adjacent ascending escalator.

'What are you thinking? You are a complete loser! I don't know why I bother. You're a total waste of time. How can you be so fucking stupid all the time!'

In spite of the fact that the as-yet-unseen origin of this tirade was evidently screeching, her voice was strangely attractive. Actress, he thought, without actually thinking. She has such marvellous projection. Her voice was raised, the volume high enough to reach several floors and yet there was no distortion, no ugliness in the tone. Only in the words themselves.

Yes, he thought. She must be an actress. And this is a performance.

Intrigued in spite of himself, he stared down at the ascending escalator, trying to find the creature responsible and the poor sap to whom the torrent of abuse was directed. Finally, after peering past swarthy men in designer stubble and bottle-blonde broomsticks, he saw her.

She was standing on the step above her victim, with her back towards him. He could see the wild raven hair, tossing around as she spewed her verbal venom, her shoulder blades tensing and shifting beneath her skin-tight jacket. He watched as her hands gesticulated wildly and seized the attention of everyone else crowded on to the escalator, as if they were her audience in a packed theatre.

With a half-smile of humiliation playing around his lips, the object of her contempt simply stood looking up at her rapt in a combination of self-loathing, wry amusement and sheer admiration. He was easily as tall as her, athletically slim with dark curly hair and a sharp nose. A handsome boy, Spencer thought. Thoroughly undeserving of this blatantly public act of humiliation. Already, he was writing the scenario, the back story that had led up to this appalling public spectacle.

As the two of them approached with agonising slowness, she suddenly turned around and their gaze met and locked. Her eyes flashed with an almost feral light, her mouth was curved in a way that was half-sneer, half-snarl. The poor fellow might have been wearing the trousers but there was no doubt about who was the Alpha creature in this relationship.

Spencer couldn't tear his eyes away. She saw him and stared straight through him, challenging him to say something. He clammed up, unable even to open his mouth. As they passed each other on the escalator, he descending, she ascending, he had the ridiculous compulsion to leap across the barrier between them and grab her, clutch her body against his and take her right there, right then, on the bloody escalator.

Christ. He hadn't had that kind of jolt for years.

She continued to stare at him, their heads twisting as they passed, as if their eyes were linked by an invisible thread. His insides felt funny, as if someone was messing about in his bowels. Eventually, she gave a kind of snort and a sneer and turned her face back towards her victim. He seemed smaller, shrunken in the process, as if some vampire had sucked his life essence out of him, leaving him a husk hanging on to the handrail of the escalator. He was, Spencer thought, ready for the sarcophagus, doubtless inspired by the elaborate Egyptian fakery of the walls and the decorative plasterwork surrounding the escalator. He was mummified, the living dead.

Poor sod.

He reached the bottom of the escalator and tried to look back up but was prevented from standing still by the avalanche of bodies coming after him; though he did catch a glimpse of her swaying raven hair as she stepped off the end of the moving staircase. Oddly, he could not see the about-to-be ex-boyfriend at all, though he should have been standing right behind her. He seemed to have disappeared. All this was academic, however, as he was immediately caught in the surging crowd and was swept out towards the front doors of the store and soon found himself standing in the street.

He wandered along Knightsbridge in a kind of dream

state for a while, idly staring into shop windows not because he wanted to but because it was expected of him. It was a kind of Pavlovian reaction. Look. Want. Acquire.

If only he hadn't 'looked' at her.

He tried to distract himself by considering the need for a pair of Church's half-brogues, reduced to the not-unreasonable sum of £160. He knew he already owned a pair of brogues but a chap can never have enough shoes. He passed on, wandering into Uniqlo and idly sorting through the skinny fit jeans that were reduced by 30% with an extra 10% discount at the till if bought today. He needed another pair of jeans like a hole in the head.

He knew what he was doing. Displacement activity, it was called. He went back into Knightsbridge and tried to urge his feet towards the Victoria & Albert Museum. Maybe culture would cure his ills.

He was just about to cross the road when he suddenly stopped moving, causing a man with a mobile phone clamped fiercely to his ear to bump into him and swear.

Without another thought, Spencer turned and started walking back towards Harrods.

Inside, he headed straight for the Egyptian escalator, pushing and shoving his way through the crowds. Once he was on and ascending, he studied every passing face. He went right to the top of the store and raced through each department, trying to retrace his steps at the same time attempting to imagine which department she was likely to have been headed for. He searched in vain and eventually wound up back on the escalator, descending disconsolately to the ground floor, taking one last desultory look at the people who passed him, ignoring their hostile glares.

As he stepped off at the bottom he saw her standing by the door, looking at him.

'Having fun?' she said, with an arch of an eyebrow worthy of Vivien Leigh.

'I thought ...' he began, changing tack halfway through. 'Where's your friend?'

'He's history,' she said, leading the way out of the store.

Shirt buttons popped and flew across the room and expensive La Perla silk tore as they attacked each other in her Flood Street flat. There was no time to think, no time to consider the folly of their union. It was crazed, sweaty, slippery-slidey-crawling-all-over-each-other sex. He drank in her odours, nuzzling her nipples into hardness and sucking on the miniature pink volcanoes. He delighted in her unshaven armpits, slick with musky sweat and felt her hand beneath his balls, pulling him inside her. In their frenzy they fell off the bed, still engaged in loin-to-loin combat, and rolled across the floor until he had her pinned against the wall, to ram into her with such force it was if he wanted to push her through the wall into the next room, or the next dimension. She had one hand on his shoulder, digging her nails into his flesh for purchase and the other on his buttock, pumping him into her. She bit his chin as she climaxed, drawing blood, and he howled as he reached his own orgasm.

After some moments of breathlessness, they subsided and he collapsed onto his back, flopping out of her. She stood and stepped over him, walking towards the kitchen. In a blur he watched the sway of her sweat-slicked bottom, admiring the shameless manner of her stride which revealed the soaked tuft of dark fur between her thighs and the way she stretched her arms upwards to ease the muscles.

He heard a bang and sat up, vaguely nervous. She

came back into the room, holding a bottle of champagne. She swigged straight from the bottle and scattered some of it over his cooling body before handing him the bottle. He drank, coughed and drank again.

'I love the Sales,' she said. 'You never know what you're going to find.'

It couldn't last, of course. Not at that level of intensity. He did his best and, to be sure, she inspired him to extraordinary feats of stamina that surprised him. She was nothing like Laura, whose enthusiasm in bed was tempered with a well-bred politeness that he now realised was a terrible turn-off. Laura always came with a delicate 'Oh-Oh-Oh!' and then immediately took a shower and brewed a cup of Lapsang.

Sekhmet, on the other hand, was an animal. She just threw on her clothes and took him out to San Lorenzo still stinking of sex, often rubbing her hand over his crotch underneath the table as he tried to eat his asparagus risotto without groaning.

'Where did you get a name like that, anyway?' he asked her, when he could breathe again after a particularly savage workout.

'I was named after an Egyptian goddess,' she said.

'That's funny,' he said. 'You don't look Egyptian.'

She struck him playfully, leaving talon-marks on his cheek.

'My friends call me Seksie,' she said.

'I can't begin to imagine why,' he whimpered as she wrapped her fingers around his aching cock.

It didn't take long for Laura to realise there was something amiss. Exhausted by Sekhmet's insatiable appetites, he was unable to fulfil Laura's relatively modest requirements. It was when she noticed a particularly musky smell on his shirt that she twigged. There were tears, recriminations and the summoning of the parents. As far as they were concerned, he was toast. He moved out of the flat they had bought together in Queensgate Place and into a rented studio in Earl's Court, which in spite of their proximity was a bit like moving from Maidenhead to Mars.

In his little kitchenette, Spencer poured a glass of Shiraz and wondered where his life was going. Clearly, he was in the throes of sexual obsession and although he felt regret at the loss of Laura and all that she represented – wealth, respectability, comfort – he was inclined to believe that he had made, albeit by default, the correct decision. Marriage to Laura would have evolved too quickly into a plateau hemmed in by a narrow circle of friends whose social circumstances kept them circling the same limited pool of interests. Charity balls, dinner parties, property portfolios, art to be collected rather than admired and explored. No, it was not for him. Boredom would have set in. It would have been far too restricting. All things considered, he was better off without her. Even so, he wondered just how long he would be able to keep up with his new companion.

He started to fade at work, exhausted to the point that his concentration ebbed. As the markets collapsed, he lost the edge he needed now more than ever to shift and sell, buy and jettison. The computer screens blurred, his mind slowed down, clotted with images of Sekhmet. Physically, he was a ruin. His body was one big bruise.

He was summoned into Sir Trevor's office.

'What the devil's going on, Spencer? Your figures are atrocious. We're all in the same boat here and we cannot afford this kind of slippage. Are you on drugs?'

'God, no. No, sir …' he stammered. 'I, just, er, I'm a bit tired that's all.'

'Tired? Tired!' exploded Sir Trevor. 'You can't afford to be tired. Nobody can these days. This is your one and only warning. Shape up or ship out.'

He went back to his station, depressed and totally demotivated.

'You wimp,' she said, when he unwisely told her of his troubles at work. 'Why didn't you tell him where to get off?'

'Because I'll never get another position like this. The market is already overcrowded. And there are plenty of younger chaps out there just itching to step into my shoes. There's a recession on, you know. In case you hadn't noticed.'

Clearly, she hadn't. Whatever it was that she did, which remained a mystery to him, Sekhmet was evidently well-heeled. Her flat in Chelsea was spectacular, filled with expensive *objets d'art* of museum quality, however she acquired them. Yet she treated everything around her with a cavalier disregard for their value. In the throes of passion, they had smashed at least two Chinese vases from the Tang dynasty and toppled a Roman sculpture, chipping off an ear – events which would have caused apoplexy in any curator. Sekhmet simply brushed the pieces into a black plastic bag and dumped them in the dustbin.

'What do you, er, do?' he asked Sekhmet as she untangled herself from the sheets and stood up.

'I'm a consultant,' she said over her shoulder and went into the kitchen to locate a bottle of champagne.

'Who are your, uh, consultees?' he asked, attempting to rise from the wrecked bed.

'Oh, you know. The British Museum. The Egyptian Museum in Cairo. Places like that.'

'I see.' He didn't.

'Anyway, why do you want to know?'

'No reason. It's just …'

'Where do you think you're going?' she asked, pushing him back down onto the bed. 'We've only just started.'

Oh Christ, he thought.

'I hope you're thirsty,' she said, looking down at him, swinging the freshly popped bottle of bubbly in one hand like a club.

'Yes,' he said. 'Parched, actually.'

'Good. Stay there and don't move.'

She lay on her back beside him, raised her hips and opened her legs. While he watched, fascinated, she spread the lips of her cunt and emptied the contents of the bottle inside her.

Oh my God, he thought, suspecting what was to follow.

She tossed the empty bottle aside, knocking an Ancient Greek amphora off a plinth onto the floor, where it smashed.

Pinning his shoulders to the bed with her strong hands, she sat astride him, sliding her wet cunt up his chest until she was sitting astride his face. Positioning herself over his lips, she relaxed her vaginal muscle and pissed the newly aromaticised champagne into his open mouth. He drank and gagged, choked and spluttered as the foaming liquid sluiced down his throat and entered his nose, virtually drowning him in a stream of vintage Bollinger and Eau de Vulva.

As it ended and he started to get his breath back, she lowered herself onto his face and began rubbing herself back and forth over his lips and nose, smothering him in her musky, salty, champagney cunt.

'Stick out your tongue,' she commanded. 'Make it stiff.'

She rubbed faster, sliming his face with a combination of juices and secretions, locating his nose with her engorged clitoris.

As she moved faster and faster, her orgasm rising from her centre of operations, Spencer felt that his features were being rubbed away and that he would end up a faceless zombie doomed to roam the city streets after dark – the erased man.

She roared as she came, clawing the wall in her ecstasy.

A little while afterwards, she flicked his flaccid cock with a contemptuous fingernail.

'Well, lover. What shall we do now?' she asked, with a cruel curve of her mouth.

Too drunk to fuck and too fucked to drink, he could do nothing but groan in reply.

Having called in sick the following morning, he looked up the number of the British Museum. Three tablets of Berocca fizzed noisily in a glass on his faux granite kitchen top.

'British Museum.'

'Oh, hello. Can you put me through to the Egyptology Department?'

'Certainly, sir. Hold for one moment, please.'

Three seconds passed.

'Egyptology.'

'Oh, yes. Hello. I am trying to trace one of your

consultants. I am doing some research and someone gave me her name as a possibly useful contact.'

'I see. What is the name?'

'Sekhmet.'

'Sekhmet what?'

'I'm sorry, I don't know.'

'Is this some sort of joke?'

'Oh no. Not at all. But I assume there can't be many people with that name working there.'

'I can assure you, sir, that there is no one of that name working here or even associated with the Museum. Not alive, at any rate.'

Spencer's scalp tingled. 'What do you mean?'

'Sekhmet is the name of an Ancient Egyptian deity. There are several extant images of her in existence. It is highly unlikely that anyone would name their daughter after her.'

'Why would that be?'

'Because she is considered the most formidable and destructive of the Egyptian gods. She is usually depicted with the head of a lion. In the Ancient Egyptian world her name is synonymous with overwhelming female power and bloodshed. She is also known as The Mistress of Dread or The Lady of Slaughter.'

'Oh, er, I …'

'Now, if you've quite finished wasting my time, I have better things to do. Goodbye, sir.'

The line went dead. Spencer put the receiver back very, very gently.

The crunch came when he failed to perform one Saturday afternoon, after she grabbed him on the sofa where he had been dozing in front of the Six Nations Championship.

She stood over him, having pulled on her jeans without

94

bothering with underwear, and sneered down at him.

'Time to go,' she said. 'The Sales are on.'

'Oh no,' he groaned. 'There are loads of sales. Why now?'

'There is only *one*,' she said.

And so he found himself standing on the Egyptian escalator as she spat her venom at him. Too tired to respond in kind, diminished and defeated, he suffered the agonies of public humiliation in a kind of bewildered daze, like a naughty little boy or a dog who had peed on the carpet.

'You're useless!' she screamed, glaring down at him from the step above. 'Call yourself a man? You're so fucking wet you should be going out with a sponge, not a real woman. You're nothing but a loser. Go back to Mummy, loser!'

Although he was dimly aware of people staring at him he just stood and took it, a half-smile on his lips.

'Look at me when I'm talking to you! See? You can't even look me in the eyes. Where is your spunk? I don't know what I ever saw in you.'

He was about to say something when she turned and stared across at the descending escalator. A young blond man with a rugged, weather-beaten face and an athletic figure was staring at them with amusement. He looked pityingly at Spencer who could do nothing but smile stupidly back and watch as the guy turned his attention to Sekhmet. Spencer recognised the look – the blond guy was experiencing the same impact that had struck him a few months earlier. Don't, he thought. Don't look. And whatever you do, don't turn back. You'll be sorry.

But it was too late. The guy was hooked.

Spencer was so weak he couldn't summon the energy

to challenge her, to resist the inevitable. Trailing behind her he could feel himself growing smaller. It was an illusion, of course, a manifestation of his psychological diminution.

All the same, when the escalator reached the top and Sekhmet walked off, she heard a woman who was standing two steps behind her comment in a conspicuously loud voice: 'God, this place is filthy. Look at that pile of dust. You'd think that loathsome little rug merchant could afford to employ decent cleaning staff.'

Not that it mattered. Spencer was nowhere to be seen. And by the time the escalator had completed its circuit, the pile of dust was gone for good.

THE STORY WAS INSPIRED by a true incident. A cut-glass bowl was indeed smashed by the over-enthusiastic sweep of my border collie's tail. I did make a trip to the store in question during the sales to try and replace it without success, though that's another story.

I was born in the East End, grew up in South London and have lived in Earl's Court, Kilburn and Chelsea. Like most Londoners, I am fuelled by an urban machismo that gives me licence to defend my city to the death against any detractors. Call me old-fashioned, but I'm with Samuel Johnson on this one.

Knightsbridge is an area that I know well as I pass through it almost every day en route to somewhere less self-satisfied. However, I am a sucker for The Sale (There Is Only One) and have flashed my plastic on more occasions than I care to remember in the Men's Dept. But when you can snap up a pair of size 12 Edward Green shoes for £99 instead of £595 it seems worth the hassle of running the gauntlet of unleashed predators who are prowling for the similar bargains.

Given the fact that London is both an ancient city and a trans-cultural metropolis it seems perfectly reasonable to suggest that ancient Egyptian deities (among other mythical creatures) would be as attracted to it as American bankers and French chefs. We live cheek by jowl with the past and while I have never met a woman quite like Sekhmet, I know plenty of people who have.

Not long ago, I spent some time with the man responsible for the extraordinary carvings and construction of the Egyptian Escalator and as a result I felt an overwhelming urge to use it as the backdrop for a story.

Apart from the opening gambit, the rest of the story is pure fiction. Cross my heart, Darling.

The Caesar Society
by Kristina Lloyd

I LIKE SOHO. IT'S horrible. It used to be worse and I liked it even better then. Black doorways and neon-lit nastiness excite and appal me. I want to slip from the street and into a world where the women are all Rimmel and skag, where the carpets smell of come, and no one looks you in the eye except for cash. I hadn't mentioned this to him though. You don't, do you? Not before a first date.

We met on a website called Looking for Crooks. No, that's a joke, it was called something else. His username was The Big Man and, if you ask me, that's going to get any girl's attention. After a few emails and a nice phone call, we arranged to meet in a bar in Wardour Street, some chi-chi place full of media types close to my place of work. It didn't really suit him. In his giant's hand, his pint glass was dainty and I couldn't get over the size of his thumb. Nearly twice the length and thickness of mine, it rested against the glass, its broad, flat nail reminding me of the head of a cock. We talked about Spain (he was very tanned and said he had a holiday home there) but mainly I was thinking how his thumb looked like a cock, albeit a rather flattened cock, and I was wondering how it would feel to have him crushing his big fingers into my cunt, his great bulk looming over me as I came.

After one drink (two for him) we left for a Mongolian

restaurant where he said we'd get the best treatment because he knew the owner. It was early autumn, an evening of people clinging on to summer as it ebbed away. Bars and restaurants gleamed with light, mellow like old apples in a hay loft or cosily orange like pumpkins and bonfires. Smokers clustered on the pavement, chatting, laughing, talking on their phones and rubbing their arms against the cold. I felt as if they all knew something I didn't, something important about clothes or films or the right thing to say. They seemed bony, fast and made of surfaces. My date drew a deep, deliberate breath, cast grandly about his surroundings, and said, 'Ah, I remember when all this was whores.'

I found him embarrassing. They fussed over him in the restaurant. Staff from the back came out to shake his hand, grinning with an enthusiasm bordering on panic as he clapped them on the shoulder. I wasn't introduced. Show-off, I thought, though I didn't know who he wanted to impress, the staff or me. En route to the restaurant, we walked through Walkers Court, a sleazy little alley top-heavy with XXX signs, its brash adverts making an urban twilight of sulky purple and cheap red neon. It got me right there, right in that place of shame and longing, but I played it cool. We passed back the same way after dinner, walking through those colours of fucking, the purples, reds and pinks bleeding into the night. I didn't know what to do or what to say about it all. I think he was watching me. I think he saw that I was bothered and aroused by the vulgarity and the soulless, transactional trash.

We had sex that night at his place, a sparsely furnished bachelor pad above a supermarket in Chinatown. It would be unfair (though not inaccurate) to call him fat. He carries some extra weight, mainly around his gut, but he carries it with confidence. He looks good – staunch and solid – because he's six and a half feet tall, and he is mighty. Naked, he's almost majestic, his torso a curve of polished pine sprinkled with dark hair, and his arms are big and strong. He said he worked in construction (on and off) and he had the body you might expect of a man who spliced hard labour with easy living.

I like fat men because I climax more easily when I straddle them. My clit anchors to their bulk as we fuck and my inner thighs bounce on cushioned flesh. It's comfy. Fat men generally know how to make a good breakfast too. My desire for the fatties, however, is pragmatic rather than erotic. I never fantasise about them. I fantasise about lean muscle, sneering thugs and men who could do me harm. But I quit chasing the bad men a few years ago, figuring it was best to keep them locked up in the safe space of my head. But I did try, really I did. I tried to find a man who could switch on the meanness for kicks then switch it off and become a person who was warm and kind, who had a GSOH and was 'comfortable in his own skin', a phrase I've discovered to be very popular on dating websites. Eventually I decided if these men exist, they're all taken.

My craziest moment was joining a fantasy-fulfilment network called The Caesar Society. Seize her. Get it? The group catered for those of us with kidnap fantasies. They made a big deal of the fact the founders were a bunch of professional women who wanted recreational sex, no strings attached. For a tidy sum, they'd arrange for you to be 'kidnapped' by guys who kinked for this but knew how to play safe and who'd been thoroughly vetted by the organisation. How, I wondered, do you get a job checking out men's kidnap skills? It sounded more fun than data analysis. I completed a detailed Caesar questionnaire, submitted to a video interview and identified a range of men who buttered my muffin.

Fat men didn't make the list. They came later when I bottled out of the whole deal. I was a nervous wreck. I couldn't sleep at night for fear someone would break in and rape me (even though I hadn't ticked that option). Walking alone was fraught with genuine danger. How could I know whether the footsteps quickening behind me belonged to a hero intent on fulfilling my fantasies, to a nasty piece of work or neither? Even though The Caesar Society stipulated sex attacks would only happen within agreed time frames, my sense of self-preservation became so skewed that I terminated my membership and decided to centre my energies on a safer option: fat blokes, big bastards. Men who couldn't run as fast as me.

Things went well with The Big Man (aka Dave) for few weeks. I had a lot of orgasms and we entertained each other, in part because we didn't have much in common so everything was news.

'Wow,' I would say, 'I didn't know you could get stuff like that past customs.'

'Javascript?' he would say. 'Isn't that some poncey coffee?'

He was in his late forties, me in my early thirties. We both knew the relationship was going nowhere but there was a tacit understanding that was cool for now. It passed the time. Then he asked me to meet a friend of his for lunch in Soho. He meant just me and the friend, not the three of us. Dave had something confidential he wanted handing over and couldn't do it himself, too busy.

'Recorded delivery?' I suggested.

'Easier if you do it, Ali,' said Dave. 'It's just this envelope. Plus, I reckon you'll like him.'

He was right about that. Mack (as in Mack the Knife) was waiting for me in an Italian greasy spoon, a poky little caff decked out in formica and plastic. Cocky and cool in a slate-blue suit and open collar, he sat with his arms on a table, steepling his thumbs, a man with money but no class. I sat opposite him on a red, vinyl banquette. In the corner, a fruit machine was winking lemons and cherries, and the cup of tea I ordered was so strong and stewed I read it as a sign I wasn't welcome back.

Mack had a handsome face, cheekily boyish but aged, and his shorn hair was an extraordinary colour, a honey-beige shining like an animal's pelt on the dome of his skull. Above one ear, a small scar of hairlessness flashed a note both tender and menacing. I thought how heavenly it would be to have his head between my thighs, his hair smooth as velvet as his thick wet tongue splashed in my thick wet folds. I pushed the thought aside, trying to focus on the task in hand.

My instructions were to conceal the envelope, on which Dave had written '3', inside a newspaper then set both down on the table. After lunch, Mack would take the paper with him. Well, I kept my side of the bargain but the subterfuge seemed pointless because after a few minutes of stilted chat, Mack retrieved the envelope and slit it open with a finger. A heavy silver watched flashed below his sleeve, pale wiry hair romping around the strap. Boy, how I love a man suited and booted with a big wristwatch on a hairy arm.

Mack grinned, removing a strip of paper to study it. I could see a line of handwriting but couldn't make out the words. After several moments, he looked up at me with fresh, interested eyes. His grin broadened.

Oh the shark has pretty teeth dear,
And he shows them pearly white
'Can I ask what this is about?' I said.
'You can,' said Mack. 'But we won't tell you.'

103

Oh, be still my beating heart! A man who takes such pleasure in his own casual cruelty is a man who can tie me up in knots – literally, if I have anything to do with it. Mack opened his book, a doorstep of a thriller with gold embossing, and slotted the strip of paper between a couple of pages, leaving the first few letters visible. He was playing games, toying with my curiosity. At first, I refused to take the bait. I picked up the menu and ordered pasta with tomato sauce. That was it; just pasta and tomato sauce. No frills here. Mack said he'd already eaten.

'You're not much of a lunch date, are you?' I complained.

When I thought he wasn't looking, I dropped my eyes to the slip of paper and read VKH. A car registration? I ate about a third of my pasta, a huge dish of spaghetti flecked with red. No one came to stand by our table with an enormous pepper mill and a gentle smile. When Mack's phone rang, he excused himself and went to take the call outside. I didn't waste a second. On the slip of paper was a string of letters that made no sense. I could see at once it wasn't a foreign language, or at least no language I'd ever seen. So either it was a reference to something I knew nothing about or it was code. I'm good at code. I'm a computer geek. I worship Alan Turing. They hadn't banked on that. Keeping an eye on the door, I rummaged for a pen, cursing myself for having no paper in my bag, then wrote the letters on the underside of my forearm:

VKH LV D SDLO RI WLWV DQG D KROE.
XVH KHU.

The woman behind the counter glanced my way. She looked too tired to care. 'I need to get back to work,' I said when Mack returned.

He reached across the table and grabbed my wrist. He squeezed, giving my skin a tiny twist, and looked me dead in the eye. My groin flushed while my mind recoiled at his manhandling of me. Rude, arrogant bastard, I thought. And also: I bet you'd be great in the sack.

'I'm sure we'll meet again,' he said, releasing me.

His fingermarks were imprinted on my wrist. I was sure of it too.

I thought about him that night when I was straddling Dave, the aroma of dim sum and crispy duck mingling with the scent of sex. Streetlight filtered through curtains as red as the paper lanterns in the restaurants below, and the film of sweat on Dave's forehead took on the orange gleam of sodium; or perhaps that was the Spanish sun.

I closed my eyes and thought of Mack slamming me hard against a wall; Mack bending me over a table, fucking me in the throat. I thought about him tugging my hair and calling me a whore; thought about him wanking on my tits as I knelt at his feet, naked and bound; thought about his cock in his fist, in my cunt, my arse, my mouth. 'You're going to take it,' he'd say, 'whether you like it or not.'

Truth to tell, my thoughts had been non-stop dirty ever since I'd deciphered their code after lunch. It was a doddle. I'd suspected a Caesar cipher; it's the one most people know, a system where messages are encrypted by shifting the plaintext letters several places further along the alphabet to create the ciphertext. Told you I was a geek. The letter D in isolation most likely represented 'a' or 'I', our only single letter words. If it was 'a' that meant a shift of three. I sat at my desk, gazing at my inked arm. The number 3 had been written on the envelope, hadn't it? I tried it out, writing the letters on a scrap of paper.

SHE IS A PAIR ...

Afterwards, I realised it would have been easier to run their message through a decoder program but nerves were clearly getting the better of me. Halfway along, my hand began to tremble as I printed out the letters. My face burned with a surge of shame and arousal.

SHE IS A PAIR OF TITS AND A HOLE. USE HER.

Me? How dare they? How very dare they? Hell, no wonder Mack had given me that interested smile. Well, the filthy, conniving, presumptuous bastards! I was furious, and yet ten minutes later, I was jilling off in a toilet cubicle, wondering if Mack's cock had been hard beneath the table in that skanky little caff. But really, how dare they?

It was only after I'd climaxed that it occurred to me the note might refer to someone else. I was disappointed, not to mention baffled. I was worried, too. I didn't want to call everything off with Dave, not yet while the sex was still OK, but maybe I was getting into territory too murky and dangerous for me.

A couple of days later, Dave asked me to meet Mack again, same place, same deal. I considered refusing. I didn't want to be a pawn in their mysterious game, but Mack was hot and I am weak, so I agreed. Trying to convince myself that maybe the pawn could become a queen, I steamed open Dave's envelope (it read '6') over the kettle in the staffroom. Back at my desk, I entered the gobbledegook into a decoder:

SNATCH HER TOMORROW. SHE FINISHES WORK FIVE THIRTY. ARCHER ST. FOLLOW HER. GET HER TO THE ROOM. MEET YOU THERE. SHE WILL LOVE IT.

My heart raced, hammering out a binary of fear and

excitement. Archer Street. It had to be me. Oh sweet Jesus, they were planning to abduct me. Until that point, I hadn't made a connection with The Caesar Society. As far as my love life went, the network was old news. I hadn't thought about it for months. But now a couple of guys were plotting to snatch me off the street and were using a Caesar shift to communicate with each other.

Eventually, I figured it had to be coincidence because I could find no connection that made sense. I racked my brains wondering if I'd ever told Dave I got off on kidnap fantasies. I imagined I probably had. I'd revealed a lot of stuff. For the most part, it seemed to amuse him. He was strictly vanilla and I felt it important for him to know that I wasn't; I was just a pervert down on her luck. So was Dave trying to fulfil one of my fantasies? Well, that was kind of him – but naïve in the extreme.

I practised his handwriting for a while – a fairly easy challenge since the note was in upper case – then encoded a different note:

SNATCH HER TOMORROW. SHE FINISHES WORK AT THREE. ARCHER ST. FOLLOW HER. GET HER TO THE ROOM. YOU ARE ON YOUR OWN. TIE HER UP. TORMENT HER. FUCK HER. MAKE HER COME. SHE IS ALL YOURS. BITCH WILL LOVE IT.

Writing that got me horny as hell, and I had to resist expanding it into a long, pornographic letter detailing exactly what I wanted him to do to me. I felt bad for Dave. It might have been fun to have him there, intensifying my shame, but to be honest, I was starting to go off him. I conceived of my interest in Mack as comparable to a Caesar shift of one. Dave was the cipher, a substitute for what I really sought, but now I'd budged one along his social circle and sussed out that my truth lay in knobbing his best mate. OK, so I realise that may sound a little screwy but we've all done it, haven't we? Used the lamest justifications to excuse our bad behaviour?

Throughout my lunch date with Mack, I tried not to act like a lust-sick loon. Oh, but he was such a perfect combination of beautiful and brute, his mink-blond crop gleaming under the strip lights, his big, macho watch glinting under his cuff. He listened to me yak on about a film I'd seen recently at Screen on the Green, his head tilted, his gaze diamond-sharp and ironic.

'Doesn't sound like Dave's cup of tea,' he said.

'No,' I replied, and I tried to explain that Dave and I don't have much in common, that our relationship is based on other stuff (he smiled slyly at that), and that Dave doesn't come to my part of town because I live in Islington. OK, so I live in an ex-council flat on the wrong side of Islington, but it's Islington nonetheless; we drink a lot of macchiatos there and Dave doesn't. Besides, it's easier if I meet Dave straight from work, and anyway I'd hate us to bump into my friends. They wouldn't understand. It would be embarrassing.

When I left work early the next day, having invented some cock and bull tale about needing to see a dentist, I was giddy with excitement. My legs were feeble and the pavement beneath my feet was made of marshmallow, the air as thin and debilitating as mountain-top air. I saw no sign of him but thought it best not to look. Instead, I fiddled with my iPod to give him a chance. Seconds later, I sensed him behind me, felt his approach, saw his shape looming over my shoulder.

And someone's sneakin' 'round the corner
Could that someone be Mack the Knife?

I spun, my heart thundering, then the world tipped as

he hooked his arm across my belly and dragged me sideways, a hand clamped to my mouth, my earphones flinging across my vision. A flash of grey sky, square high windows, street lamps, bollards, cobbles and yellow lines collapsed into one jagged scene as I stumbled with his brogues into the windowless recess of an office doorway. He pressed my back to the wall, his hand still covering my mouth, and fixed me with a cold grin.

My breath pumped hot and hard against his palm. He leaned close. Over his shoulder, below a security keypad, were the names of the businesses who occupied the building, too small for me to read. I don't know what goes on behind the closed doors around here. Mack's voice was low and scratchy. 'Consider yourself kidnapped, bitch.'

My legs practically gave way, a whoosh of horniness flooding my groin. I'd grown so used to dreaming of being overtaken that the intensity of the experience knocked me for six. It was real, it was happening, no cipher substitute.

'Don't say a word,' he warned. 'Don't even try.'

His hand over my mouth made me feel paradoxically safe, reminding me of bitterly cold schooldays when I'd wait for the bus, feeling pleasantly cocooned with a scarf wrapped over half my face, my breath making a pocket of humidity against the wool. Mack edged closer, angling his body to shield us from passersby. We probably looked like a randy couple or maybe a pimp sorting out his tart. Either way, no one paid us any attention.

He ground against me with deliberate, intimidating lechery. I could feel his erection jutting against the soft cloth of his suit. In a whisper, he said, 'You're gonna get this big dick inside you soon. How about that, eh?'

I groaned into his hand. It's a miracle I didn't simply

slump to the floor and melt into a puddle of lust. But a jolt of fear kept me bolt upright as I suddenly realised I hadn't thought this through. Oh, Alison, you idiot! Too late now. Because supposing this wasn't about me at all? I'd been so blinded by fantasy, I hadn't considered the scenario from any perspective but my own. Supposing what they had in store for me went beyond anything I'd imagined? I thought I knew Dave, we'd been dating several weeks. But on the other hand, he was just some bloke I'd got off the internet, wasn't he?

'You're going to be very good,' murmured Mack. 'Aren't you?'

I nodded.

'Now I'm going to remove my hand and you're not going to scream or shout or do anything stupid. OK?'

Again, I nodded, and when he took his hand away I was as quiet as a petrified mouse. Mack's eyes were steely, his voice stern as he warned me to act like a girlfriend, to take his hand, keep my mouth shut and simply follow him. Funny kind of girlfriends you've had, I thought. But I said nothing and slipped my hand into his, both of us hot and clammy as we headed northwards through Berwick Street market. I wondered if we looked strange but the market, with its apples, oranges, knock-off jeans and household goods, and not a sliver of artisan cheese in sight, is such a throwback that no one would bat an eyelid at a meek, nervous girlfriend trotting loyally alongside her man. Me and my geezer, we were perfectly at home in the mish-mash of Berwick Street where old Soho rubs shoulders with the new.

He took me to a hotel. It was nothing special but all the same it must have cost him a whack.

'What the hell's going on?' I hissed.

'Don't ask questions.' Mack locked the door, cool as a

cucumber. He'd already checked in and had a few bits and bobs scattered around the room: a laptop on the dressing table, a jacket on the chair back, leaflets on the bed which was smooth and angular as hotel beds always are.

'Hey, I've every right to ask –'

'If you don't shut your fucking mouth,' said Mack, strolling towards me, 'I'll shut it for you.'

I folded my arms. 'Meaning what, exactly?'

Mack touched his thumb to my chin, tipping my head back to meet his eyes. 'Meaning one more stupid question and I'll gag you.'

I jerked away from his thumb. 'What sort of stupid question?'

'That sort.' He suppressed a smile. He knew I was goading him. 'Take your knickers off.'

'No.'

Mack gripped my face, pinching my cheeks so hard they hurt. He glowered at me. 'Take your fucking knickers off. Now. Or I'll tear them off.'

I obeyed, unsteady on my feet as I stepped out of my underwear, slipping the silkiness and lace over my best suede boots. Mack crossed the room to draw the curtains, blocking out the jumbled backsides of buildings and fire escapes peeping through the slatted blinds. He switched on a wall lamp above the bed, enclosing us in a small anonymous world where the light was soft and transporting. I could be anywhere, I thought, and anything could happen here.

Mack gestured for me to hand him the knickers then in one swift, evil movement, he scrunched the fabric into a ball and crammed it into my mouth. I spluttered in shock as he whipped a tie from his pocket and strapped it twice across my stuffed mouth, securing it at the back with a knot.

'Hands behind your back,' he said, grabbing my wrists and giving me no choice in the matter.

I twisted around to see him binding my wrists with a short length of rope. 'There.' He went to stand a few feet in front of me, hands deep in his pockets as he surveyed me. My breath came hard and fast. I felt his attention like a touch, sliding beneath my clothes and grazing my skin, squeezing my breasts and invading me with a gleeful disregard for my wishes.

'Gotcha,' he said, smirking. 'You're all mine now. And I'm going to use and abuse you till I'm bored, use that sweet little body of yours.' He shrugged off his jacket, slung it onto the bed, then turned back his shirt sleeves with neat efficiency, his watch winking as it caught the light.

He stepped forwards. 'Let's have a look at you, then.'

My pulses rushed as he set two hands to the top button of my blouse, my cheeks burning. I moaned behind my gag, implying I didn't want him to touch me but he continued, unfastening one button, then another. Between my thighs, my lips fattened and a beat hammered in the swelling flesh. I tossed back my hair in a gesture of disdain as he undid the third button and the fourth. Pushing my blouse open, Mack bared my pale cleavage and brown and blue bra which, had he cared, he would have noticed matched the knickers in my mouth.

'Nice tits,' he said matter-of-factly. He shoved my blouse further back so it was halfway down my arms then swooped a hand above my cleavage. He dipped his fingers into a bra cup, watching my expression as he found my soft, pliant nipple.

'Ah,' he sighed, swirling his fingers. 'I knew you'd like it.'

I shook my head, feeling the looseness of my nipple shrivel to tightness beneath his touch. After a short while, he withdrew, reaching round to clutch my arse. He pulled me close, rubbing his hard-on against my belly. 'Want some cock, do you?'

Again, I shook my head.

'Course you do,' he said. 'I have it on good authority. Bitch is gonna love it. Let's hear you say 'yes', shall we?'

I protested into my gag. He merely laughed and reached behind me to unfasten my bra, pushing it down to join the crumpled mess of my blouse bunched around my waist. The air was cool on my exposed breasts and, half undressed, I felt more naked than naked. Taking a nipple in each hand, Mack pinched lightly between thumb and forefinger. I inhaled sharply as he intensified the pressure, squeezing and twisting. The pain rose higher and higher and he held me there on a plateau of suffering until tears pricked my eyes. When he released me, the pain was slow to ebb away. I heaved for breath, panting through my nostrils, so stunned that he'd done that to me. So stunned and so aroused.

It was my Patti Hearst moment, the point where I started to bond with my captor, grateful for his acts of apparent kindness.

'Again?' he asked.

I gave a nod, reluctant and ashamed. He twisted my nipples once more, pulling and lifting my breasts. The pain ballooned and peaked, and he smiled at the stream of tiny bleats echoing in my throat. When he released me again, the pain receded to leave me shot through with sensation, my cunt throbbing at the centre of it all.

'Like that do you?' He reached for the hem of my skirt, hitched up the fabric and cupped my groin. He scoured the heel of his hand against my pubes then trailed

113

a finger along my slippery crease, spreading my lips. 'Ah yes, I can see that you do.'

I was wet, so wet and hot, and my juices spilled as he drove two fingers inside me, curling them onto my sweet spot. I tottered then steadied myself, my entire body fizzing with pleasure as he rubbed me there. Bowing his head to one breast, he took my flesh in a gentle bite, his tongue fretting the stiffened bud of my nipple. The room was silent save for my stifled moans and the soft clicks of my wetness being stirred by his fingers. I ached to stroke his velvety head and yet I loved that my hands were trapped and I couldn't. I could do nothing. All I could do was be done to. And Mack really did me.

When I thought I was on the brink of collapse, he ushered me to the bed, ordering me to lie back and spread my legs over the edge. My bound hands raised my buttocks and Mack dropped to his knees between my thighs. I closed my eyes, giving it all up to him as his supple lips fluttered over my folds and his clever tongue danced on my clit. He shoved his fingers into me when I was close, packing me with solidity, and I came in a rush with his lips on my clit, wailing into my gag as I shuddered and jerked.

Mack moved away from me. I lay there, bombed out on bliss, vaguely aware of him undressing. Moments later, he clambered onto the bed, kneeling astride me. 'Good girl,' he said, edging higher. 'I knew you wanted it. You want this as well?'

Half dazed, I struggled to understand where he was coming from. He was still there, still horny, still chasing it, whereas I was on cloud nine, my body glowing with the most delicious heat and exhaustion. Then I saw his nakedness towering above me, his cock big and virile in his fist, his flat belly rising to a broad chest whose pecs were taut and furred with gold. How could I have ever wanted a fat man? Mack straddled my shoulders, biceps flexing as he jerked his cock above my face, his balls leaping as his weighted sac hitched below his fist.

'You want some of this dick inside you, huh?' He angled himself to skim my lips and chin, his cock's glossy crown an obscene violet-red like the neon lights in Soho. The nearness of him, the smell of his musk, the hint of his power before my gagged mouth had me writhing in frustration.

'Go on then,' he said. 'If you want it, take it. Turn around. Get on your knees.'

I wriggled against my bound wrists, grunting into my gag, trying to show him I was helpless.

'Oh, come on,' he mocked. 'Don't give me that. On your knees. Show me your cunt. Come on, you little slut. Show me your cunt and I'll fuck it for you.'

Fire blazed in his cheeks, eyes bright, face twisted with passion. He wanked himself as if it were a threat, hurrying me to roll onto my belly and wriggle higher up the bed. He wanted it as badly as I did. Gathering my knees beneath me and using my shoulders as leverage, I managed to struggle into position, head to the bed, arse in the air, my neck in grave danger of getting a crick. I thrust back, searching for him, desperate to feel his penetration.

'That's right,' cooed Mack. He grasped my buttocks, steadying me as he slid the heavy bar of his cock up and down the wet split of my lips. My need for him was agony but clearly he liked making me suffer. He nudged at my entrance and for a terrible moment I thought he was going to keep doing that till I passed out with wanting. Then he rammed me with a sudden, sure bang, slamming himself to my core. I gave a muffled howl, grunting over and over as he began powering away at me, his hands

115

clutching my hips.

Inside, I was tender and swollen from coming and the fat thrust of his cock edged me to new heights. I felt loose and half-delirious, my mind spinning strange trippy patterns as he pounded me. Soon, he grew more frantic and he clasped me above the elbows, lifting my upper body so it was at right angles to his. I jerked like a rag doll on the end of his cock, shuddering and shaking as he drilled like a man possessed. Moments later, he released a series of rough, exuberant grunts then peaked on a half-roar of bliss, lodging himself deep as he shot his load.

He held me there as he caught his breath before gently lowering me to the bed. He removed my gag first. I ran my tongue around my gums and waggled my jaw.

'You OK?' He untied my wrists and stroked hair away from my face. 'Was it good for you?'

'Amazing,' I breathed.

'Likewise.'

We lay on the bed, feeling very pleased with ourselves. Outside, a car honked its horn several times, and I thought how great it was to have kidnap-sex in the afternoon when the rest of the world is busy and stressed.

At length, Mack said, 'A shame Dave couldn't make it.'

'Oh, I dunno. I quite like it this way, just the two of us.' I sat up, remembering I needed to text Dave to tell him I was at the dentist. I didn't want him turning up at the hotel and spoiling my one-on-one abduction.

'I know we should've played by the rules and arranged this via The Caesar Society,' began Mack, 'but I thought –'

'Via who?'

He gave a dismissive flap of his hand. 'You know, the usual shit. Pay through the nose, agree on the scene, fix a time, report back to – '

'I don't know what you're talking about,' I said.

I'm not sure if that was when my pawn became a queen but I did enjoy seeing Mack's face turn a little pale.

After a few emails, I got to the bottom of it. Turns out my membership had been mistakenly reactivated when another woman by the name of Alison Harris had signed up. I don't know who she is. I worry she's still hanging around some dingy street corner, waiting to get kidnapped. Anyway, Mack's a member of the Caesar society too and when he spotted me out with his mate, Dave, he recognised me from my old Caesar profile. Mack being a dodgy bastard thought he'd cut out the middle man and arrange a threesome with Dave's involvement – except he hadn't counted on me intercepting their messages and uninvolving Dave.

And the codes? 'Just a laugh,' said Mack. 'Spice it up a bit, you helping to arrange your own kidnap and not having a clue. 'Cept you did have a clue cos you're smarter than us.'

You can say that again. I got on to The Caesar Society and kicked up an almighty fuss about their error. Result? Major financial compensation for me and Mack, plus heaps of gratitude for our 'discretion'. In other words, they bought us off, terrified I'd go to the cops.

I like Mack. We understand each other. Best of all, we've decided to blow the money on a holiday to Sweden. He's going to snatch me in the capital and hold me hostage in our hotel room. And we're going to play out our very own Stockholm Syndrome, my abductor subjecting me to all manner of unspeakably sexy acts as I fall increasingly in love with him. And I'm going to send a postcard to Dave, labelled '2', and it will say:

OCEM JCU MKFPCRRGF OA JGCTV
Which means: Mack has kidnapped my heart.

About the Story

ABOUT TEN YEARS AGO, I worked in London's Soho as a sub-editor on a couple of adult magazines. Our offices felt isolated from the local hustle and bustle, and the job was fairly dull to me. Most of my days were spent in a small fourth-floor room adjoining an open-plan office. There were bars on the windows.

I got to know Soho's streets during my lunch hour or when I was sent out on strange errands. I remember one morning trawling sex shops for a pair of size-three stilettos which I then had to deliver to a nearby studio where a model and photographer were waiting to do a shoot. Sex shops at 10 a.m. are absurd, joyless places. Many aspects of Soho feel like that during office hours whereas in the evening, when the neon is glowing, a sleazy darkness comes alive. You can sense the contained excitement, the furtive lusts and shame. Risk hangs in the air.

I'm horribly fascinated by magic's tendency to become bleak and cracked in the cold light of day. I see that degeneration as laying bare desire's power to push us to do preposterous, and sometimes dangerous, things. I'm equally captivated by secrets and seediness. So much of Soho takes place behind closed doors and is never spoken of again. The selling of sex – or rather, of women and women's bodies – ranges from the blatant to the covert. The brightly advertised strip clubs and cinemas are easy to spot but look closer and you notice ordinary-looking doorways where only a handwritten note advertising French girls alerts you to the existence of a brothel.

It's interesting to see that shady world co-existing with the hipper, slicker world of media and publishing. In some ways, having a job on a top-shelf mag put me in both camps but I never felt I belonged in Soho. The area encourages anonymity; it feels like a city at its most intense. I don't think you can ever really know it; so much is unseen. In *The Caesar Society*, I was trying to capture that sense of feeling close to something hidden, hence the use of codes, the suggestion of clandestine networks and a criminal underbelly. I also wanted to draw on Soho's atmosphere of menacing masculinity and transform that so it became about active female desire. I think it's quite a romantic piece – in a sleazy, brutish kind of way.

The Champagne Whore
by Lily Harlem

SLUT RED, THAT'S THE only way to describe the shocking colour of my new lipstick; sticky, shiny, slutty red.

Perfect.

My working dress is also slut red, a daring halter-neck that leaves my slim, golden shoulders bare and the cleavage open to an inch below my rather modest breasts.

Clicking my patent slut-red heels through the grand lobby I especially like the way the soft material moves around my legs. It swishes just above my knees, not in a tight clinging way, but in a gentle flowing way that gives just a hint of the toned thighs and hips beneath.

I'm wearing fishnet stockings, a tight mesh that suits my small frame; hold-ups as opposed to a suspender belt, can't have lumps and bumps ruining the sleek lines of my figure.

The overall look is just as I intended, it befits a high-class whore and suits the exclusive Grosvenor House Hotel on Park Lane; the venue I've picked for tonight's sales pitch.

I glance at the display of exotic flowers flooding an antique mahogany table and sense the concierge looking my way. I strut a little more confidently, as if I belong, as if I am entitled to be here. I am – why shouldn't I be? I'm performing a service the same way he is.

Before me heavy double doors are propped open and a gold sign overhead reads 'Champagne Bar' in black writing. I walk in and the atmosphere mellows from the stiffly formal lobby to a distinguished but relaxed lounge. A huge fire blazes through subdued lighting and an excess of contemporary leather seating is dotted about.

There is a sleek bar and three middle-aged men in suits lean casually against it, drinks half-drunk, chatting in a familiar way. One of them looks at me; turns, comments, then they all scan me up and down. I give just the barest tilt of my lips and step around them. The floor here is thickly carpeted and my trip-trapping heels fall silent.

'Good evening,' one of the men says as I draw parallel.

'Hi,' I say. I quicken my pace and choose a stool around the far end of the bar. Behind me is a window, a huge expanse of black glass which glistens as the lights of Park Lane traffic fractures through the millions of raindrops streaking its surface.

The barman is attentive and I've barely seated myself and placed my slut-red purse on the bar when he's over. 'Champagne, madam.' He stands a tall flute of golden bubbles in front of me. 'Compliments of the three gentlemen.'

I raise the glass, smile and mouth cheers to the three men who are staring at me with hopeful expressions. But I don't let my attention linger, they're not my type, a bit old, a bit samey, not at all hunky.

I'm fussy – really fussy.

I can afford to be. I have a roof over my head, money in the bank and two kids doing rather well at private school. Being discerning about customers is a luxury I allow myself.

The bar is half full and as I savour the deliciously dry bubbles popping on the roof of my mouth, I check out the clientele. Several couples sit cosy on over-stuffed sofas, a few groups laugh with reserved mirth so as not to disturb the gentle ambiance and a pianist tinkles away near the fire; something lazily jazzy, un-intrusive and mellow.

There are two single men; one reads a broadsheet in a bucket chair by a table lamp and the other has a laptop on his knee and a glass of red wine in his hand. Neither looks my type, but it's OK, I know I'll get lucky if I bide my time.

I take another sip of champagne and my attention is caught by a shadow looming in the double doorway. A big bulk of a man is briefly silhouetted before he strides onto the carpeted area. He wears a charcoal-grey suit which fits his wide, six foot-plus frame to perfection and my heart does a happy flip of hope; he's so my type.

I've always had a thing for men with that overdosed-on-testosterone look. Big, burly chunks of muscle do seriously funny things to my stomach, my knees and somewhere else in-between. I find myself hoping his wallet is deep enough for me to have a good time as well as him. Not just a request for a quick blow-job – that's not my style. My rate is for the night, not individual acts, unless it gets kinky, then it's an open court for discussion and depends on my mood.

He stands at the bar beside the men who sent me champagne, dwarfing them as he catches the barman's attention. I lip-read his order of bottled beer, exactly what I'd have predicted, then I pout and run a hand through my long dark hair as his brooding gaze scans my way.

But his glance hits me so briefly and with such lack of interest I wonder if he's even noticed me summing him up. I try not to crease my forehead into a frown, reach into my purse and pull out a gold compact and my slut-red lipstick.

I keep my eye on the hunk.

He signs the drink to his room and the sight of his big-man hands tip me over the edge. That's it. He's my target for tonight; no one else will do. It's him or nothing.

He moves to take a seat nearer me, but not at the bar, a creased brown leather armchair next to a Tiffany lamp and with a view of Park Lane. I settle into re-applying lipstick and peer at his face over the compact. He has a strong, square jaw that protrudes slightly, giving him an air of pride, his nose looks like that of a rugby player, or a boxer. His mouth is wide and soft. I watch fascinated as he licks a drip of beer from his bottom lip and leans meaty shoulders back into the chair.

'Another champagne?' A quiet voice at my side jolts me from my study. I re-focus and see the shorter of the three men from the bar standing at my side.

'No, I'm fine thank-you,' I say watching his thin weasel moustache twitch.

'Perhaps a night-cap, a brandy perhaps, the hour is getting late.' He nods at the over-sized clock behind the bar which shows eleven.

'No, really, I'm fine.' I tuck away my compact and lipstick. 'Thank you so much for this one though.' I hold up the nearly empty glass.

'Well,' he says, and leans in so close I can smell his musty aftershave. 'I'm sure we could come to some sort of arrangement for you to say thank you properly.' He places a clammy hand on my bare arm.

I swallow tightly.

This is not what I want. Not by a long shot.

'The lady said no.' A deep voice growls.

Weasel man turns and comes face to chest with the hunk I'd been happily admiring until a few moments ago. 'What's it to you?' he questions in a squeaky voice.

'She's my date.' Hunk moves closer and Weasel side-steps around the corner of the bar to avoid becoming trapped. 'You got a problem with that?' Hunk adds with a scowl.

'No, no, not at all, I just thought she was alone … you were sitting over there.'

'Not any more.'

'OK, OK.' Weasel holds up his hands as if in surrender. 'No harm done, sorry mate.'

I watch with relief as he heads back to his friends giving a forced nonchalant shrug as he goes. 'Thanks,' I say releasing a genuine smile up at my rescuer.

I get one raised eyebrow in reply.

'Would you like to er … join me?' I ask.

He bangs his beer on the bar, pulls up a stool and sits down – very close. 'I'd better now I've told them you're my date.'

'I really appreciate it, unwanted attention can be a hazard for a woman like me.'

The same thick black eyebrow lifts again as his eye-line drops to my displayed cleavage. 'I'm guessing you want attention wearing that dress.'

'Oh, yes.' With a dainty flick of my tongue I lick my freshly glossed top lip. 'But I only like attention from a certain type of man.'

'And what type would that be, no …' he holds up his palm. 'Let me guess … the rich type.'

'Rich works, so does …' I pretend to be thoughtful, rest an index finger against my temple. 'So does … handsome.'

He snorts and rocks his head back. 'That rules me out then.'

I make a show of slowly dropping my eyes from his buzz-cut dark hair, over his slightly stubbled, rugged face and then down his suit, all the way to his shiny leather shoes, one of which rests on the gold bar of his stool. 'Another glass of champagne and I think you'd be very handsome to a woman like me.'

'Champagne it is.' He holds a hand up to the barman and using sign language orders two glasses. 'You gonna tell me your name?' He turns his attention back to me.

'Ruby.'

'Ruby.' He nods slowly. 'And tell me Ruby, what do you do for a living?'

'Can't you tell?' I reach for the fresh champagne the barman has placed next to me.

'I want to hear you to say it out loud.' His knowing eyes bore into mine; they're so dark they have no gap between pupil and iris.

'You want me to say it?'

'Sure, then we'll know where we stand and I won't make a cock-up that'll earn me a slap.'

'OK.' I tip my head and hold eye contact. 'I'm a whore.'

He grins and flashes a neat row of white teeth. 'A whore.' He rolls the word around his mouth. 'A whore. Ruby the whore. I think just whore is a better name, forget the Ruby.'

I shrug. 'Whatever turns you on …er …?' I extend the sentence wondering if he'll offer his name.

'You don't need to call me anything.' He lifts his champagne to his lips and takes a deep sip. His silver wedding band twinkles in the headlights of a passing Bentley. 'You want to set up a deal, Whore,' he says.

I like him calling me whore; he says it with such deliciousness; he savours each syllable and ekes out the 'r' at the end. His mouth plays with the word and I hope he wants to play with me that way. 'A deal,' I say, knowing I must stop fantasising and think business. 'What have you got in mind?'

He leans his head to mine, moves my long hair with the back of his hand and whispers into my ear. 'A quick fuck in the toilets.'

The request doesn't even deserve a response so I tilt my chin in the air with a haughty flick.

'Too downmarket for a whore like you, eh?'

'I could have had that with them.' I nod at the three guys at the bar ordering more drinks. 'I'm not up for that, not with you.'

'So what are you up for?'

'The whole night or nothing. Sex, foreplay, a soap down in the shower. Eight hours from the time we get to your room.'

'How do you know I have a room?' He frowns.

'I saw you sign your tab earlier.'

'You were watching me?'

'Why not? You look like you have deep pockets.'

A deep rumble of laughter spills from his lips. 'Not all I got in my pocket,' he says as he shifts his weight on the stool.

I smile but stay in business mode, cross my legs and hook a heel on the bar of my own stool. 'Fifteen hundred for the night.'

The smile slips from his face. 'You must be joking, you got a gold-plated pussy or something?'

'I never joke about money.'

'Me neither, seven hundred and fifty.'

'Thirteen hundred.'

'How do I know you're any good? You might shag like a sack of potatoes.'

'I can assure you I've never had complaints before, the odd heart attack yes, but no complaints.'

He props an elbow on the bar and leans in close. 'One thousand,' he murmurs. 'For the whole night, my rules, I'm in charge – you do what I say.'

'That could work.' I pretend to mull it over and try not to look too excited at the deal about to be struck and what delights might lay ahead. His cool water aftershave and his intensely primitive stare are making me wet for him already.

'But one thing first.' He straightens and his suit jacket stretches across his chest.

'What?'

'Uncross your legs.'

'Pardon?'

'You heard what I said – I want to sample the goods before I cough up a grand.'

'You want to sample the goods … here?'

'Oh, yeah, right here, right now, my rules, remember?'

I unfurl my legs and slide to the edge of the bar stool, grateful that apart from a few drivers whizzing along Park Lane I'm hidden from view to everyone in the Champagne Bar. He stands, nudges my legs further open and reaches back to pull his stool closer; sits back down.

I take a sip of champagne and feel a thrill as a cool finger sneaks up the hem of my dress on to my fishnets. I make a point of not reacting to the burst of pleasure as he winds higher and higher on to the warm flesh of my thigh. The material of my dress is bunched and rucked around his wrist and his wandering fingers find and sweep the silk gusset of my lace panties.

I don't look down though I know I'm on show, exposed, instead I hold a serene, confident expression as his unblinking eyes drill into mine.

'You're hot,' he whispers. 'Are you wet, too?'

'Just for you.' I squirm onto his inquisitive finger.

'Dirty little whore,' he mouths, a twitch catching his upper lip and a wicked glint sharding through his eyes. He pulls the elastic of my knickers aside and a single thick finger strokes up the soft folds of my now hyper-sensitive flesh and flicks over my buzzing clitoris. Just once, just enough to tease and make me want more.

I pull in a sharp breath and try not to let out a whimper as the barman walks over and removes our empty glasses.

'Would you like more champagne, sir?' he asks.

The exploring finger heads lower and begins to slowly push into my emptiness, filling me just a little. I can barely register what the question has been.

'We're fine thanks,' Hunk answers for me as he slides all the way in. I feel my spine soften and curl forward. I need more of what he's doing but I can't have it now, not here. I look up at the barman and see a fleeting, unreadable expression cross his face before he turns his back on us.

The finger pulls slowly out, knickers realign, and my dress is straightened to my knees. 'Well?' I ask, feeling a flush of colour rise on my cheekbones as I re-cross my legs, pretending the whole thing never happened.

My brooding client props his elbow on the bar and the light catches my glistening juices spread on his middle finger. 'Let's see.' He opens his mouth and pokes his long, moist finger in up to the knuckle. Then closing his eyes he withdraws it very, very slowly letting out a small murmur of approval as he does so. 'I think ...' he says, hardly opening his hooded eyes. 'You'll do very nicely, but I'll warn you, I don't spend a thousand pounds lightly, I'll be getting my money's worth. You think you can handle that?'

I practically melt into a boneless heap at the thought of him making sure he gets his money's worth out of me. 'I can handle plenty,' I say with a jut of my jaw that belies my jubilant butterflies.

'Good,' he says standing up. 'Let's go.' He waits as I pick up my purse and then threads his fingers with mine. He leads me past the three men and out into the bright lobby.

'You like my dress then?' I ask conversationally as we head to the lift.

'Not nearly slutty enough,' is his gruff response.

We step into the waiting lift. The second the door rolls shut he's on me. Pushing me against the smoky mirrored wall with his big, powerful body and slamming his erection into my stomach. His mouth presses down on mine and his insistent tongue probes and explores. 'No,' I manage to breathe as I twist and remove his tongue. 'No kissing on the mouth.'

'What?'

'No kissing on the mouth, that's the rule, stick to it or the deal is off.'

He steps back and his weight is gone, I miss it already. A flash of disapproval, or maybe hurt, crosses his face and he runs a hand over his short, sharp hair. I have no time to explain it's standard whore practice because the lift door pings open and an elderly, well-dressed couple step in.

'Good evening,' they say.

'Evening,' he replies through a strained voice.

I smile and smooth my hands down my dress to remove tell-tale creases.

We alight at the fifth level and he stops at the first door on the long, windowless corridor.

'Next to the lift?' I say with a frown. 'It'll be noisy all night.'

'You'll be too busy working to notice,' he mutters,

130

slotting in the key card, clocking the green light and shoving at the door with a wide, flattened palm.

I step in, move past the bathroom and glance around the high-ceilinged room delicately bathed in the buttery glow of a brass floor lamp. It's a perfect square centred with a Queen-sized bed draped in a bottle-green eiderdown and bursting with pillows. A desk containing phone, TV, hairdryer and writing paper stands at its base with a minibar slotted neatly underneath the shining surface. On the far side of the bed a royal-blue sofa overflowing with densely embroidered cushions blocks drawn checked curtains. Two wooden occasional tables sit either side of the sofa; one of them is adorned with a bunch of citrus-coloured flowers.

'It's nice,' I say.

He shuts the door without responding. Walks past me, chucks his suit jacket on the bed and folds his tall frame onto the sofa. 'Stand in front of me.'

I place my purse by the TV and saunter with a practiced roll of my hips to where he's gestured.

'Take a step back,' he says, shifting as if settling down to watch a long movie.

I do as he asks and wonder where the softness has gone from his face. He seems all business now. I guess it was the no kissing on the mouth thing, perhaps I should have forgotten that rule for tonight, after all, he is pretty hot – a good snog would have been nice. But no, I can't let him think he's anything special to me.

'Take off your dress,' he says. 'Slow, real, real slow.'

I let a hint of a smile tickle my lips as I raise my arms and undo the knot at my nape holding the top half of my dress in place. I don't wear a bra, I don't need to. As soon as the material is free it falls to my waist and exposes my pert breasts and dark, puckered nipples.

131

I see a muscle twitch in his cheek as his eyes devour my tits. I can almost feel his hands on me, can almost imagine that long thick finger brushing across the tight nubs of my nipples and flicking them harder still. I feel my body respond just at the thought and the slight weight of my breasts doubles with need.

I wiggle my hips and tug the soft skirt over my behind. When I know gravity can take over I straighten and let it fall. It lands in a heap and I step backwards over it, hook it onto the toe of my pointed stiletto and send it through the air towards him.

It lands on his knees and produces a hint of a smile on his solemn face.

I place my hands on my hips and jut to the left. Raise an eyebrow in a 'bring it on' kind of way and arch my back to show off my slim waist.

'Take off those slutty red pants, whore.'

The rumble of his voice saying such dirty words vibrates right through me. I hook my fingers into the elastic and feel a tremble in my own excited skin as the lace rolls into a thin band of material.

Once removed they too are tossed alongside the dress. He reaches for them, screws them into a ball and shoves them into his pocket. 'I reckon for a thousand quid I get a souvenir.'

I nod and run a hand over my narrow landing strip of dark pubic hair to make sure it's at its fluffy best.

'Turn around,' he instructs, undoing his belt buckle.

I do as he asks and bare my naked behind for him to get off on. Not my best feature, it's a little on the round side, but I'm guessing from the straining bulge in his trousers he won't be too critical.

'Take off your shoes.'

I bend my knees and squat to the floor to undo the

132

silver buckles at my ankles.

'No, no, not like that,' he snaps. 'Stand up. Bend from the middle, touch your toes and shove that whore's arse in the air, I want to see you poking out from behind.'

I straighten up and feel my pulse quicken. The blood rushes to my head as I double at the waist directly in front of him and give him a good view of my most intimate hole, my plump, needy lips and the juice that's collecting just for him.

'Very nice,' he says as I struggle with the second strap. 'Perfect in fact.'

When the shoes are off I straighten and turn to him wearing just my black fishnets. I step right up between his knees and look down at him chilling on the sofa. 'Tell me,' I say in a husky voice. 'What do you want me to do next for you?'

He reaches out to my pubic hair and slips a finger through the curls to my clitoris. My knees suddenly feel whacked from behind and I struggle to remain upright. But he pulls his hand away and the feeling is over before it's had a chance to begin.

'Get me a whisky,' he says. 'From the mini bar.'

I catch my breath, hardly believing he can think of a drink at a time like this. I'm so turned on I feel like I'm travelling in another dimension. 'A whisky?'

'Yeah, a whisky. I'm gonna drink it while you blow me off.'

I move to the minibar, pull out a whisky bottle and slosh it into a glass.

'Get your lipstick too,' he orders.

I return and thrust the drink at him, impatient to get to the main event.

'Hey, slow down, I'm running this show.' He sits forward so his face is inches from my breasts. Dips a

133

finger into the amber liquid and slowly traces a wet circle around one nipple and then the other.

I sigh at the touch I've been longing for. Clench my internal muscles and put a hand out to his rock solid shoulder for support. I want him to lick the whisky off, suckle me into his mouth.

He doesn't – instead he blows and the icy cold wetness makes my nipples pucker to bursting point. I let out a low moan and my eyes flutter shut as he switches attention from one to the other.

All too soon he leans back into the cushions and I'm forced to remove my hand from his shoulder. He takes a long, appreciative sip of his drink and shifts his pelvis towards the edge of the sofa. 'All yours,' he says taking a deep breath. 'But I want more slut-red lipstick first.

I sink my knees between his legs and undo his suit trouser button; slide down his flies straining with the erection beneath. He lifts his hips and allows me full access by shoving at his own undergarments. His penis springs out, dark and solid, the shaft heavily veined and the head shiny and wide. I reach forward and spread my flattened tongue over the top.

'Lipstick,' he growls over my head.

I pull back, roll up my lipstick and make a show of applying it ridiculously thick – I don't stay within the borders of my mouth I just shove on as much as possible. His eyes are wide, his breath finally catching the same pace as mine as I take his shaft in my hand.

I lean forward and with my slutty red lips swallow him deep over the base of my tongue. 'Oh yes, Whore, do it, do it, Whore.' He tangles a hand in my hair and applies a steady, dominant pressure. I begin to bob up and down, letting his thick, smooth head hit the back of my throat every time. He moans, sighs, shifts his hips upwards and I hear him slosh back a gulp of whisky. I revel in his reaction to my skills.

Just as I taste a delicious salty hint of pre-come he pulls out of my mouth and tips me back on my heels. 'Not like this … inside you.' His voice is tight as a violin string and he holds his enormous body tense as if the slightest movement might tip him over the edge. 'Get on the bed.'

I stand, my own legs giddy as I feel an anticipatory spasm of pleasure surge through my body. The thought of him inside me, filling me, shoving hard and fast into my core has me furious with impatience.

I lie on the bed but before I've even positioned myself he's above me, desire surrounding him like a dark, heavy cloak. He whips off his plain grey tie and I feel my arms hoisted above my head. Thin silky material binds my wrists and he knots me to the slatted oak head-board.

'Hey,' I make a feeble attempt at protesting.

'Shut up, whore,' he says, removing his shirt.

I'm distracted from my complaint by the sight of his sculpted chest, patterned with thick coarse curls of hair looming inches above me.

'This is my show and I'm paying you good money to do it my way,' he says and shucks down his trousers, toes off his shoes and socks and mounts the bed beside me.

I can smell him, taste him, I want to feel him. I manage to raise my head and kiss his chest, but he beats me at my own game and heads for my tits. Finally I get to feel the roll of his tongue, the suckling of his mouth, pulling me in. I groan and shut my eyes, arch my back and hope his hand will travel lower.

It does and I feel him parting my slick flesh like he did in the bar, delving into my moist pussy. 'He could see us you know,' he says, as he swaps breasts.

'Who?'

135

'The barman.'

'What, how?' My eyes ping open and I catch his wicked grin.

'The reflection in the window, he could see my hand in your cunt.'

'Oh, shit.' I'm mortified.

'You won't be able to work The Grosvenor again.' He laughs at my ruination.

'It's not funny,' I say, but then catch my breath as he puts not one but two long thick fingers right inside me and begins to urge my g-spot into a state of euphoria.

'I didn't notice the depth of the reflection until we left.' He goes to kiss my lips. I turn away and screw up my eyes.

He pushes more urgently, circles my clitoris with his thumb and I feel the start of an orgasm building. 'Get inside me,' I say tugging trapped arms in frustration. 'I want you.' I pull at the tie and it sinks deeper into my flesh; my hands tingle with lack of blood.

'It's not about your fun.' He nudges my legs apart with his and climbs on board. 'You're at work, remember, you're doing this for my pleasure not yours.'

'Whatever, just be a man will you?' I give up politeness – I'll say anything to feel that hulking big penis hit the spot. 'Fuck me now, damn it.'

He obliges by removing his hand and with one long, deep thrust penetrates my swollen, aching hole with his glorious cock. His pubis rocks up against my hungry clitoris and his shaft whacks against my g-spot with scary accuracy. 'You feel so good for a dirty old whore,' he grunts into my hair. 'So good.'

I want to wrap my arms around him, hold him close, but I can't, I'm tied up and at his mercy. The best I can do is twine my stockinged legs around his thighs and force myself into his scratching, heaving chest, position my pelvis so it hits just right. 'Don't stop,' I grunt but know instantly it's a mistake as I feel him withdraw.

I'm flipped onto my stomach. Arms stretched above me, backside in the air. I whimper a protest; I can't even get my hands down to do it myself.

'Patience is a virtue,' he mutters. His hand slides a lazy journey from my shoulder blades, into the dip of my lower back and then on through the crack of my buttocks. I feel his fingertips pause and begin to ring the ridged skin around my anus.

'That'll cost extra,' I manage, though right now I'm not really bothered about negotiating, I just want it any way I can get it

'How much extra?'

I pluck a figure out of the air. 'Five hundred.'

'Fuck that,' he says removing his finger and sending it lower. 'There's a perfectly good hole here, lubed and paid for, waiting just for me.'

Head on my forearms and up on my knees, I remain submissive, restricted by the tie. I feel big hands wrap around my hip bones as his thighs edge between mine.

'You're gonna take it all now,' he says.

'Oh, yes.' I wriggle my butt; invite him in.

'I'm gonna fuck you really hard, reckon you can take it, whore.'

'Yes, yes, I can take it.'

'No more Mr Nice Guy, he's gone.'

'I don't want Mr Nice Guy,' I say as I feel his fingers parting me and his dick sliding in. 'I want it hard ... now.'

His grunt is pure Neanderthal as he shoves in to the hilt and his hips jar against my buttocks. I can feel him pushing at my womb and I let out my own howl of pleasure. He is amazingly thick and long, filling me to absolute capacity and rubbing all the best spots in just the right way.

I pull at the tie, once again wanting to get my own hand down to my clit. Fortunately he takes pity on my struggle and sends the pads of his first two fingers around to rub me. It's exactly the right pressure and combined with the thrusting feels like Nirvana, Paradise and Heaven all calling me at once.

His breaths are coming thick and fast, same as mine. He has one hand pinned to my hip bone keeping me steady as he shunts forward with increasing power and determination. I brace hard with my arms straight out and clutch the slats the tie is looped around. 'Oh, God, don't stop.' I hear myself beg into the eiderdown. 'Don't stop, Jack, don't stop.'

'No fucking names, whore.' He slams all the harder for my mistake and I feel his hand move from my hip bone and begin circling my anus again. I whimper with delight and let myself catch the orgasm roller-coaster, no longer needing to search it out because it's here, taking over, covering my body in liquid pleasure, and the moment he shoves not just one but two fingers up my back passage it all splits apart; roars through my veins like an earthquake. Every hole filled I can do nothing but surf the spasms of pleasure, clench and tremble and scream out in ecstasy.

He curses violently overhead and I feel him bashing high up inside me, urgent and desperate. His cock is as hard as any cock can possibly be. He's near to the edge and I let myself be impaled by his pleasure. Use it to eke every last drop of satisfaction from my glorious climax as he comes within me; pours his seed into my body and lets out an unholy praise to the Good Lord above as he does so.

I keep my back arched as he trembles and shakes for

several long seconds. With his fingers deep inside me and his penis pulsating within I can't remember when I last had such naughty fun.

'That was …' I don't bother to raise my head as I speak. 'Intense.'

'Just a bit,' he replies, removing his fingers from my arse and his dick from my swollen folds.

He flops on the bed next to me and I twist my neck to look at him. A sheen of sweat glistens on his forehead and tiny droplets have formed on his top lip. His eyes are shut and his breaths are still fast and jagged. I look at his chest and see his dark curls of hair matted and stuck like miniature coils. He's truly a fine specimen of a man and this is the best I've seen him all evening. It makes me hot for more. 'Untie me,' I say quietly.

He rolls to his side and reaches for the constricted knot. 'Bloody hell, you pulled this a bit tight.'

'You were teasing me.'

He pokes it loose and it slides from my wrists. 'Sorry about that.' He rubs the reddened skin as though he can erase the marks of our passion.

'It's OK, it'll be gone by morning.' I flex and un-flex my hands to encourage a return of blood flow.

'I hope so.' He drops back down and scoops me against his chest with those big, beefy arms. I can hear his heart beating; pounding strong and steady against his ribs.

'I take cash or cheque,' I say as I finger the curls around his flat nipples. 'Either is fine, but with a cheque I require a banker's card.'

A rumble of amusement bubbles from his stomach and I raise my head to look into his eyes. 'What's so funny?' I question with a frown.

'I'm afraid I've already spent your earnings.'

'What.' I push up and glare at him. 'On what?'

139

'Well you know that trip to Florida you and the kids have been on about for ages.'

'Yes ...' I tilt my head and can't help the smile of hope.

'Well it's all booked, we go next month.'

I whoop with delight and hurl myself on top of my husband. 'Oh, Jack, I can't believe it ... you've really booked it, really ...'

'Yes, really,' he laughs and rolls me over to contain my excited wriggling with his body weight. 'It's the least I can do after you agreed to act out my fantasy.'

I grin and give him a deep, lingering kiss on the lips. 'Well, it was hardly a chore was it.'

WHEN I WANDER CENTRAL London I play a private game. I try to view things as a tourist might; the imposing streets, the grand palaces and the eclectic mix of people. Doing this always gives me a sense of ownership and pride even though I actually own nothing in this glorious, sprawling city.

In my early twenties I did live in London with a cute boyfriend (who went on to become my husband) for a short while. We were poor, it was cold and grey, but we were happy. I remember one night we went to bed with the luxury of a borrowed gas heater and woke up covered in sticky floral wallpaper. It had literally slid from the walls overnight because of the extreme dampness in our flat – which six months later was condemned and pulled down!

Having progressed from those meagre student days, a few years ago said husband took me to a charity dinner at The Grosvenor House Hotel. I knew very few people, and as he chatted with colleagues I was content to sink into a leather chair in the Champagne Bar and indulge one of my favourite pastimes – people watching.

The ambiance was muted; men kept their voices hushed and ladies sipped golden bubbles with little fingers poised. A pianist tinkled in the background and the sombre bar staff were attentive yet discreet. It struck me that with all the elegant dresses and finely suited men, a passing time traveller would have had difficulty guessing the year, or even the decade, we were socialising in. There were no mobile phones, no bluetooths and no ipods on show, just chic people on their best behaviour.

Perhaps a glance out the window at cars slicing through dark puddles would have given a clue; limos, Lexuses, Bentleys and Mercs, rushing the rich and famous, royalty and celebrity to the other Park Lane venues surrounding us.

As people arrived in the Champagne Bar and greeted one another it became hard to tell who was catching up with old friends and who was being introduced for the first time. I studied my husband in his pristine tux holding a perilously thin flute of champagne. He laughed at something someone said, nodded his head and then turned and caught my eyes. I returned a smile and wondered what it would be like if 'we' we're just being introduced for the first time.

I'm pleased to say if we had just met at that moment, I'd still fancy him like hell and still want to have his babies. But what would it be like to play a game, come back and fool everyone? Could we in fact fool anyone? Or would people guess by our familiar body language that we were a couple and knew each other's deepest, darkest desires? And what about the genteel staff in this sophisticated hotel, would they be so crass as to challenge our behaviour if we thought up the naughtiest way possible to become acquainted? It got me thinking!

Woke up with that Hampstead Blues Again
by Maxim Jakubowski

THERE'S LONDON.

Then, there's the real London.

And then again, there is the unreal London, a world of shadows, imagination and a well of loneliness.

That was the London he'd inhabited since Julie left him.

He often wished he had the power within him to make things fade away, the subtle art of erasing memories, feelings, associations, but that was an ability he did not possess. Sometimes he even felt he had no talent whatsoever, and was ever amazed that he had reached this stage in his life when material and professional success and the admiration of others was a given. All a facade, he knew; others could not even guess at the desolation inside.

I am a hollow man, he reflected. Without her, I am nothing.

But, in the meantime, life had to go on.

He worked, he lectured, he attended glittering parties for the launch of books at the Groucho Club, Soho House or The Horse Hospital, film premieres on Leicester Square, the opening of exhibitions in shiny art galleries in Bond Street or South Molton Street, he commented on the radio on matters artistic, or even sometimes became a talking head on late-night television on subjects intellectual, and watched as his bank account steadily grew in size.

Which brought him little pleasure or satisfaction.

There was the London in which he functioned, an artificial stage on which he lived, but like a dark cloud following his every step, there was also Julie's London. The places they'd been together on her only visit here. Locations he could not deliberately avoid for ever: the cavernous galleries of the Tate Modern, the counter at the 3rd floor bar where they could overlook the ant-like commuters trooping up and down the Millennium Bridge below while sitting on their high stools; the Tesco supermarket in Finchley, where he had uncovered her amusing craving for Hula Hoop snacks; the restaurant in Coin Street where they had shared a bad meal; the coffee concession at Luton airport before she had taken the escalator to the departure lounge, clutching the John Lennon box set of CDs he had given her (or was it the Clash box? or had that been on a separate occasion and not in London?); the black shelves of the Notting Hill branch of Waterstone's where he had proudly pointed out to her a well-fingered copy of his only book which had been sitting there gathering dust for ages now, this after a stroll down Ladbroke Grove and the Portobello Road Market which she had found terribly disappointing (one day he had promised to take her to Camden Town if she ever came back to London); the rippling waters of ... Enough now! It was over. She would never return. She was now with another, others, somewhere; she had moved on. And he was the one still encased like amber in the unforgiving past. Enough. Over and out.

He banished Julie from both his life and dreams and entered another London, one with which she held no connection.

At a concert at the Roundhouse, he met Aurora, the Spanish girl. Beirut were playing, Balkan brass, hints of klezmer and gently fey Americana, a combination that spoke to all his sensibilities. In the crowd at the bar, during the interval, he had accidentally knocked over her glass and bought her a replacement. Diet Coke to his Classic Coke. An hour or so later as the concertgoers were filing out of the venue on Chalk Farm Road, he brushed shoulders with her as the stream of human traffic met a brief bottleneck descending the stairs from the balcony. He was about to apologise, but she turned her head towards him and recognised him. She smiled. He smiled back. Of such minor things, life is made.

It was raining outside, quite heavily. He had an umbrella in his ever-present tote bag. She visibly hadn't, he noticed, as she momentarily stood outside on the pavement clearly unsure as to her next step: walk to the tube station, wait in the rain for a cab, step back and shelter for a while in the theatre?

'Do you live far?' he asked, as he deployed the umbrella over the both of them.

'No, West Hampstead,' he noted her accent. 'It's not very distant.'

'I know … look … I have a car parked near the Lock. I can give you a lift. My own flat is just beyond Hampstead Garden Suburb, so it's not out of my way.'

As if to encourage a positive response, the pouring rain intensified in ferocity.

'OK,' she agreed.

They became lovers one week later.

It would have been earlier, but she had a flatmate who worked as an intern for an Aids charity, and she had to wait for her friend to go away to Brighton for the weekend for an educational conference. She wanted their first time together to take place on familiar ground.

Aurora had curling, dark auburn pre-Raphaelite hair and alabaster skin.

'Come to the bedroom,' she asked. They'd been having coffee after she'd invited him back, after catching a Lars Von Trier film at the Everyman. The choice of the cinema and its plush double sofas sitting two had not been his. It was the only screen in North London showing the movie they'd both agreed to see together.

Sitting so close to her with no divider, he could feel the heat her body generated in the darkness. They both fidgeted a little, either because of nerves or the fact the double-seater did not restrict them each to a single position. He unfolded his leg and as he did so her thigh brushed fleetingly against his.

'Sorry,' he whispered, just as she was about to say the very same thing. They looked at each other and laughed. Someone in the row behind shushed them. They both fell silent but their hands moved closer and touched. He took hold of hers. She did not resist the deliberate contact.

Aurora leaned against him, and he caught a drift of her perfume. She whispered in his ear 'your hand is so warm …'.

'I know,' he said. Julie had always been telling him that. His feet too … Martin, the human radiator!

'A penny for your thoughts?' she asked him, spinning him out of his reflections.

'They're not even worth a fraction of that.'

'Ah.'

'I come dead cheap,' he joked.

Later, she'd put a record on, ambient piano music by

146

Ludovico Einaudi. But the constant thrum of the traffic streaming towards Kilburn High Street outside the first-floor flat muted the sounds. Melodies morphing into an indistinct wall of confused sounds. Julie had been a fan of The Clash. He hadn't. Julie's hair also curled like a Medusa-like web. But it hadn't been red. Julie wasn't here. He was. With Aurora. And he was no longer sure whether he really wanted to make love with her, to her.

She reached towards him.

'So when do I find out if you are equally warm in bed?' she smiled.

'As long as you don't expect me to be much else, too. I'm no multi-tasker!'

He took her hand and they made their way to the bedroom.

'Are you sure?'

'Yes. Absolutely.'

'Then I want you to keep the light on,' he ordered. 'And I want to be the one to undress you.'

Her shape was on the right side of voluptuous and her rose-coloured nipples were attractively puffy. She knelt topless on the shag carpet and assiduously took my cock into her mouth. She was visibly experienced in the craft and care of men's cocks, blending loving tender care with the ideal and correct amount of roughness. And just the right touch of saliva in her oral caress, that clever slip and slide of pliant, warm lips, of tongue and teeth. Moving in agonising laziness from tip to stem to balls, lingering here, concentrating there, a finger and then another teasing the demarcation line between my perineum and my sphincter, clenching, releasing, wetting, sucking, licking the whole ridged geography of my penis and the bodily territories that bordered it.

I closed my eyes.

Thought of another blow job. A yearning remembrance of things past. Julie one night after we'd walked down towards the ravine of the Vale of Health. The moon's pale rays reflected across the rippling surface of the small pond. The heat of her mouth. The maddening tangle of her hair beneath me. The uneven and disturbed texture of the tree against which I was leaning, which I was polishing with the palm of my right hand while my other hand kept hold of Julie's head, guiding her mouth's steady movements around my cock.

'I can't hold on much longer. I have to come.'

'It's OK.'

'Are you sure?'

'Yes, come into my mouth, my love.'

The Hamsptead night around us was punctured by my deep moan, the obscene sound of my release, the flow of my spend inside the cauldron of her mouth, her throat.

The croaking of a frog, or was it a duck, somewhere across the pond.

The hiss of Julie's breath as she swallowed me.

'You taste sweet.'

'Really?'

The memory faded and I was back in the room with Aurora.

'You've done this before, I see?'

'Yes,' she nodded, allowing my hard cock to slip from between her dark lips. She gripped it between her fingers and continued the up and down motion with mechanical precision. 'That previous lover, the older man, the mathematician, sometimes wanted me to suck him for hours. He trained me. I told you about him, didn't I?'

Maybe I hadn't been listening properly at the time.

'Trained?'

'He was an older man. I was younger then. Naive. It was when I was doing my degree. He would take me to these clubs, fetish, BDSM, and have me pretend I was his slave. He wanted me to suck him in public, while others watched. At first, it was hard but I learned to blank it out.'

'Just sucking?'

She drew back as her own memories no doubt flashed back.

Flushed ever so slightly. 'Not always ...' her eyes avoided mine.

My neglected cock hardened again. 'Come here,' I indicated, and pulled her jeans off. 'On your knees. Face the wall. Yes, like that.'

Her regal and generous arse positioned itself at the right angle. Just the way Julie had grown to place herself to greet my vector of entry as our bodies had once so quickly become accustomed to each other and the geometry of our couplings. I squinted and peered at the flank of her left thigh. No stain.

The eye of her anus shone in the unforgiving brightness of the light bulb above, surrounded by the darker shadows of her pale Mediterranean skin.

I hesitated one brief instant as I adjusted myself to the myriad differences between her and lost Julie. My hand caressed her firm rump, tracing imaginary longitude lines across her ample orbs, inveigled itself between her crotch, still dry, and spread her even further. She drew her breath.

'Did he also spank you?' I asked Aurora.

'Yes,' she replied. 'How did you know?'

'Just did, I reckon.'

Spanking had never quite been my scene but right there and then, a stone's throw from Kilburn High Road and technically still in West Hampstead with this fragile young Spanish woman voluntarily at my mercy, the compulsion to hurt her, mark her, swept uncontrollably over me.

I smacked her hard, three or four times in succession until the shape of my fingers peered back at me like a pattern imprinted across the white skin of her arse cheeks.

She began crying.

I spat into my right hand, still stinging from the assault on her flesh, and lathered my cock and entered her from behind in one single, brutal movement.

Aurora shrieked.

'That hurt,' she protested.

'But you want it this way, you like it, don't you? I can feel it …'

'Yes,' she sobbed. 'Yes.'

I had known the odd intrinsically submissive woman during the course of my past feeble erotic adventures. Somehow I was drawn to them. Could almost identify them in a crowd. But didn't quite understand what drove them. And all too often craved to experience what made them tick, how they felt. A thoroughly dangerous curiosity.

Her reply encouraged me and I began to fuck her with all the anger that Julie had left simmering inside me. As if I was taking revenge on her by proxy. There had been nothing submissive in Julie; on the contrary, what I most adored about her was her rebellious, gypsy streak.

Inside Aurora's cunt, I could feel my cock harden even further, grow within her holy heat as her tears ebbed and flowed and soon poured alongside the rhythm of my thrusts.

'That hurt,' Aurora later said, shrinking away from me as I attempted to cuddle her in the exiguous single bed.

'I'm sorry,' I said.

'I'm sorry I'm not her,' she added.

'I …'

'Don't say anything,' she interrupted my stillborn protest. 'Look, I want to sleep now. You can stay. Or you can go. Up to you.'

'I'll stay,' I had no wish to drive home right then, winding my way up the Finchley Road and past the Heath Extension lost in thoughts that would make me feel bad about myself or evoke yet more unwelcome memories.

The doorbell to her flat rang in the middle of the night. I drowsily checked my watch. It was past three in the morning. She rose from the bed, dragging the top sheet away from me. I noticed that she had, at some stage while I slept, slipped her cotton knickers back on. I heard muffled voices at the door. I stayed in bed. Aurora shouted out 'It's just a friend. He wants to talk. We'll stay in the lounge. Don't worry.'

I dozed off.

Later, half an hour? An hour? Alone in her bed, I recognised familiar sounds on the other side of the closed bedroom door that led to the rest of the small flat. Moans, sighs, indecipherable words. Sex. Aurora and her visitor were having sex. On the couch? On the floor? I was already forgotten. And not even an invitation to join in, I wryly reflected. Strange how old boyfriends emerge from the woodwork at the worst possible time. Or was there ever a right time?

Early in the morning, with delivery vans rushing up Kilburn High Road with their daily freight, buses now criss-crossing North London again after a night's rest, I tiptoed over the entwined bare bodies of Aurora and some bearded guy with a pony tail sprawled across the lounge floor and made my way out of the flat in silence. Another ghost from the past. Her past. Unlike me, she felt the need to hold on to him after the sex. Spooning, touching,

151

maybe still embedded within each other. Giving her what I couldn't.

My car was parked across the road. The pavements had dried since the previous evening's showers. I started the engine.

All too soon, it was summer again. My first without Julie.

She was driving across the Baltic States and then Poland in her camper. I knew this, as I spied on her FaceBook page and had mastered Google Alerts to keep an eye on her newspaper filings. Towards the end of August she would be going to the Venice Film Festival, keeping the expense down by parking the camper van at one end of the Lido.

My own destinations were somewhat less exotic and distant, lazing in the sun in Golders Hill Park, eyeing the female tennis players hopping about in their unbelievably short skirts and tanned thighs, watching small kids feed the farm animals behind their wire enclosures or flying kites over the green wide open manicured fields towards the top end of the park, while munching on salmon and cream cheese bagels I had picked up earlier from the Carmelli Jewish bakery on Golders Green Road, and listening to the balmy afternoons waste away and the sound of my longing heart. At any rate, there were worse ways of cultivating a good tan.

I didn't want to hear about the gold chains her lovers now wore, or the dull words through which they burrowed under her skin, the petty offerings they bestowed on her, the love they stole.

Her skin, her hand upon my neck.

This skin, her fingers on my skin.

Her kiss, her heartbeat her breath.

Her heart, her heart her gypsy wilderness.

And here I was a prisoner of the Hampstead triangle, circumscribed between Camden Town to the south, the A406 to the North, Highgate to the east beyond the lush open-air vastness of Parliament Hill Fields and the dirt of the Edgware Road to the furthest east. Here I stewed, here I yearned in this summer of longing. In the home of the so-called bourgeois novel and overvalued properties. Unable to venture beyond those parts of London I associated with her, the roads we had walked, the museums, cinemas, supermarkets we had frequented, the beds we had fucked in, the pavements on which she had walked, the alley where she had squatted down and peed under cover of darkness when caught short while I stood red-faced as a lookout for passers-by, the cafes where we had slowly sipped espressos, the flower stall where I had bought her a single rose, the tapas bar where she had introduced me to cold potatoes with sour cream and chilli powder (or, come to think of it, maybe that had been in Barcelona … The mind wanders so …).

But summer in London seldom lasts long and soon the implacable waltz of the seasons had drawn to an end and autumn came, or fall as the Americans called it.

I tried to venture out of my Hampstead fortress, cleverly concealing some form of temporary visa inside my heart. One step at a time, one further stop daily on the Northern Line. Mornington Crescent. Take a deep breath. Euston. Warren Street. Control your emotions. Goodge Street, once the battleground for another disastrous campaign some ten years back. Tottenham Court Road. Leicester Square, gateway to Soho …

The man he met at the Groucho Club was a friend of a friend of a friend. Martin had been vouched for, somehow.

'You'll still have to be vetted by a couple of the others,' the other man said.

'I quite understand,' Martin answered.

He gave a phone call and one hour later they were joined by two others. Well-dressed businessmen, suited and tied. A few drinks later he was formally approved.

'How do you find them?' he asked.

'Chat rooms, ads, by personal recommendation ...'

'Recommendations?'

'You'd be surprised.'

'Jesus ...'

'All quite normal women. No money changes hands, ever.'

The spokesman for the group was in his early fifties, slight in stature, his beard streaked with white. Earlier in the conversation, he'd mentioned he'd returned just a few weeks back from his holidays, sailing his boat along the coast of Turkey. Another was a surgeon, and the third had some unspecified job in the City.

It was agreed Martin would be able to join their next session.

They met in the cellar bar of a big impersonal hotel right by Victoria train station. Two of the other men in the group were already there, nursing beers, when Martin arrived.

The young woman walked into the bar ten minutes later, accompanied by the group's leader. She was barely out of her teens. She appeared at first hesitant, even shy, but, after a few drinks, she relaxed and loosened up. She was a student nurse. On later occasions, they would gang-bang an older bank assistant manager who'd travelled up for the occasion from the South Coast, and on another occasion a single mother who wanted to be a poet and who, having discovered his media connections, would later mail him some stories she was working on; they were actually quite good. Sometimes, the group booked the hotel in Victoria, but sometimes they used another hotel near Old Street. And, one time, the basement of an empty store on Old Compton Street which one of the guys had access too through his job. The hotels were principally chosen for their busy nature and the fact that five or six men entering the lift to the upper floors together with a single woman would not attract undue attention.

'Your first time?' he asked her. This was still at the bar. Two of the other men had walked over to the bar to pick up another round.

'Yes,' she said.

'Me too,' he attempted a smile.

'That's nice,' she replied.

'Why are you doing it?' It wasn't quite what he wanted to ask, but the right words couldn't quite form on the edge of his lips. She looked so young.

'You know, a fantasy. I think all women have them. Just want to know what it would feel like. Silly, no?'

'No, not at all.' The others returned and their one-to-one conversation came to an abrupt end.

A few weeks later he would discover that following that initial evening she had continued to see some other members of the group and been taken to a swing evening at a private club, and later dogging in a lay-by off the M25 where she was shared with total strangers in the dim light of the car beams. But he was not invited to those follow-up events.

Once finally in the room, the young nurse was summarily stripped. She had lovely, round breasts. High and firm. She had been ordered to shave herself below and had followed her instructions to the letter. She wore no panties, just hold up black stockings.

The leader of the group unzipped his trousers and presented his cock to her, forcing her down to her knees. She took him into her mouth. This was a signal for the other men to all undress. He looked around at the ocean of male flesh now crowding him. They came in all shapes and sizes, and he was glad to see he was not the smallest, or the fattest either.

While she hungrily sucked on her first cock of the evening, others began to finger her other holes, greedily exploring her, forcing her, feeling her up like a prime cut of meat. Cocks hardened, jutted. His eyes took in the room, the scene of the crime. The window looked out on a dull panorama of city roofs. On the bedside table, a small pile of condoms and various tubes of cream and lube. On a desk near the fridge, someone had brought a couple of bottles of wine. Both red. Three glasses and a mug. A few sex toys were scattered around, including a monstrous two-headed dildo that surely wouldn't fit into any woman's openings without tearing her apart, he thought.

It did fit, he would later observe, as two of the men, an hour or so later, after all her holes had been used by every man in the room in succession and on some occasions together, busied themselves stuffing the black dildo deep into her vagina while the other extremity was, inch by inch, forcibly buried into her anus. The young nurse breathed heavily as the operation took place, on all fours on the bed, her mouth impaled onto the thick cock of a heavy red-haired man.

'Good girl,' someone said.

By then, he was already spent. He had ventured inside all her offered holes, once even felt her gag on his hard cock as it hit the back of her throat as the black doctor thrust into her from behind and the motion threw her involuntarily forward more than she had expected.

The others kept busy. Between fucks, they would hand her a glass of wine, or later water, which she requested, and some would gently mop her brow when the sweat began to drip from her fevered forehead. She never complained or asked for a break. He looked at the scene, trying to place himself in the skin of a dispassionate observer. One of her stockings was badly torn and the one on her other leg was bunched up around her ankle. She was ravaged, but still rather beautiful. The men in the group circled the bed, their damp cocks bouncing against their thighs as they moved along to play with her.

The cocks.

Thick and thin, conjugating every possible geometrical angle, smooth and veiny, bulbous, heavy.

He gazed at the other men's cocks. Wondering what it must feel like to have a penis in one's mouth, what it would taste like, how it would fill his insides. What it would feel like to be a woman. And experienced a brief flash of yearning. And envy.

Right there and then, at the heart of his first gang bang Martin momentarily understood what it would be like to be submissive and knew that if he were a woman, he would also be a woman who would gift herself to men. To strangers.

There could be no greater gift.

The young nurse shrieked. Someone had pushed too far. Somewhere.

'Enough,' she protested.

But her blushing face was radiant, ecstatic even.

The men respectfully moved away from her. She slipped off the bed and the tangle of bodies.

Spent condoms littered the hotel room carpet.

'I think I need a shower,' she said.

Looked at the circle of bodies surrounding the bed.

'Wow! That sure was some party,' she laughed and headed towards the bathroom.

They all dressed and one by one left the hotel room, leaving her behind with just the group's leader who had initiated the original contact with her and escorted her there.

Martin attended a further five gang bangs organised by the motley group. None of the men involved ever knew each other's' name. Those were the rules. And he soon came to understand the other unwritten rules of the game. Because it was a game, consensual, lustful, sexual. The group provided a need and, surprisingly, some of the women even returned on a few occasions.

Every time, he told himself he wouldn't attend the next event. Feeling shameful, guilty, angered by his own frailty and cowardice. This was not the Hampstead way, surely? But every man is led by his dick and, even if he left it to the last minute before confirming his attendance, he would be present at the pub or the bar where yet another new girl would be introduced.

At the final gang bang he attended, back at the hotel near Victoria station following a few forays into different areas, he reached the depths of abjection.

The woman was a librarian from High Wycombe and they had liberally taken their pleasure with her, when a stray member of the group, taking a break from their activities had gone to the hotel bar downstairs to get some extra drinks and returned with another woman he had somehow seduced in record time or at any rate convinced to join them all in the room. She was not taken back by the spectacle of six naked men writhing lewdly around the pale body of the younger woman, cocks at attention, hair in disarray. She announced she would not participate but wanted to watch.

Right then, the woman who was the evening's main attraction was on her knees on the edge of the bed where Martin sat with thighs wide apart, feeding on his cock. He was tiring, losing his hardness. The woman from the bar watched them both, nursing a glass of gin, her eyes eager, her lips moist as she observed their congress. He avoided her gaze and pulled the librarian's face away from his crotch, and raised himself slightly so that her face was now looking straight into his rear hole. He spread himself.

'Lick me clean,' he ordered the young woman. And took hold of a belt which just lay there on the bed, abandoned earlier as part of another sexual variation and placed it around her neck.

She buried her nose and mouth inside his crack and beavered away, held in place by the belt.

The woman from the bar snickered in her nearby corner as Martin was rimmed.

For just a moment, he left his body and became an observer of the scene, watching it all from afar, detached.

And felt sick inside.

How could he fall any lower?

Ten minutes later, he was dressed and racing through the hotel lobby and signalling for a cab.

'Take me to Hampstead,' he asked the driver.

'Where in Hampstead?' the cabbie asked, 'It's a big place, Hampstead is.'

'I'll decide when we get there.'

The night traffic was sparse and they soon crossed the Marylebone Road, cruised through Regent's Park and reached Camden Town and then Belsize Park.

'Take right, past the Royal Free,' he said.

'You're the boss, mate.'

He ordered the taxi to stop when they reached the pond

by Jack Straw's Castle.

His mind was bubbling with confusion.

On the one hand he felt downright disgusted at what had become of him these past months. The senseless sex, the indifference, the emptiness. Images of the women, the men, the cocks repeatedly breaching openings in full Cinemascope close-ups against the large screen of his conscience, the animalistic sounds of unfeeling lovemaking, the cocks, the hard, warm cocks …

For a moment, he was tempted to enter the woods by Jack Straw's Castle's car park, an area notorious as a gay cruising ground. He stepped one way, then another, hesitated, and finally walked slowly towards home.

He didn't reach the stone steps leading to his flat until well past midnight. He could have hailed another taxi, but the walk had calmed his nerves.

There was a half moon above the imagined Hampstead map of green.

Someone was sitting, bunched, on the highest step, just by the door.

It was Julie.

She looked up at him and the pleading in her eyes just broke his heart.

'I'm back,' she said.

'I always knew you would return,' he said.

About the Story

ALTHOUGH I WAS BORN in London, my parents moved to France when I was still very small. I was regularly shipped back to London during school breaks, to stay with my aunt in Bayswater, but my appreciation of London was long limited to much-awaited visits to Hamley's on Regent Street and Saturday morning movie shows and I never truly came to know my own city until I finally returned in my mid-twenties.

I now live a few miles from where I was born and, despite a few years in Italy and the temptation of New York, I wouldn't want to be anywhere else. London is not just a city, it's a hundred different places, each with its own personality, shopping centres, parks, character, geography. It's also so wonderfully diverse and easy to live in (I'll make an exception for the transport system) and, when it comes to culture in all its shapes and sizes, offers a veritable and inexhaustible cornucopia of offerings you would never tire of, but then we don't have the extremes of temperature so many other places suffer from. But nowhere is perfect.

There is a joke, perpetuated by *Time Out's* occasional North/South issues with different covers, that you are either from North London or South London, and never the twain shall meet. The joke has some grounding in reality and there is an element of truth in the fact that Londoners are very 'regional' and make only rare forays into neighbouring zones, let alone across the river (I'll make an exception as a Northern denizen for the South Bank arts complex and the Jubilee Walk from the London Eye all the way to the Globe

Theatre, but then being by the Thames, it's barely in the South, is it?). Which is the genesis of this story. Yes, I do live close to Hampstead, long ago the jewel in the Bohemian crown of London, and now all too residential, expensive and fashionable, and also for ages the heart of the middle-class English novel. So the idea of a love story circumscribed by invisible London frontiers came to mind. The rest is, of course, strictly the product of my imagination.

Rain and Neon
by Elizabeth Coldwell

WHEN HE DASHED INTO the café that night, collar turned up against the steadily falling rain and sketch pad under his arm, I thought he was just another art school know-it-all. Heaven knows we'd had enough of them in Vettori's over the years. They would commandeer the big booth in the corner and sit there for hours, occasionally ordering more cappuccinos or a toasted teacake which a couple of the girls would split between them, and sit there bitching about their tutors and the ridiculous amount of work they were expected to do. They had opinions on everything from music to the cost of living in London to sex – but mostly sex – and they were all utterly convinced they were going to be the next Damien Hirst. They were too loud, too attractive, too confident, and they reminded me of how I had been before life had got in the way of my dreams.

It was because of the students that we set a minimum charge over lunchtime, to stop them hogging tables when we were at our busiest. On the whole, I preferred the perpetually harried runners who worked for the nearby film production companies: they dashed in, ordered four coffees, a Danish pastry and a couple of egg-and-bacon baps and dashed out five minutes later in a tangle of styrofoam cups and grease-spotted paper bags. Tonight, however, it was quiet. Not that Soho is ever completely deserted: even at three in the morning you'll find some lone soul wandering the streets. But the rain was doing a pretty good job of keeping people away, so if Sketch Pad Boy chose to linger, I was in no hurry to chase him out.

When I went over to take his order I was surprised to see that his pad was actually open, and he was drawing something with rapid sweeps of a soft pencil. Though it had barely taken shape yet, I could tell his subject was the building across the street, which had been a pub favoured by heavy metal and Gothic types until it had been sold for redevelopment about six months earlier. I didn't say anything then, but when I returned with the cup of strong tea and the tuna mayonnaise sandwich he'd asked for, I commented, "I've never seen anyone take so much interest in a boarded-up pub before."

Without even pausing in what he was doing, he answered, "That's because you see a boarded-up pub where I see an old Soho landmark."

I was right, I thought. Just another art school know-it-all. And then he looked up from his pad and I found myself staring into the bluest pair of eyes I had ever seen.

"I'm sorry," he said. "That was rude, I know, but I've never liked being interrupted when I'm working."

"That's fair enough." I turned to walk back behind the counter.

"No, hang on," he said. "Let me show you, if you've got a minute." I had more than a minute; apart from old Joe, one of the regulars, who was methodically working his way through a plate of liver, bacon and chips, the place was empty. Papa Vettori wouldn't like it if he knew I was sitting chatting to a customer, rather than wiping down tables and restocking the display of chocolate bars by the till, but he was away tonight, visiting his wife who

164

was in the Royal Marsden. So I perched on the seat beside him, ready to spring up if a customer walked in or Joe wanted to settle his bill.

"I'm working on a project," he explained. "I want to capture the real spirit of Soho before it finally disappears. I mean, you look at the beautiful Victorian tiling on the front of the pub. When the bulldozers move in, that'll all be gone. And what will replace it? Probably some tiny, overpriced flats with all the architectural merit of a shoebox."

He was warming to his theme, startling me with his passion. I was so used to students who only worried about how everything affected them that it made a real change to listen to someone who really seemed to care about his wider environment. But then he'd never actually said he was a student. I only assumed he was because of his boyish looks and the raincoat which would once have been just another charity shop purchase but now came with the label "vintage".

"Take a look at these," he said. He flipped through his sketch pad, showing me scenes I walked past almost every day: the stalls on Brewer Street market; the Patisserie Valerie on Old Compton Street, its window a riot of elaborate gâteaux; the entrance to a strip club on Archer Street, a curvy woman lurking enticingly in the doorway. Places and people alike were rendered with an accurate yet sympathetic eye.

"They're good," I told him, meaning it.

"Yeah, everyone knows these places, but they'll be around for ever. Even the strip club, though I'm sure the council would like to see that close down just like the pub over there. They're taking all the dirt from underneath Soho's fingernails, you know. So many places have shut in the last few years, or been gentrified beyond all recognition ..."

I wanted to laugh. The way he talked, you'd have thought he'd been working in the area as long as I had. I'd certainly seen the changes he mentioned over the years. Not all of them were bad, despite what he said: no one really mourned the passing of the clip joints, where gullible men were overcharged for watered-down drinks and paid for sexual favours which never materialised. But the old Marquee club, where everyone from the Rolling Stones to Joy Division had played, that was a loss, and so were some of the speciality shops and cafés, pushed aside by the imported coffee shop chains with their comfy sofas and their unlimited wi-fi access. Popular as it was, Vettori's was part of the past, and when Papa Vettori died, or decided he'd had enough, I doubted whether any of his sons or daughters would really have the heart to keep the business on.

I could have happily argued the point with him, but it wasn't just the possibility of more customers which was distracting me. A couple of times as he flipped over the pages of his pad his arm brushed against mine. The contact sent little sparks of sensation through me and I pulled back. It had been a while since any man had aroused such a sudden, physical reaction from me, and I couldn't understand why. He wasn't my usual type: I liked slightly rough-looking men who worked with their hands. He was too young, too pretty, too soft. But I'd been on my own for a while now. My last boyfriend, Tamas, was a Polish builder who I'd met while I was on one of my rare nights out with the girls. He was wiry and muscular from hard manual work, he had a dirty, cigarette-roughened laugh and incredible stamina in bed. I'd really started to think we had a future together, but once work had started drying up for him he decided to go

166

back to Gdansk. My body was obviously missing what had been great and very regular sex and was reminding me it was time I did something about it.

Not that I was going to have the opportunity to do anything about it tonight. From behind me, Joe called, "Excuse me," and by the time I'd dealt with him, a group of men had come in who had seen a write-up of Vettori's on a website devoted to classic cafés and wanted to see if the food and ambience were as good as the author claimed. Four orders of egg, bacon, chips and beans later, I looked round to see that Sketch Pad Boy had gone, leaving behind enough money to cover his bill plus a generous tip. Clearly, he had enjoyed my company, but he hadn't even told me his name.

Two nights later, the rain was back and so was he. Same table, same order, same intent concentration on his sketch pad. I didn't think I would get a moment to talk to him this time; Papa was in, and though he was in a good mood as his wife was responding well to treatment, I was still aware of the need to look busy in front of him.

When I went over with Sketch Pad Boy's sandwich, I realised that he was actually drawing Papa. The man was ripe for caricature, with his saggy jowls and the black, bushy eyebrows that contrasted so strikingly with his white hair, but the sketch had somehow caught the essence of him: a mixture of pride at everything he had achieved, coupled with an evident weariness. Disappearing Soho, in all its glory.

"Are you going to show it to him?" I asked.

"Not till it's finished," he replied. "And then I'd like to draw you, if you don't mind."

"Why, am I an old landmark, too?" I couldn't really object if that was the opinion he'd formed of me. After all, I had been working here so long, I sometimes felt as though I was as much a part of the furniture as the chipped formica tables and the brown leatherette booths.

He shook his head. "I wouldn't be drawing you here." He scribbled something on a scrap of paper and pushed it over to me. His name – Andrew – and an address. "Come and see me on Sunday. Wear your uniform. I'll explain."

His cool assumption that I was free, or would drop any plans I had made in order to go and see him, should have been infuriating, but something about him intrigued me. I was curious to know how he saw me, how he would render me on paper. And, more than anything, I wanted to be alone with him. I didn't say anything, just stuffed the note he'd given me into the pocket of my overall and went to clear tables.

Andrew had an apartment above a wholesale jeweller's on Berwick Street, which explained his familiarity with the area. It didn't strike me as a typical student residence, and I thought again how little I really knew about him. He soon put that right, filling me in on his background over coffee which he had laced with a generous amount of brandy. He'd left school with a good set of A-levels and joined an investment bank, but had quickly grown tired of the pressurised environment and the boorish culture that surrounded the job. When the financial markets began imploding, the bank had looked for people prepared to accept a generous redundancy package. Andrew immediately put his name forward, knowing he had enough money behind him to go back to college and take a foundation course in Fine Art.

In return, I told him how I'd married too young, to a man my parents didn't really approve of. Phil and I had had an explosive sex life, but once the initial physical attraction had worn off we had realised that was pretty much the only thing which was keeping us together. The sensible thing to do was to go our separate ways so we could both start afresh. In the immediate period following the divorce, I had found the job at Vettori's, intending it to be a temporary thing while I sorted my life out. Obviously I hadn't sorted it out all that well, because I was still there, still waiting on tables, nearly twenty years later.

"I always meant to move on, but they're like family to me now," I told him, finishing the last of my coffee.

"And that's why I want to celebrate places like Vettori's," Andrew said, "because they've been important in people's lives for so long. And then one day they'll be gone, and you'll walk past the sushi bars that have replaced them and struggle to remember what was there before."

I knew he could talk about the changing face of Soho all day, but that wasn't why I was there. "So how do I fit into all this?" I asked. "And if you're so desperate to draw me, why can't you do it in the café? Papa loved the sketch you did of him. I'm sure he wouldn't object."

"Because if you posed the way I wanted you to, we'd both get arrested." Andrew stood up. "Come with me."

I followed him into what I suspected had originally been a bedroom, but had been converted into an artist's studio. The big windows let in plenty of natural light. A blank canvas stood propped on an easel, and finished paintings hung on the wall. I was drawn to another of the street scenes Andrew loved. Its centrepiece was an American-style diner, painted on a rainy night, its reflected neon sign seeming to melt into the wet pavement. I couldn't understand how someone who clearly had so much talent had ever been attracted to a career in investment banking.

"That's not what I wanted to show you," he said. He produced another sketch pad and handed it to me. As I leafed through it, I found myself looking at a series of nude studies, some of a man who must have been in his sixties, the rest of a younger, rather overweight black woman. "I did those in life modelling classes," he said. "I enjoy drawing nudes, but I've been wanting to find a subject who isn't a regular on the circuit." He gestured to a sketch of the old man posing in the lotus position. "Bill's a good old lad, but there's only so many times I can look at his scrotum."

Sudden realisation hit me. "And you want me to pose for you. Naked."

"Not quite," he said. "But as soon as I saw you, I thought how much I'd love to paint you half-out of your uniform."

In a club, after a few drinks, that line would have sounded like a sleazy come-on. Here, in Andrew's studio, it was a proposal that was both flattering and sexy. I was beginning to become aware of the erotic tension between us once more; Andrew must have noticed it as well, but he just watched me, waiting for my answer.

"What would it involve?" I asked.

"Well, I'd produce some preliminary sketches of you today, and then you'd come back a couple of times while I worked on the actual painting. We'll work round your shifts at the café – I take it you usually get Sundays off?"

"You're being a little presumptuous here," I told him. "I haven't actually said yes yet."

"But I know you want to, Geri."

He was right: perhaps I was looking for an ego boost; perhaps I wanted to do something which was utterly removed from the routine I had fallen into, but whatever the reason, I was suddenly eager to pose for him.

"So what do you need me to do?" I asked.

He smiled. "Well, first of all you can help me move the sofa."

Once we had manhandled his wicker sofa into the studio, Andrew told me to go behind the screen in the corner of the room and take my underwear and tights off. When I returned, barefoot and with my uniform overall fastened over my nakedness, I saw that Andrew had draped a soft grey wool throw over the sofa, to make it more comfortable for me to lie on.

Suddenly feeling incredibly self-conscious, I went to lie down, waiting for instructions on how I should arrange myself. Instead, I felt Andrew take hold of the neckline of my overall and pull the poppers apart roughly, baring most of my body to his gaze. Then he gently contorted my limbs into the position he wanted. By the time he had finished, I had one arm sprawled above my head, and one leg slightly bent. Posed like that, I knew my pussy would be visible and a prominent part of his painting. I hadn't been expecting that, but I didn't object or try to close my legs. Not when Andrew was looking at me with such obvious lust and admiration.

"Right, turn your head to look at me," he ordered. "Yes, that it's it. You look fantastic, but let me know if you start to get uncomfortable, and we'll take a break."

He reached for his sketch pad, and began to work with the same concentration I'd seen him display that first night in Vettori's. Despite his concerns, I found I was able to hold the pose for quite a while; the room was pleasantly warm, not some draughty pre-Raphaelite artist's garret, and the throw kept the wicker beneath it from pressing into and marking my skin. When I finally rose from the sofa after an hour, limbs just a little stiff, and padded over to where Andrew was sitting, I was stunned by what I saw. Like almost every woman, I'd never been entirely comfortable about undressing in front of a man for the first time, and, as I'd grown older, I had become conscious that my breasts weren't quite as perky or my stomach as taut as they had been when I first married. But in the strokes of Andrew's pencil I saw a body that was soft and enticing, rounded in all the right places and subtly framed by the open flaps of my overall. It was a startlingly erotic image, with my bare breasts and my rudely parted legs, but one which was a celebration of my femininity.

"I – I don't know what to say." This wasn't like me. I was never speechless; I could deal with the occasional obnoxious drunk who stumbled into Vettori's, or the customers who complained about everything from the strength of their tea to an egg yolk that wasn't runny enough, but looking at Andrew's beautiful drawing had completely thrown me. Finally, I managed to add, "Apart from thank you, obviously."

"I'm glad you like it, but this is just the beginning," Andrew replied. "When you come back, we'll get into the real meat of the work."

As I was leaving the flat, on impulse I gave him a hug. It was the only real physical contact we'd had, apart from when Andrew had arranged me in the pose he wanted. For a moment, he pulled me tight to him; I could feel the solid bulk of his cock trapped against my body, more erect than I might have expected. Our lips met, and we kissed with a passion that left us breathless. Andrew's hands cupped the cheeks of my arse, gently squeezing them. And then I reminded myself that Andrew was a good fifteen years my junior, and I pulled away. "I have to go," I told him. "I'll see you next Sunday."

A hundred yards down the street, I turned and saw him standing in the doorway that led up to his flat, looking utterly bereft. I stepped up my pace and didn't look back; it was the only way to avoid the temptation of going back and letting him fuck my brains out – which, I told myself firmly, would be a very bad idea, however obvious it was that we both desperately wanted each other.

There were a couple of moments during the course of the next week when I wondered whether I should ring Andrew and tell him I'd changed my mind and wouldn't be returning for a second sitting after all. Maybe I'd just imagined the fervour of his kiss and the strength of his erection pressing into me. Even though I'd heard female customers talking in Vettori's about their conquests of much younger men and proudly referring to themselves as 'cougars', I thought there was something sad about women who went chasing toy boys. It was as though they were so determined to hang on to their disappearing youth, they didn't care how ridiculous they made themselves look in the process. I couldn't deny that I found Andrew really attractive, but even though I spent that Sunday evening with my fingers in my knickers, fantasising about what it would have been like to let him fuck me in that airy studio of his while I brought myself to a hot, breathless orgasm, I wasn't going to make a fool of myself over him.

And what if he'd decided I was some kind of prick-tease and no longer wanted anything to do with me? For all I knew, once he had gone back into his flat, he had crumpled up the sketch he'd made of me and thrown it in the bin. So it was with some trepidation that I found myself standing in front of that doorway on Brewer Street, hoping he would let me in.

To my relief, when I buzzed the entry phone he answered at once. "Hang on, Geri, I'll be down in a second."

"I'm sorry I had to dash off like that last time," I said, as I followed him up the stairs.

"Don't worry about it," he replied. "Come on, let's have a drink and then we can get down to work."

Again we hauled the sofa into the studio, and I changed behind the screen, though this time when I emerged I did so with my overall already open, no longer quite so concerned about being half-naked in front of Andrew.

I settled myself on the sofa, taking up the pose Andrew had previously asked me to adopt. I had expected him to start painting on a blank canvas, but to my surprise, he pulled a cloth off the easel to reveal that he had already copied the outline of my body from his initial sketches.

He fussed around with tubes of paint, holding a couple alongside my overall so he could choose the shade which most resembled the real thing. It was hard to keep my composure, having him so close to me when I was so scantily dressed, but I did my best not to react when I felt his hand accidentally brush the top of my thigh.

It was strangely soothing to lie there and watch Andrew at work, squeezing paint on to his palette and dabbing at the canvas. It was an unseasonably warm day, and the window was open; I could hear voices and laughter from time to time as people passed on the pavement beneath us, but apart from that all was quiet. Andrew kept looking over at me, making sure every detail was accurate, and occasionally our eyes would meet, making me shiver with desire.

Eventually, Andrew put down his palette, stretched and said, "I think that's enough for today. Do you want to see how it's coming along?"

I got off the sofa and went over to the easel. Andrew had filled in much of the background colouring and was beginning to pick out the streaks of honey-blonde in my hair where it fanned out over my red uniform, working with broad, definite strokes.

"I can't wait to see it when it's finished," I told him.

"I'm pleased you like it," he replied, and then we were in each other's arms, mouths locked together in a fierce kiss.

Andrew thrust me up against the wall and pulled the overall down off my shoulders. I loved his aggression and his desire to take control, but even so I stilled his hands before he could strip me completely. "We shouldn't be doing this," I said. "Think about it, I'm old enough to be your mother."

"Do you think I have a problem with that?" he asked, tracing his finger along the soft skin beneath my eyes, where the first crow's feet were starting to form. He was no longer looking at me with an artist's eye, but regarding me in the manner of a man who wants to imprint every detail of the woman he's in love with on his memory.

"No, but what would people think if they knew?"

He snorted. "Who gives a fuck what they'd think? Geri, you must know how I feel about you – it's in every brush stroke on that canvas, for God's sake …"

And with that he dragged me back over to the sofa, pushing me back so I sprawled in much the same wanton, abandoned pose he had had me adopt for the painting. I didn't resist, not now I knew how much he wanted me. Instead, I lay back waiting, my body open to him.

He dropped to his knees and began to kiss his way up the insides of my thighs. He deliberately took his time, so I was squirming with anticipation and impatience as he neared my pussy. At the first touch of his mouth on my lips, I couldn't help but groan; the soft, sucking pressure felt so good. My fingers snagged in his shaggy dark hair, keeping him in place while he licked and teased me. Suddenly, it didn't seem to matter that Andrew was so much younger than me, or that he was ambitious and passionate about the bigger things while I was stuck in my safe waitressing rut; on this level, at least, we were perfectly matched.

Andrew kept on eating me, his tongue occasionally straying down to lap at my arsehole, till I was bucking my hips into his face, half-crazed and on the verge of coming. That was when he stopped, rising to his feet so he could strip off the T-shirt and torn, paint-spattered jeans he was still wearing. When his underwear came off, his cock stood up from his groin, hard and tempting. I tried to reach out a hand and touch it, but he slapped it away with a grin, telling me not to be so greedy. I watched, fingers idly dipping into my pussy to keep my arousal gently stoked, as he fished a condom from his wallet, rolling it down over his erection. Once he was safely sheathed, he turned me over forcefully, placing me on all fours with my rump sticking out towards him. I clung on to the arm of the sofa as he played his cockhead along the length of my slit. For a moment I felt it pressing against the entrance to my arse, and I trembled at the thought that he might be planning to fuck me there. And then his cock slipped lower, butting at the entrance to my cunt, and I reached down underneath myself and helped to guide him in.

This was a moment which should be captured on canvas, I decided. The glorious moment when the tight muscles of your pussy willingly cede possession to a thick, probing cock. I could only imagine how Andrew's talented brush work would capture the expression on my face, eyes closed and head thrown back to expose the pale length of my throat, as that big shaft thrust into me.

His hands gripped my hips, pulling me back so he was almost completely inside me. It was a long time since I had felt so full, so overflowing with hot male flesh, and I was glorying in the sensation. My fingers found my clit again, rubbing frenetically as he pushed and withdrew, pushed and withdrew. Andrew's breath was harsh in my ear, his movements more forceful, and I knew he was as close as I was. He stuffed a couple of his fingers into my mouth and I sucked on them, vaguely tasting linseed oil and my own juices. All too soon, he held me tight as he shot his seed into the condom and then I felt my own pleasure crest, colours dancing behind my eyes as vivid as those on the canvases which hung round the room.

It took another couple of sessions before the painting was finished to Andrew's satisfaction. Every time I visited his flat, we would end the afternoon having wild, uninhibited sex. He took me into the bathroom so we could watch ourselves in the big mirror as I rode him, and to celebrate the completion of my portrait, he fucked my arse in the studio. I glowed with the satisfaction of good sex as I went about my job, and with Papa in an elated mood as it appeared his wife was going to make a complete recovery, I felt happier at Vettori's than I had in a long time. Even the art school know-it-alls seemed to have lost their power to annoy me.

Andrew submitted his collection of paintings and drawings of Soho for his final coursework assignment. Entitled *Rain And Neon,* it was displayed alongside all the work submitted by the other students on his course at a special viewing for family and friends. It seemed as though he was going to pass with one of the top marks in his year, and the reaction to his paintings and drawings from college staff and invited guests was suitably enthusiastic. From the comments I heard as I mingled with everyone there, it seemed as though he had succeeded in his ambition of getting people to look at the area with fresh eyes. I had been taken along by Andrew even though my contribution to his project was conspicuous by its absence. That was because the painting was hanging proudly on my bedroom wall, where Andrew and I could see it every time we fucked – and as far as he was concerned, that was the only audience it needed.

LIVING IN A RATHER unexciting area of East London, I knew if I was going to write about any part of the city which really interests me, it was going to be Soho. It's one of those places everyone has an image of in their head, but the reality is so different from when I first moved to London, over twenty years ago. Then, it still seemed quite seedy but, like the area round King's Cross, it's turned into somewhere much safer, but it's also lost a lot of the individuality it had. The characters and the quirky little shops and pubs are still there, but you really have to seek them out. Like Geri, the narrator of the story, I walk round there and I'll notice a new branch of Starbucks or a noodle bar, and not be able to remember quite what it replaced, and that's where the idea of trying to capture the spirit of a place before it disappears came from.

The café is based on a real greasy spoon in the area, as is the derelict pub Andrew is sketching, which people who know Soho might realise was the Intrepid Fox. Geri is very much part of this old Soho, not entirely sure how she'd fit into the new, homogenised version, while Andrew has the idealism and vision of the young newcomer. I'm writing quite a lot of older woman, younger man fiction at the moment – perhaps it's just the age I've reached! – but I didn't want Geri to be the stereotype predatory cougar; I felt she needed to be as unsure about the relationship and the changes it would bring as she was about the changes in her immediate environment to make the story work.

Rain And Neon is the title of a track by Bill Nelson, and it just seemed to fit the mood I was trying to create – late-night Soho in the rain, like an English version of Edward Hopper's *Nighthawks*, with the feeling that anything could be about to happen and you just have to trust yourself enough to let it …

The Tourist
by Clarice Clique

I WALKED PAST THE air hostess, ignoring whatever standard processed words she spoke to me. I walked down the clanging metal steps and into the English rain, across the puddled grey concrete and down the never-ending corridors. I queued to present my passport, waited for my black case to spew around to me and then I walked through customs and out into the main airport as I had done countless times before and would do countless times again until the day I finally retired. I walked past the drivers with their bored faces and lazily held up signs, past the families with their expectant smiles, past the tired travellers sipping at badly made coffee, and then I stopped walking.

She was leaning against the wall, her hair looked as if at one point it had been scraped back into a perfect pony tail but now dark curls had escaped and rested against the pale skin of her face. She was dressed casually, a long brown skirt, some sort of blue top with lace edging round the bust, a dark coat hanging open. Either she was so aware of her youth and beauty she knew she didn't need clothes and cosmetics to enhance it, or she was trying not to draw any more attention to the curves of her body. The only concession she had made to the Boots beauty counter was long dark crimson nails.

I knew it was her. The pain deep in my stomach told me it was her. It had been years, no, not years. It had been twenty-one months since I received that last e-mail from her, when she finally accepted I was a happily married man and I wouldn't carry on corresponding with her. She was married too and had children, but she never made any claims to happiness.

She'd sent me one photo; I had never sent her any. In the midst of the time when we were e-mailing each other ten or twenty times a day she blessed me with one image of her. She was naked apart from a pair of black stockings. At the edge of the photo lay a pair of discarded stiletto heels; metal handcuffs rested by her outstretched hands. I'd stared as much at those handcuffs as at the curves of her breasts hidden under the waves of her hair. Now the woman from that photo stood mere feet away from me.

'Catherine?' My voice betrayed nerves I didn't realise I was feeling until I spoke.

She didn't reply and I was fully aware of myself as a middle-aged man approaching a beautiful young woman on the basis that she resembled a photo an e-mail flirtation had once sent me. But it was more than a resemblance. And it had been more than an e-mail flirtation, so much more. Then she looked me up and down and laughed.

'If you like,' she said, her brown eyes sparkling in a way that separated her from the weary atmosphere of the airport, as if everything surrounding her was just a video playing in the background.

I wanted to think about her answer, digest what each of the three words could mean but her long legs were already striding away from me. I trotted after her, more puppy than man.

'I want to see everything,' she said in a low husky

voice.

The heat rose to my cheeks, the first time I was conscious of blushing in my life.

'I want to be a tourist,' she breathed into my ear. 'Find a hotel, then show me everything.'

She didn't say another word on the tube journey into central London and I had no idea how to ask her if she was the woman I thought she was, it somehow felt rude seeing we were already travelling together. I noticed that she was not wearing the wedding or engagement rings that had graced her long slender fingers in the photo and there were no marks betraying that she had worn any rings recently on her naked fingers. I gazed at our almost invisible reflections in the window opposite and the more logical part of my mind questioned what I was doing sitting so naturally next to this woman, but the majority of my mind was too busy acting out mini porn movies. Every time the movement of the train pushed her knee or arm against my body a thousand nerve endings responded and pulsed straight to my groin. I was a teenage boy again unable to control my excitement, getting a hard-on at the slightest stimulation. I imagined bending her over the seat, pulling her skirt up and fucking her roughly regardless of the other passengers. I visualised sharing her with the other men, varying gang bangs and orgies with being the only man allowed near her while the others looked on in envy with their hands fumbling in their pockets.

When we reached the hotel I had mentally fucked her dozens of times and was too aware that it was only in my mind that she'd permitted me to touch her. The hotel itself was part of one of those generic characterless chains, which was the main reason I selected it, no chance of bumping into anyone I knew. To be entirely certain I took her to the one in Southwark muttering something about it being a good location for tourist attractions as we walked into one of the blandest red-brick buildings it was possible to build. She didn't say anything, staring at a nondescript painting in the reception as I booked us into a double room.

The room was everything you'd expect and nothing more, but it didn't matter, my whole body was shaking as if it had reached a place where I could no longer control it. I sat on the bed in an attempt to steady my nerves. She was standing by the door, about as far away from me as she could be in this small room. All the things Catherine had written in those e-mails flashed through my mind, I remembered words and images I had once vowed to forget.

I will suck every drop of cum from your body

I want to ride your big fat cock until I collapse with exhaustion

Say the word, or click your fingers, and I will be on my knees in front of you spreading my ass cheeks for you

Fuck me. Fuck me. Fuck me. I am begging you to fuck me. Please Fuck me

I have fallen in love with you. I am in love with you. Please love me

I took a deep breath and walked towards her. I raised my hands to caress her face, she grabbed my wrists and held them an inch away from her skin.

'I want to see London,' she said.

'There's a lot of London to see,' I said when we were again outside. 'Where in particular do you want to go?'

No answer.

Catherine had never mentioned anything about London, or about cities in general, she wrote of country walks; fingers sticky with blackberry juice; trying not to scratch her nettle stings; her favourite dog who never came back to her no matter how long she spent calling and searching for him. I would read her words and look out of my apartment window at the traffic and noise and imagine rolling around with her in some country field with only the rain covering our skin.

I took her to the London Eye, queuing to buy a combined ticket with a river cruise, while she stood staring into the green brown darkness of the Thames.

The pods moved slowly. I chatted constantly to dispel her silence, pointing out the landmarks that she must know as well as I did; trying to be a bit more risqué by mentioning it was possible to hire a private night time trip on the Eye (although I left unspoken my desire to penetrate her while looking down on the bright lights of the unknowing city); finally, I resorted to the most clichéd topic of all, and began to discuss the weather.

'It's still very grey but at least the rain has stopped,' I said.

'I like the rain,' she said, 'it washes everything away.'

My heart stopped. I'd said that to her once. Not quite the same but close. I'd said that London suited clouds and rain, if Paris was springtime then London belonged to winter with all the sins of summer hidden and forgotten under a barrage of constant rain. Was it similar enough? Was she giving me a sign?

I moved to put my arm around her waist, she walked away to stare at London from a viewpoint furthest away from me. I sat down on the hard wooden bench and waited for the pod to finish its circular journey.

The boat trip was filled with the same tension, although the tension was only on my side. She appeared perfectly calm, staring out at the drops of rains disappearing into the mass of the Thames, oblivious to both the commentary from a depressingly cheery guide and to my presence at her side.

Catherine's e-mails had always been so unique, so chatty, she could and would talk about anything and everything. It was the first thing that struck me when we first encountered each other so innocently on a chess internet site. She was the only person I knew who could entwine topics as diverse as world economics, blow jobs and gardening. The woman sitting next to me sat in silence.

'That was nice,' I said when we stepped off the boat onto the damp London pavement. My own voice was chalk scratching a blackboard. If she had asked I wouldn't be able to recount a single thing about the trip, I could have described in detail the subtle hints of jasmine in her perfume, or the beauty of her naked face devoid of all make-up, or the way her slightly parted lips made me want to tenderly kiss her, and how when her tongue darted out over them I yearned to pull her head down onto my cock.

'Train stations are nice,' she said.

She pronounced 'nice' mimicking my voice. The colour rose to my cheeks for the second time in the day, but it was also a rush of pleasure to think that she was at least listening to me however distant she appeared.

I'd been thinking whether she might want to go to either the nearby London Aquarium or the Dali place but instead I followed her to Waterloo Station. She stood underneath the big clock for one hour. I stayed by her side for a little while before going to buy her a cup of tea and a sandwich overflowing with Mediterranean filling. She took them both off me but only sipped the tea when it had grown cold and she dropped the sandwich into a bin.

'Soho,' she said drawing out the two syllables so they sounded like two different words.

I took her to Piccadilly Circus, she didn't even glance at the bright signs but she paused by Eros.

'When he was first constructed there was controversy about having a nude statue on public display,' I said with a smile.

She walked off without looking at me. Catherine in her e-mails had loved facts, always asking questions, always wanting to know more.

It was now me following her as she led the way up the grand London streets to Soho. She looked straight ahead even when she crossed roads. Soho looked the same as any other district in the daylight, not how I remembered it from late-night stag nights when I was a younger man. She walked straight into a shop and I went after her. The staff looked as bored as they do in so many shops in London but my eyes were wide as I took in the array of sexual paraphernalia lined up so casually on the shelves; whips, dildos, blow-up dolls, repulsive-looking plastic pussies boasting on their packaging of their teenage tightness.

She was caressing the ersatz cocks as if they were real flesh; my own body ached as I watched her. For the first time she showed an awareness of people around her, smiling at the female shop assistant, winking at a male customer furtively fingering the sealed magazines on a rack in the corner. And she turned to me, laughing at me as she had done when I first approached her. She took my hand and led me up black metal stairs.

'Men tell me they prefer me in heels, what do you prefer me in?'

I remembered the pair of heels laying at the edge of the photo Catherine sent me, my voice caught in my throat as

187

if it was a physical object I could choke on. 'I … you … haven't … didn't … don't.'

She walked away from my mumblings and ran her thumb down a red stiletto heel. She slipped out of one of her flat black pumps and stepped into the shoe like an erotic version of Cinderella. A male shop assistant brought over the other shoe without her having to ask. Then my phone rang. Some classical tune that had seemed right at the time, but blaring through the hush of this shop I realised how wrong it had always been. She looked at me with a raised eyebrow and that one gesture from her gave me no choice but to answer it.

'Hello, darling, where are you?'

Hearing Heather's matter-of-fact, straight-to-the-point, voice, there was no guilt in me, just extraordinary pity. How could Heather, who would find even the suggestion of going to a sex shop together shocking, compete with this woman twenty years her junior who I couldn't keep my eyes off? Not that there was any competition going on, if Catherine wanted me, she could have me, it was as simple as that.

'Just got caught up a little bit, nothing serious.'

'What happened? Your flight arrived on time.'

So she was already checking up on me; somehow that was a relief, it was less of a betrayal if she didn't completely trust me.

'You know how work is. It'll be easier for me to stay an extra night or two in London than to commute.'

'You know best, love. Now, what do you think about the dinner party on Thursday, should I buy the new dinner set? Do you think Eva would be insulted if I didn't use the one she gave us?'

Disappointment.

I'd spent almost all my adult life with her and she

either didn't know or didn't care that I was lying to her. I desired to be loved and wanted by someone who knew me completely and accepted my flaws as readily as my money. Heather had never been that someone. I spoke to my wife about what various acquaintances would think about her purchasing some new china while I stared at another woman revealing more and more of her flesh as she tried on a pair of black leather boots and thought maybe this is what marriage comes down to.

When I clicked the phone closed Catherine smiled at me.

'Can you answer yet whether you like me in heels?' She was holding her long skirt up, to show the tops of the boots clinging to the white flesh of her thighs. She turned around pulling her skirt up higher to reveal that she wasn't wearing any knickers, my cock responded to the glimpse of her full buttocks making my whole body physically ache for her.

'I like you,' I said. The timing was wrong, I knew that. It must have been obvious to her and everyone in the shop that I'd been talking to my wife, but she let go of her skirt and stepped towards me, brushing her hand against my cheek.

'Show me how much you like me. On your knees, lick the heel of my boots.'

The shop assistant showed no surprise but smirked as I dropped to my knees and ran my tongue down the heel of her boot. Maybe this was her game, maybe she knew London better than me and the whole tourist thing was a ruse to bring random business men to this shop and humiliate them. That made more sense than the forces of fate and coincidence delivering a woman I'd had a cyber fling with to the airport at the exact time I arrived. In that moment breathing in the scent of new leather and the tantalising closeness of her sex I didn't care who she was and what she wanted to do to me.

'Take these boots off me, I don't like them any more,' she said, 'they've been sullied.'

I unzipped them and peeled the leather away from her smooth skin, fighting the urge to stroke her beauty. Her feet were perfection, high arched softness with crimson painted toenails and I couldn't resist stroking the heel of her foot as I pulled the boot away from her. She looked at me with something akin to pity and stroked my hair.

'Buy me that pair of shoes,' she said pointing to a shoe with six-inch see-through heels.

I obeyed running my fingers over their contours hoping she would let me do the same when they were on her feet. She put them on and walked out of the shop leaving her original shoes discarded on the floor.

She moved with as much ease and grace as when she was wearing the flat footwear. Except now in the moments when she turned to me she was looking me in the eye, staring at me with a gaze that I never wanted to escape from.

'I want to see something big now,' she said.

There was no teasing or innuendo in her voice, nothing that encouraged me to do what I so desperately wanted and put her hand on my cock. So we went back on the tube and I suffered through the airless heat of too many people in too small a place, her body continually brushing against mine and the thought of trains going into tunnels. Trains going into tunnels. An agonising image.

I took her to the Monument waxing lyrical on Sir Christopher Wren and the Great Fire of London.

'Is burning a bad death?' she asked.

I stared back at her, all the dates and facts and figures I wanted to impress her with fading away as I looked at her.

190

'I think, I've heard, anyway, that it is the smoke that kills you, not the flames. It is suffocation rather than heat.'

She nodded, it was an acknowledgement of the fact I was choosing to ignore her question and the too obvious pain in her eyes.

We looked away from each other and stared up at the 202 foot high stone monument strutting into the grey sky in commemoration of people who died hundreds of years ago.

'Something else now,' she said turning away.

We walked up to London Bridge. She did not pause to look at it.

'I like the other one,' she said, 'this one is nothing.'

'Shall I take you to Tower Bridge?' I asked. 'Is that the one you mean? The one you see on all the postcards?'

'No,' she said. 'Somewhere else.'

I took her to Canary Wharf hoping that it might fit her earlier remit of something big and my vague impression that all females like to shop. She walked out into the street, took one look up at the UK's tallest building and then walked back to the train station without giving me a chance to regale her with any of the facts I had been mentally preparing for her.

I followed her back onto the train, she got off at the Cutty Stark station. The old Tea Clipper was hidden behind boarding but she didn't seem to mind as she stood staring at it.

'There was a fire a couple of years back, I think,' I said, 'I recall something about it on the news.'

She looked at me and I stopped speaking remembering her odd question at the Monument.

I felt a strange relief when she walked on and we began the hike up the park.

'I don't really know this part of London so well,' I said, settling down next to her on the grass at the peak of the hill. 'Of course as a kid I did the whole trip to the Royal Observatory but that was a long, long time ago.' I laughed, silently hoping she wasn't aware of the difference in our ages as much as I was.

'Shut up. Enjoy the view,' she said.

I looked ahead at a city I didn't know, old grand buildings taking their place in the skyline alongside new functional upstarts. It wasn't just looking at London from a different side, the strangeness came from the fact she was beside me. The fact I wasn't at home listening to my wife empty her head of all the little things she'd been saving up to tell me. I was here sitting on the grass in Greenwich with a woman who was either a total stranger or someone I flirted with online a couple of years ago. Everything had an air of unreality, even the ancient stones of London had a surreal quality.

Then my thoughts disappeared, my breath caught in my throat and I dared not release it, her hand was on the crotch of my trousers, undoing my fly. I fought the urge to look down as her fingers wrapped themselves round my cock. I was a superstitious kid again making up rules in my head, if I don't stand on any of the cracks in the pavement my mum won't really be dead, if I don't move then this beauty by my side will really be touching me.

Except this time it was true, Catherine's had pulled my erection out of my trousers, the coolness of the air was touching my heat, making me feel alive. Catherine's hand was working up and down my erection with a speed that I couldn't fight against. I came hard, spunk flying in the air making me feel like I had fired my juice over all the distant buildings, my cream had landed on the spikes of the Millennium Dome and drowned the arrogance of

Canary Wharf, the whole of London was touched by my seed.

The release was short-lived, she zipped me up and wiped her hand on my trouser leg.

'Let's go somewhere else,' she said.

I followed her around as she walked the streets of Greenwich and then beyond, following the path of the river. I wanted to say something to her, but what could I say? 'Thank you for the hand job, but please can I have a bit more, Miss? Sorry I came so quickly, I normally last a lot longer than that, you can ask my wife if you don't believe me. I promise I'll do better next time if you'll be so kind to give me another chance.'

'It's getting a bit nippy,' is what I said, rubbing my hands together as if she needed extra signs to understand me.

It was getting colder, but what concerned me was the way darkness was falling in around us, apart from being somewhere in the midst of London I had no knowledge of, I recalled a recent dinner party discussion about London being the most violent city in Europe. She was too beautiful to be wondering around at night with only me for protection.

'Maybe we should start finding our way back to the hotel?'

She answered me by pressing me against a brick wall, her body pushed into mine, the heat of her breath warming my lips. Her hand was on my fly releasing my desire to the cool air again. She gazed into my eyes as she wanked me with the same expert speed as before. I tried to hold back, think about something else, but my lust had increased, not abated after her earlier attention. She was too close to me, her stare was too intense, I came again.

She stepped away from me at the precise moment my pleasure exploded leaving my cream to spill onto the pavement.

We both looked down at the white puddle.

'Lick it up,' she said.

I dropped to my knees and lapped my come up. I thought of the millions of people who lived in London, the number of feet that must have passed this way through time, and I was in the midst of all that population and all that history, tasting my spunk for the first time because she had ordered me to.

When I had cleaned every last droplet she turned and walked on. I followed after her, almost forgetting to make myself decent in my fear that she might disappear into the night. She turned away from the river and within a couple more turns we emerged back into the noisy, lighted hub of the city. I followed her onto a bus and then a tube as she took us back to the hotel. Re-entering it, I had to remind myself why I had chosen it, all the glamour and pampering that was available in London, why had I taken this beautiful, amazing woman to a place like this. I wasn't the man I was this morning, I didn't care who saw me with Catherine, nor who they told.

'Let me take you somewhere else,' I said.

She shook her head and I was struck by the fear that she had no intention of staying with me, but she came with me to my room and sat down on the bed with her legs stretched out in front of her.

'Do you want something to eat?' I asked.

She shook her head.

'What would you like? What can I do for you?'

'You want to fuck me,' she said.

Her saying the word 'fuck' made my cock struggle against the material of my trousers.

194

'Would you like me to? I want to make you happy,' I said.

She laughed, a hard mocking laugh that somehow made my cock yearn for her more.

'Do you think the fake chivalry makes you a good English gentleman?'

'It's not fake,' I said, 'it's who I am. I don't want to fuck you if you don't want me as much I want you.'

She continued with her laughter. 'Do you believe the truth of your own words?'

I opened my mouth to protest, but realised there was nothing I could say.

'Fuck me.'

I climbed onto the bed feeling like a virgin as I edged her skirt up her thighs and revealed her sex, dusted with dark, nearly black, hair. I gently pushed her legs apart and moved to bury my head in her haven. She grabbed a handful of my hair and pulled my head towards her.

'Don't waste time,' she said before releasing me.

I fumbled with my belt and removed my clothes while she watched. I wished I could do as my wife did and turn the light off, but my embarrassment was worth the view of her beauty. She did not undress but still lay with her skirt where I had raised it to her hips and her feet enclosed in the shoes I had bought.

'Fuck me,' she said.

I lowered my body on top of her, hardly daring to breathe as my sex was at her entrance and her velvet passage was parting to let me in. I thrust into her gasping as our bodies met on this cheap hotel bed. It humiliated me how excited I was that she was so much younger than me.

Take that you little cockteaser, my mind yelled as I pounded into her.

She yawned.

'I want to be fucked not tickled,' she said and effortlessly rolled me over onto my back so that our positions were reversed.

She ground into me with a fury, her nails digging into my chest. Her body squeezed round my cock, sucking my cream out of me. She screamed as I jetted up into her, I had no idea whether the sound she made was from a place of anger or pleasure, it was a primal roar from somewhere hidden deep inside the human psyche. It continued for an eternity, she ground against me with more fury, uncaring of the fact that I had reached my orgasm. She ripped the lace edging of her top, pulling it down to reveal her full breasts. I reached my hand up and gingerly touched her orbs but the look in her eyes showed me what she wanted. I pinched at her beautiful flesh and pulled on the dark circles of her nipples. I twitched inside her and responded to her passion and rage with my own.

'Fuck me, slut,' she said, her words echoing my thoughts.

I bucked up into her and she pushed her weight down into me. I was screaming back at her, a low moan growing into something monstrous. It felt like the room couldn't contain us, our lust was spilling out onto the streets of London mixing and being heightened by all the unfulfilled desire of the city itself.

Sweat was dripping down her face between her breasts. I leant forward and licked the salt off her skin as her breasts pounded against my ears. My heart was thumping so hard. This is death. This is death, I thought. Her nails were in my back and I was clinging onto her as if she was life itself.

I came, an explosion, my whole being draining into her. I collapsed back on the bed, my eyes closed, bathing in the scent of her sex. I rested my hand on her hips and breathed deeply as droplets of her sweat fell on my body. I opened my eyes to look at her and saw it wasn't sweat but tears falling from her face.

She turned away from me.

'I thought London would be a good place to get lost in. Somewhere you could spend all your life walking through, surrounded by crowds and never seeing anyone.'

'At the airport were you leaving or arriving? I didn't know, you had no luggage with you and you came with me, I didn't know why you were there. I don't know.'

She rested her head on my chest, moving so that I still knew the warmth of being inside her.

We fell asleep like that, or I did. When I was aware of her breathing it was heavy and even. During the night our bodies merged more times, our limbs twisting around each other as we sweated our lives out onto the hotel bed.

'Who do you want to be?' she whispered into my ear at some point in the darkness when my hand was pressing between the flesh of her buttocks. 'You called me Catherine, who do you want to be?'

I almost said my real name, but I remembered the name I had used online.

'Ed,' I said. Ed had sounded like a man who could write the things I wrote to Catherine.

There was a moment's silence as my fingers delved deeper into her.

'Short for Edward or Eddie?' she asked.

'Just Ed.'

'Ed, Ed, Ed, Ed,' she breathed as I pushed my way into the tightness of her ass.

I woke up with my head resting on her chest and my hand feeling the moistness between her legs. I flicked over her clit on my way to her stomach where I traced over the faint silvery lines of stretch marks. Perhaps she had had children like my Catherine. Perhaps she was my Catherine.

'One moment,' she said.

Her body rolled out from under me and she walked to the bathroom. I admired the rear view of her hourglass figure, the smooth expanse of her back curving into full and shapely buttocks, then I reached for her handbag. There was a small hardback book written in one of the Latin languages I couldn't read, her place marked by a downturned page. Next I looked at her iPod, she had been listening to *Amore o grillo* from *Madama Butterfly*. I played a couple of seconds and then flicked through the rest of her selection, more opera, many bands I wasn't familiar with and then all the usual suspects: The Rolling Stones, The Beatles, David Bowie, Oasis, Radiohead etc. I replaced the iPod and then looked at the things that interested me most, her purse and her passport laying innocently in her bag and both containing her real identity.

I removed her passport, there seemed something seedy about opening her purse. I ran my thumb over the red passport cover. As I began to open it, my hands were shaking. I looked up. It was one of the moments when I knew what I would see before I saw it. Catherine was standing there staring at me. She was naked but I couldn't look at her, my eyes stayed on the carpet as she came over to me, took her passport and her handbag from me and began to get dressed.

'I am sorry,' I said. 'I needed to know.'

'You don't need to know anything.'

'I wanted to know.'

'You don't want to know.'

I swallowed hard and looked at her, I was scared I would start crying. She was already dressed, complete with torn top, stained skirt and the lapdancer shoes I had bought her yesterday.

'I had a fantasy,' she said, 'you won't understand. I wanted to submerge myself in the Thames, I wanted someone with me, inside me. I thought you could be the one. Something about you I thought matched something about me.'

'You wanted to drown yourself in the middle of London with me fucking you?' I said, my voice sounding too high, reflecting too much of my shock.

She shook her head. 'I told you you wouldn't understand.' She put her handbag over her shoulder.

'Don't go. Please don't go. Let me buy you some new clothes, I can't let you go out like that. Don't. Don't look at me like that. I had a right to look in your bag for fuck's sake, I licked my spunk off the street for you in the middle of God damn London.'

'I mistook you for someone else,' she said and left.

I stared at the closed door.

'I thought maybe you were this girl I met on the internet. I hoped you were her, because I fell in love with Catherine within moments of her talking to me. I lay awake at night every night dreaming of her. During the day no matter what I was doing I couldn't stop thinking of her. I wanted her more than I wanted to breathe. So I ended it as I was married and I was sensible and didn't believe you could fall in love with someone without meeting them. I mean, I didn't even believe in love. I believed you met someone you were sort of compatible with and made the best of it. But Catherine made my heart beat. You made my heart beat. I am sorry,' I said to the empty room.

I went back out into London a few hours later but still as dishevelled as when she left me. I thought if I walked along the Thames for long enough I would find her again. I looked up at Bankside Power Station protruding into the grey sky. It had been transformed into the Tate Modern now and was considered a thing of beauty. That was where I would start my search for Catherine.

About the Story

LONDON HAS ALWAYS BEEN a city I've felt attached to. I've walked its streets with men who have been born, bred and worked their whole lives there, and can transform all its grandeur into an everyday story; with men dissecting it with giant cameras into postcard pictures; with men who fall in love with it, and with men who are indifferent to it. Each time I've felt the same wonder of being in a place where each landmark is engrained in my mind as part of my childhood legacy but I still feel like a lost stranger. My story was inspired by this sense of dislocation which I thought could be reflected in the complexity of an internet relationship where people can reveal their greatest passions and most intimate selves without ever being certain of each other's true name.

The freedom and release of being with a stranger can be directly connected to the atmosphere of London, a big city where no one cares about you or what you do as long as it doesn't interfere with them. The easiest way to traverse London is by the underground, disappearing into the airless false light, bodies packed together but no eye contact socially permitted and then a few minutes later emerging somewhere completely different but permeated with the same feeling of London. My London is a place of darkness and shadows. Whether walking in the sun in Hyde Park, listening to the soaring human beauty of opera singers at Convent Garden, or staring up at the green-blue majesty of St. Paul's Cathedral, for me London always has a greyness, a sense of the mystery behind millions of hidden consciousnesses living in close proximity.

In London history and modernity are forcibly juxtaposed, a Tesco's Metro next to a quaint old building calling itself a *boulangerie* in its current incarnation, the Neon lights of Piccadilly overlooking Eros, and winding through it all the murky River Thames, a natural wonder, somehow unchanging despite all London's history of pollution. There is something in the way it is all bound together that states 'this is what man was, this is what man is'.

Being in London is knowing how small and insignificant I am and this sense has lit up some of my greatest liaison in anonymous hotel rooms which will hold no memory of anything I do.

West End Girl
by Carrie Williams

DINAH CIRCLED THE AD with her pen then placed it back on the table and took another sip of her pint. She would need some extra cash for Christmas presents and parties, and this sounded like it might be easy money. It had to beat selling mail-order organic turkeys, at any rate. She sat back, lit a cigarette and scanned the words once more:

'Actors required for living tableaux, prestigious central London store, December.'

Dinah couldn't imagine what a 'living tableau' might be, but the term intrigued her, somehow conjuring up decadent scenarios in her mind's eye. It sounded like it might even be fun. Taking a long drag on her cigarette, she reached for her mobile in her coat pocket and, glancing back at the newspaper, punched in the number and secured herself an audition for the following week.

Two months later she was being frisked by a handsome security guard at the staff entrance of Paley's. It felt strange, going behind the scenes of this upmarket department store where she had spent so many hours browsing the rails of designer clothes she couldn't afford, or ogling exotic goodies in the food hall. Almost immediately, a lanky, bug-eyed girl with blonde hair slicked back into a supermodel-esque ponytail introduced herself:

'Erin March,' she said. 'I'm in charge of window displays. If you come this way, you can meet the others.'

She strode purposefully across the room, in a corner of which a gaggle of young men and women stood chatting. Even if Dinah hadn't known it, she would have recognised them a mile off as fellow aspiring actors – markedly more attractive, in the main, than the usual run of mortals, they had the studied, rather self-conscious gestures and overloud voices common to thesps.

She turned to Erin. 'How will we be assigned?' she said.

The girl shrugged. 'This first evening we suggest you go in random pairs, to whatever window takes your fancy – first-come, first-served. We did intend to make a detailed plan, but it never happened.'

Dinah's eyes moved over the assembled party. Should she move in now, she wondered: find someone who looked her kind of person and scoop them up? Or should she be a little more relaxed, just go with the flow and see who she ended up with?

'Depending on how that works out,' she heard Erin continue, 'you'll either stay with the same person in the same window, stay with them but change window, or there'll just be a huge swap around to keep things fresh.' She flicked at a loose scrap of varnish on the end of one of her talons. 'The important thing,' she concluded, '*obviously*, is that you don't get bored.'

Dinah nodded. She'd been excited about this ever since the audition, when they'd explained to her that Paley's was planning special Christmas window displays featuring live models in place of mannequins. It wasn't to be a living tableau in the strictest sense of the word. Dinah had looked that up on the Internet in the interim and discovered that it was a translation of a French term, *tableau vivant*, denoting theatrically posed groups who don't move or speak during the display, as if they were in a painting or a photograph. It had been popular just prior to Edwardian times, both in upper-class drawing rooms and proper theatres, and sometimes – using naked or semi-naked actresses – as an erotic entertainment at private clubs or fairground sideshows.

No: in Paley's displays the actors would move and talk, as if they were in their own living rooms or in bars or nightclubs. Basically, Dinah had decided, she would get paid to sit around doing bugger all for entire evenings, dressed in designer gear, some of which she might even get to keep afterwards. It was the kind of kooky job she loved.

Erin clapped her hands to snare the attention of the small crowd.

'If you could please separate out into guys and girls,' she rasped, 'there are clothes here waiting to be chosen. Find something you like and then, when you're dressed, select a partner with the same kind of look – casual with casual, couture with couture, and so on. That's how we'll play it this evening at least.'

Dinah stepped up to one of the rails, picked out a silver Versace mini-dress. She had little interest in fashion, and almost invariably wore blue or black jeans teamed with a dark polo-neck sweater. But tonight she thought: *To hell with it.* This might not be the Adelphi, but if she was going out there to play her West End role, she might as well try to lose herself within it.

As she was turning away from the rail with her hanger, she felt a hand at her elbow.

'Dinah,' came a familiar voice. 'It's been yonks.'

'Suzy!' she exclaimed. 'How *are* you?'

They kissed each other lightly on the cheeks, established that they hadn't seen each other in about five years, since graduating from Goldsmiths, and agreed that, yes, didn't time fly?

'If you haven't chosen a partner yet,' said Suzy, 'why not come with me? I'm sure we've got plenty to catch up on.'

Dinah readily agreed: she'd always liked Suzy and often regretted that they hadn't stayed in contact. Happily, since Suzy had picked out a slinky black Moschino dress, the pair were sartorially compatible. She followed her friend over to a corner, where they changed and checked their belongings in with Erin's assistant. Then they, together with their fellow actors, followed Erin out through the shop.

At the front of the store, Erin drew back a dark curtain behind one of the perfumery counters and gestured inside.

'How about you two first?' she said, jutting her chin towards Dinah and Suzy. 'Versace and Moschino would go great in here.'

The pair followed her in. A chaise longue stretched the length of the window, swathed in aubergine velvet and littered with cushions in chocolate-covered silk. In front of it was a low chrome and glass coffee table set with two margarita glasses full of a deep red liquid.

'Pomegranate juice,' said Erin at Dinah's raised eyebrows and hopeful expression. 'Sorry girls, but there's no drinking on duty. Now, if you could just drape yourselves elegantly over the chaise longue and look as if you're guests at a glamorous cocktail party, that would be fabulous. I'll check in with you later.'

She let the curtain drop behind her on her way out, and Dinah and Suzy looked self-consciously out at the shoppers streaming up Regent Street. A few of them had already noticed the girls and were shooting them quizzical glances.

'So is that really it?' said Suzy. 'We just plonk ourselves down and chat away for a few hours?'

Dinah let herself tumble back onto the chaise longue, glad that she wouldn't have to stand a moment longer in the Perspex stilettos she'd chosen to match her outfit. Suzy plumped herself next to her and reached for the glasses on the table.

'Cheers!' she said with a little peal of delighted laughter. 'This is the life, huh?'

Dinah was already giggling: as her friend had leant forwards, her not-inconsiderable cleavage had spilt forth, and already a small fan club had congregated at the window – a group of three or four teenage boys, ties loose, rucksacks pulling their school blazers out of kilter.

'Christ,' said Suzy, when she saw where Dinah was looking. 'That didn't take long, did it? I don't think I'll be wearing this little number again tomorrow, somehow.'

They didn't need the margaritas, as it turned out: within an hour the two were drunk on talk and laughter and were wondering aloud how they could have ever drifted apart. After two hours they had declared themselves best friends and were talking about the possibility of sharing a flat together. At eight they clocked off and made up for the fruit juice with a bottle of red in a wine bar just off Carnaby Street.

Afterwards, as she jumped on a bus at Piccadilly Circus, Dinah waved her friend goodbye.

'Roll on tomorrow night!' she shouted as Suzy threaded back into the mêlée of Christmas shoppers.

The second evening, Erin declared she had decided that everyone must swap both partners and windows, 'to keep things interesting'. Dinah was disappointed, but the feeling dissipated when the most gorgeous of the boys in the group – and there were *a lot* of gorgeous guys – approached and asked if he could team up with her.

·'Why not?' she said, smiling coolly, but her pussy pulsed a little. She looked over at Suzy, who was gazing at her enviously.

'Threesome?' Dinah saw her mouth, and she had to purse her lips hard to stop herself laughing out loud.

She was led, together with her new partner – whose name, she learnt, was Rupert – to one of the large corner windows. She was dressed a bit more casually this time, in a black rubber dress that ended just above the knee, with short sleeves and a high neckline. Judging that it was posh clubbing gear, she had matched it, with Erin's consent, with some black designer trainers, Rupert was wearing brown leather trousers and a simple white shirt, open at his muscular throat. The trousers were a very snug fit, and Dinah was embarrassed to keep finding herself sneaking glances at his ample crotch.

This time the window contained a bar area at the back, in front of which stood two white-leather stools. In the centre a mirror ball revolved slowly. Several people were already almost pressing up against the pane of glass from the outside, peering inside curiously. Dinah pulled herself up on one of the stools and sipped from a highball glass of fruit juice.

'So what have you been in I'd know?' she heard Rupert ask, but before she had drawn breath to answer he had begun to reel off his own achievements.

After half an hour, Dinah wanted nothing more than to go home. What Rupert had in the looks department didn't translate into any form of personality, and she was bored. She'd counted the glitter ball around so many times she was dizzy, but she couldn't look at Rupert's smooth, tanned, glib face any more, and over and over in her mind she heard Erin's admonition:

'Whatever you do, don't hold their stares – the punters',' she'd said. 'Cause then you'll laugh and it will all be over.'

Dinah inspected her nails for the umpteenth time, wondering if she'd ever met anyone with an ego the size of Rupert's. OK, she knew that thesps were a self-regarding bunch – it came with the territory. But this guy had talked of nothing but himself since they got in here: his walk-on parts, his role as an extra in a soap opera, his voiceover. It was driving her berserk. Suzy was welcome to him.

She shifted her weight on the stool, jiggled her shoulders to loosen them. It was uncomfortable here, too, and she pined for the spacious chaise longue with its deep cushions. For a moment she closed her eyes and succumbed to blackness as she moved her head from side to side. It was when she opened them that she saw *him* for the first time, eyes blazing into hers.

Afterwards, she realised how strange that was, given the number of people who had been standing much closer to the window. He, by contrast, was a good twenty paces away, leaning against a streetlamp, a curious half-smile flitting about his lips.

She couldn't take her eyes off him, and Rupert's words became mere background noise. In comparison with her colleague, the observer was plain, physically unremarkable, with regular features set in a pale complexion, and clad in jeans and a dark corduroy jacket. But something about the way he was looking at her made her suddenly want to touch herself in her most secret places.

'Is something wrong?' Rupert's voice jolted her back to the display, to her role, to her job.

'I'm sorry,' she muttered. 'I'm just – I need the loo.'

She stood up, pushed her way through the curtain, heart pounding. What was happening to her? she wondered as she rushed for the staff toilets, where she doused her face with cold water. She looked at her reflection in the mirror. Was it someone she knew but hadn't recognised right off? If not, why was he staring at her that way, with that weird smile on his face? And what was it about him that agitated her so?

She spun round, marched into one of the toilet cubicles and, sliding the bolt behind her, yanked the rubber dress up around her waist and thrust her hand into her panties. Her pussy was sodden, had been for a while now, and her fingers slid easily over her aching clit and the frill of her lips to her hole. She slipped two fingers inside, then three; with her thumbs she massaged the hard little bead of her clitoris.

Her legs began to tremble as she felt her climax approach. Turning around, she lowered herself onto the toilet lid, then raised both legs and pushed her feet against the door to steady herself. By now she cared little whether there was anyone in one of the other cubicles: her desire to be sated was all-consuming. As she felt all resistance give, she threw back her head and yelled out as pleasure jagged through her like an electrical storm.

She'd gone back – she'd had to – but he wasn't there any more. Perhaps, she told herself, he'd never been there at all. Perhaps her brain, desperate for relief from Rupert, had made him up just to give her something else to think about.

Still, the orgasm-swoon was still with her as she

climbed onto the stool again. It pleasantly numbed her, so that Rupert's noise was just a susurration beside her, like the sound of the sea. The remaining hour and a half passed relatively quickly, and then Dinah caught the bus home to Finsbury Park and dreamt of eyes, thousands of pairs of eyes, all of them on her. When she woke the following morning, she felt a strange mixture of fear and elation.

That night, Erin announced that, having had chance to get to know all of her 'living dolls' and observe them interacting, she had come up with some pairings of her own. The following evening, it would revert to choice. She'd chop and change at will, after that, to keep things 'buzzing'.

Dinah was looking out for Suzy when Erin led a tiny Japanese-looking girl over to her.

'Dinah, this is Michiko,' she said. 'I'd like you two to take the Babyfoot window tonight. So I'll need you in jeans and trainers – there's some Diesel and Pumas over by the rails.'

The girls changed and headed for the window. For the first time since she'd started, Dinah wasn't to be on one of the main windows facing out onto Regent Street but on the side street running left of the building. She bit her lip: she imagined there'd be less chance of seeing the man again there.

Almost as soon as the thought had presented itself, she shook her head. What was she talking about? A passer-by had caught her eye but there was nothing to make her think he would return – unless, of course, he always walked that way home. She bit her lip again.

The Japanese girl was ducking under the curtain, holding it open behind her. Dinah had already established that her colleague had a limited command of English, and she was relieved that she wouldn't have to repeat her experience of the previous evening with the garrulous Rupert. She smiled back at Michiko as she stepped into the window and positioned herself behind the table football machine so that she was the one who faced the street. Just in case, she said to herself. You never know.

It was fortuitous that they had the table football, as Dinah and Michiko soon found that they didn't have a great deal to talk about even taking the language barrier into consideration. They just didn't hit it off, somehow. Not like Dinah did with Suzy. She wondered which window her friend was in, whether she was having a good laugh with somebody else, and felt the pang of a little girl missing out on a birthday party.

Every so often, the pair would halt their game and sit on the brown suede sofa behind it and face the spectators gathered at the window, taking care not to catch any of their eyes. It seemed that the novelty value of these live window displays would never wear off; even positioned where they were on this side street, Dinah and Michiko drew a constant crowd. Scrutinise it as she might, though, Dinah didn't see the face that she sought.

At last it was time to go home, and Dinah turned from the window and pulled back the curtain. Letting Michiko go first, she glanced back over her shoulder on a sudden impulse and felt a thrill run up through her, making her skin tingle. He *was* there, standing back from the window again, his posture suggesting aloofness but his gaze scorching her. She swallowed painfully; her throat was impossibly dry all of a sudden. Then, almost without thinking about it, she broke into a run, racing back through the shop towards the staff quarters, fighting the urge to strip off her Juicy Couture hooded top as she ran.

Once there, she changed breathlessly and took the exit onto Argyll Street at a jog, thrusting her pass at the friendly blue-eyed security guard, oblivious to the slight look of hurt that traversed his boyish features. Bearing sharp left, she raced along the side street. She knew it was unlikely he would still be there, but this might be her only chance.

In front of the table football window she halted briefly and gauged the exact spot where he had been standing. Then she sprinted up to Regent Street. There, the sheer volume of pedestrians persuaded her of the futility of continuing her search.

Back in the changing room, where she had left her shoulder bag, Dinah splashed some water on her face and stared at herself in the mirror. What had come over her? She was actually like a schoolgirl becoming deranged over some distant crush. She didn't know the first thing about this man. What had she thought she was going to say to him?

'Penny for them,' came a voice behind her, and arms insinuated themselves around her waist.

Dinah smiled. 'Hey, Suzy,' she said to the face in the mirror, its chin resting on her shoulder. 'How was your evening? Fancy going for a drink?'

They linked arms and strolled out of the building and down Regent Street to Heddon Street. A jazz band was playing beneath a string of Christmas lights, and they were able to find a cosy table on a bar terrace lit by gas burners.

After spending a few minutes vainly trying to work out the spot where Bowie had shot the cover image for *Ziggy Stardust*, they talked of their partners in the displays, exchanging experiences. Then Dinah lit a cigarette and looked her friend right in the eyes.

'Have you noticed anything funny about the people who watch you?' she said.

'Funny? Like how?'

'Oh, I don't know. Just, well, sometimes staring maybe a little too hard?'

Suzy laughed. 'Oh, I *see*. You got yourself some unwanted attention? Don't worry, I guess it's bound to happen.'

Dinah looked down, traced the frosted rim of her glass with her fingertip. She wanted so much to confide in her friend, but how could she even begin to explain how she felt, to tell her that a stranger's gaze had sent her running to the loos to pleasure herself, had sent her dashing out into the street on some crazed quest?

No, she thought, lighting another cigarette. There were some things that were best left unspoken. It would be best, she told herself, if she didn't see him again the next night. With any luck that was it. That was what she wanted, and also what she was frightened of.

As she and Suzy had agreed, they were partners again the following night. Shortly after they'd arrived, Erin had told them she wanted them to be in the main window, which meant dressing up as sexy elves in little red Lycra hotpants and crop-tops, and sitting in a sleigh next to a waxwork Santa, while fake snow fluttered down on them.

Though she didn't say anything to Suzy, Dinah was secretly pleased by the allocation: it meant that Erin rated her performance so far. Which was all the more reason to keep her eye on the ball and not allow herself to be distracted again.

As before, the time flew by when Dinah was with Suzy, and there was soon a large gathering at the window, watching them frolic on the huge wooden sleigh, tossing presents around, sipping at glasses of would-be champagne, showing all the signs of festive cheer. Dinah found herself wishing she could be with Suzy every night; she couldn't imagine them ever running out of things to talk about.

There was only a half-hour or so to go when Dinah spotted him, positioned well back from the crowd so that he was almost off the pavement. His gaze was almost appraising, she felt. Heart in her throat, she dived out through the curtain without a word to Suzy and ran blindly towards the main exit. Pushing through a mass of shoppers and into the revolving door, she spun out onto Regent Street.

The cold spanked her bare legs, and it was only at that moment that she remembered that she was wearing next to nothing. Folding her arms across her bra-less breasts, more as a reflex to stop them jiggling around than to hide her bunched-up nipples, she carried on at a run. Her quarry, too, was on the move, but he hadn't made it far, and though Dinah wasn't particularly fit she gained ground rapidly and pounced, fingers closing around his shoulder.

'Just stop, will you?' she panted as he turned towards her. Even then, face to face with him, she couldn't pinpoint what it was that had impelled her to run after him. He wasn't ugly, certainly, but there was nothing obvious that made him stand out from the crowd. Yet as they carried on looking at each other, both shocked by this sudden confrontation, there was something in his eyes, some need, that made her legs shake under her.

It was now that she remembered the window displays, and she glanced back over her shoulder, afraid that Erin might be stalking down the street with an irate look on her face. Dinah needed this job, and she realised how rash her

215

behaviour had been. She should, she told herself, have thought of Suzy too: her friend would be worried about her.

'Listen,' she said, panicked into breaking the silence. 'I know you've been watching me. I've seen you, every night.'

The man lowered his eyes.

'It's OK,' she said. 'It's fine. It's a fucking window display, after all. That's what I'm there for – to be looked at.'

He raised his gaze, looked at her full-on, and then spoke to her for the first time.

'I'll be there when you've finished tonight, at the back entrance,' he said in a low voice.

She paused, the space of a heartbeat, then heard herself say, strangely assertively, 'Great.' She turned around and ran back up the street.

She'd been lucky: Erin hadn't found out about her absence, and Suzy, assuming that Dinah had answered an emergency call of nature, had somehow managed to keep going alone – largely, it seemed, by holding a one-way conversation with the inanimate Santa. Realising she owed her one, Dinah decided to come clean about the whole incident.

When she'd finished the story, Suzy was looking at her with concern.

'You mean, you're just going to go off with this guy you've barely even met, who you know absolutely nothing about?' she said. 'Some creep who's been staring at you?'

Dinah shrugged. 'It's nothing, Suze,' she said. 'We'll just go for a drink, see if we still like each other.'

Suzy frowned. 'OK,' she said, 'but if he tries to make a

move and you don't feel one hundred per cent comfortable, just get the hell out of there. Call me, if you like. I'm meeting some friends nearby.'

Over the public address service came the announcement that the store was about to close, and the girls clambered down from the sleigh and crossed the beauty hall. In the changing room they dressed and hugged, and then Dinah hurried out past the security guard, who flashed her a bright smile she was too anxious to return, and into the night.

For a moment she didn't see anyone, and she felt empty inside. Then, in a taxi waiting on the opposite side of Argyll Street, she saw a face at the back window. She lifted a hand and ran across the street.

Inside, the door closed behind her, she found that she didn't know what to say. As soon as the man had instructed the driver where he wanted to go, unable to think of what else to do, she threw herself upon him, forcing him back onto the seat. Pushing his lips apart with her tongue, she probed his mouth, not caring that their teeth were clashing.

As she kissed him, her hands tugged his shirt out from his trousers. Her pussy was deliquescing deliciously, and she had an almost overwhelming urge to tear off her knickers and mount him right there in the speeding cab. She had never known such an appetite in herself, and adrenalin coursed through her veins.

Their journey wasn't long, but she took little heed of the route, noting only that they passed several famous hotels as they traversed Mayfair and then swung right onto Park Lane. She was too busy trying to ignite some kind of spark within him: he was curiously passive beneath her, and every so often he'd murmur, 'Wait, wait!' and try to sit up, before giving way again to the persistence of her caresses. Each time, he'd swoon back onto the seat of the cab, eyes closed, and she had the bizarre feeling that he had almost abstracted himself from the scene.

In a dimly lit street in the strange territory where Bayswater segues into Paddington with its budget hotels and cheap trattorias, standing at the man's front gate as he leant into the cab window to settle his fare, she looked up at the impressive white stucco house and was disturbed to see a figure standing in darkness at the first-floor window. For a moment the mad thought fluttered through her mind that his reticence in the taxi was down to his having someone waiting for him at home: maybe he'd fancied a threesome but had grown nervous on the journey back. As she carried on looking, however, she saw that the figure was uncannily still. This was no spying spouse, it dawned on her, but a shop mannequin. She had to admit that, as a deterrent to burglars scoping out the area, it probably served quite well.

The man was walking towards the front door now, and she followed him, rethinking her strategy. It was clear that she had been too full-on for him, and she decided that inside she would play it cool: a chat over a cup of coffee, or a G&T if he offered her one, would give her the chance to assess the situation a little more clearheadedly. Perhaps, in jumping him in the cab, she'd given him the impression she was a bit of a nympho. Some men, she knew, didn't like the feeling that their women had been round the block a few times.

He opened the front door, ushered her inside and then reached for the light switch.

'Please,' he said, gesturing through a door, 'make yourself comfortable. Red or white wine?'

'Red, please.'

Dinah edged into the living room, where another lurking figure made her jump, until she realised that this was a dummy too. Dressed in an elegant black silk dress and a hat in a similar fabric, it looked impassively back at her. Discomfited, she turned away. Partition doors into a dining room allowed a view of a garden. She wandered through, dragging her fingertips along the dusty glass of the dining table, and spotted another two – naked this time – in each corner of the garden, limbs entwined with the foliage of the evergreens that surrounded them. A spotlight over the back door illuminated their pale torsos and limbs. She shuddered slightly, turned back to the room.

He had stepped inside silently, was watching her, a large glass of red wine in each hand.

'Nice house,' she blurted, and immediately felt foolish.

He smiled indulgently. 'Thanks,' he said.

She advanced back towards the living room, wondering why she had come here. It seemed like it was going to be hard work. Did she have anything in common with this man, or even any kind of physical chemistry, or had she just been flattered by the insistence of his gaze? If so, then more fool her.

'I see you have a thing about dummies,' she said as she took the glass he proffered, looking over towards the front window. 'Where did you find them?'

He smiled again. 'I liberate them,' he said enigmatically. At her confused stare, he added: 'There are more upstairs, if you're interested.'

She felt her knees go weak, her pussy throb again. Her excitement mounted when it registered that he wasn't going to wait for her answer, that he had already turned and was walking up the stairs. She took a large gulp from her wine, then another. She immediately felt lightheaded, and she remembered she hadn't had anything to eat since breakfast. Head beginning to spin, she went after him.

At the top of the stairs, she risked a peek into the bathroom as they passed it, and clocked another mannequin at the window. Then she followed him into the bedroom. The dummy she had seen at the window was turned away from them towards the street, but from closer up, even in the darkness, she could make out that it, too, was wearing some kind of dark, close-fitting dress.

The man turned, put his hands on her shoulders and moved his mouth to her neck. She felt his breath on her, then his lips brushing her skin, and wondered if her legs were going to give way beneath her. With one hand he played with the loose strands of hair at her bare nape that had worked themselves free from her ponytail.

Fearing collapse, she turned him around and let herself fall back against the bed, bringing him down on top of her. One of her legs was between his, and against her upper thigh she could feel his cock straining within his trousers. She fumbled for his belt buckle, then unzipped him and pushed his trousers down as far as his knees.

From out of the blue he pushed himself up from her. She looked at him searchingly: she'd been following his cue this time, was reacting to his ardour. Or so she'd thought. Was the wine addling her brain?

He was standing now, pulling up his trousers and heading for the window. She watched him as he drew the curtains, then rested her head back against the pillow, eyes closed. Why the interruption? There was no chance anybody outside could see far enough in to get an eyeful of them fucking, and in any case the light was off. No, he was stalling again.

'I'm just going for a wash,' she heard him say, and she opened one eye in time to see him leaving the room.

'Well, fuck *you*,' she thought. 'Or not, as the case may be.' As she listened to the sound of running water, she let her fingers play around her wet pussy. His libido might have died a death, but she wouldn't be able to concentrate on anything until she'd had some satisfaction.

Sliding out of her jeans and knickers and pulling up her top and bra so that her breasts were exposed, she began strumming at her clit. With two fingers of the other hand, she tweaked at one nipple, felt it pucker at her expert touch. Who needed a man when she could make herself feel this good? Her juices were in full flow, coursing down over her onto the duvet cover as she twisted her hips from side to side, obeying her internal rhythm. The pace accelerated as she moved her hand down from her breasts and bunched four fingers to push them up inside herself. She arched her back to meet her climax, pushing her breasts up towards the ceiling as if displaying them to an invisible observer.

As she came, legs spasming, she rolled her eyes to one side and met another pair. She clutched at her searing pussy with excitement, for the moment it took her realise that she was under the blank gaze of the mannequin. It took another moment to remember that the last time she'd looked, the doll had been facing out from the room and not in.

On the way back to the Seven Sisters Road, she resolved to put it down to experience. The guy was obviously fixated on these perfect, impossible women with their alabaster skin and figures that no mortal could ever attain, no matter what Primrose Hill diet or fitness craze they embraced. In Paley's living tableaux, he must have believed he had found something to give him what his mannequins couldn't. But faced with a real woman, a woman who under the designer gear had freckles and lumps and underarm fuzz and even a touch of cellulite, whose breath smelt of garlic from the pizza she'd had at lunchtime, whose hands were a little rough from the washing up, he'd chickened out. Who could ever match up to his dolls?

She smirked: she'd had her fill, in any case, and her blood still buzzed from the orgasm. Only one thing still niggled her: when she'd turned her head and believed she was being watched, the intensity of her orgasm had risen to a new level. What was that all about? As an actor, she aspired to make her living from showing herself to people. But was there something deeper that she'd never tapped into? She rested her head back against the seat of the bus and dreamed.

It was almost too easy. He'd been flirting with her a little anyway, every time he frisked her when she clocked on for work in the evening, and when she whispered to him of her plan, he was happy to go along with it without too many questions. And so, as the store had closed, he had signed her out and then let her slip back into the staff rooms, in which she'd found a hiding place until it was safe to cross the deserted beauty hall.

She'd wondered about the Santa window, but decided it might be just too visible. There were limits after all. So she'd headed for the cocktail window, and sat for a while on the chaise longue looking out at the dwindling number of shoppers trailing up Regent Street. The windows were still lit – would remain so until the early hours, she imagined – but no one stopped to look at her. She was perfectly still, breath held in her throat, blinking only when she was utterly sure no one was looking her way.

At the appointed hour – an hour when the scant

passers-by were mainly drunks or couples too wrapped up in themselves to see the world around them – the curtain drew back. She was pleased to see he was still in his uniform: it emphasised the honed contours of his chest and upper legs. He looked at her. *What's this all about then*? his eyes seemed to say.

She lay back on the chaise longue and drew up her skirt. She'd already divested herself of her knickers. He moved across to her, kissed her fully before lowering his face to her pussy and nuzzling her, then gradually beginning to explore her with his tongue. She arched again, nipples chafing against her bra in their erectness.

Sitting half up, she reached down and took a firm hold of the solid baton of his member, gave it a playful squeeze. Why had it taken her so long to understand? He had been there for the taking, and she'd been wasting time on some doll-fixated weirdo.

He responded to her grasp by sliding his hands beneath her buttocks, digging his fingers in. A feeling of masterfulness took hold of her, and she pushed him up and away from her, then stood up. Pushing him into a seated position on the chaise longue, she straddled him, slotting herself down over his smooth cock, coating him with her nectar. He began pumping, gently to begin with, and her clit rubbed against the hair on his lower belly, driving her into a frenzy.

She threw herself forwards, and as he parted her buttocks with his hands once more, splaying her for all the world to see while he plunged in and out of her, she risked a triumphant little glance over her shoulder. She couldn't be sure, but she imagined she could make out a pair of eyes trained on her from about twenty feet away, witnessing her in all her marvellous imperfection.

About the Story

HAVING MOVED TO LONDON after university followed by a long period of travelling, I spent nearly 15 years becoming ever-more intimate with my adopted city, reviewing restaurants, hotels and shops for guidebooks and local magazines. Whether reporting on the latest designer eatery, scouring the streets for undiscovered vintage clothes boutiques, or exploring the museums and art galleries, I came to know the city more closely than any other place on Earth.

I'm no longer based in London full-time, but I still regard it as my true home and continue to set much of my fiction there. My first Black Lace novel, *The Blue Guide*, saw tour guide Alicia Shaw become embroiled in a love triangle while introducing flamenco star Paco Manchega and his wife Carlotta to the city's sights. From luxury hotel suites to sybaritic spas to the erotic artworks in the Tate Modern, there was no end of sexy metropolitan locations to provide a sizzling backdrop to my story.

After an excursion to India with my second Black Lace novel, *Chilli Heat*, my third saw a return to London. In *The Apprentice*, aspiring writer Genevieve Carter hopes to give her career chances a boost by taking a post as a live-in help for her literary heroine, Anne Tournier. Little does Genevieve realise that Anne, who lives in Bayswater, has a more complicated in role in mind for her assistant – one that will take Genevieve beyond any limits she ever imagined for herself.

In real life, I gradually gravitated towards Marylebone from my first base near the Portobello

Road, along the way renting a top-floor bedsit with an oblique view of Hyde Park on Moscow Road in Bayswater – an area that continues to exert a fascination on me. In Bayswater, the seedy meets the luxe and there's a dangerous decadence to the air. It's a strange, schizophrenic twilight zone between the full-on swank of Mayfair and the trustafarian faux-bohemianism of Notting Hill. Hence my choice of it as the setting for part of this tale, 'West End Girl', as the home of the Dinah's mysterious voyeur.

Dinah herself, of course, is both me and not me. For a time I worked in the beauty hall of a top West End department store, although to my chagrin I never graduated to any live window displays that might have taken place. As to whether I seduced or was seduced by one of its security guards – well, that would be telling …

Strawberry Pink
by Kevin Mullins & Marcelle Perks

GARY CAN ALREADY FEEL the morning sun heating up outside. A compassionate glow envelopes the white walls and gleaming wooden floorboards of his small, tidy flat. It feels good, sitting there polishing off the last of the organic muesli that he has pro-vitamined with slivers of fresh strawberries. But then it needs to. At five hundred quid a week he wants it all ship-shape, *in ordnung* as his German colleagues would say. Although it costs Gary 70% of his net income to keep the overheads ticking on this Primrose Hill London pad, his persistence in holding out for just the right place has paid off. Ester, he thinks, is the one he's been waiting for. And already she's sleeping in the next room.

Ester is a find. True, she's a blonde, when really he prefers slinky redheads, but she's got luminous very blue eyes that startle everyone that he introduces her to. They stare through you in the same way that Persian cat's eyes do, almost spookily unnatural. It gives her the impression of knowledge. And there is so much he doesn't know about her, yet. But she is captivating; everyone says so. His colleagues use words like *enchantee* to describe her. In every imaginable way she is extraordinary.

Although, of course, they are quite different as people. Mustn't forget that. She likes to sleep late, and so even though she works from home she tends to be fiddling around with words for deadlines when he returns from the office. She only works part-time now and then, but still. You'd think she'd organise herself better. Sometimes when he leaves in the morning there is a faint odour of sour milk, or a furred moggy smell in the kitchen.

Heading for the door, he senses the postman outside. He feels the invasion of privacy, even though he wants his mail. The hinges snap back aggressively and a brown envelope falls onto the mat. He can see it is an old-fashioned one, foolscap outsize, rather than A4, just like the other ones. His muscles involuntarily clench, and an acidic flame creeps up his stomach. But he must pick it up. Or she will.

As before, the postmark is smudged and the address hand-printed. It doesn't matter. He knows where it's come from. Sweat from his fingers soils the surface. It's getting more difficult each time one comes. He looks warily at the bedroom door, but he knows she will be asleep for another three hours yet. Can he resist opening it? He can't help noticing that the new white leather sofa that they've just bought on Tottenham Court Road is pleasing. Why can't his life be normal, like everyone else? Especially now that he has the found the right one. His hands are shaking as he opens the envelope.

'Fuck!'

It's just a single photograph. A woman's vagina, pink and swollen, framed by moist straw-coloured hair. From such an extreme close up, he can't possibly tell who it is. But Gary knows. And he cries as quietly as he can.

Ester is curled up cat-like in the broad divan bed. When the front door slams it prods at her consciousness.

'Shit.'

227

He's banged it yet again. Just because he wants to slope off to the office for a 7 o'clock start, doesn't mean that he has to wake up the whole street. Ever since the new colleagues arrived from Frankfurt and she'd had to run the gauntlet of meeting them, he's been rising earlier and earlier, then coming home unpredictably mid-afternoon. Ester finds it weird and tiring, and it means that any work that she might have put off doesn't get done. No matter that London's creatives don't even check into the office until 10 a.m. Or that, historically speaking, she's done her best work at night. No, no, Gary assumes the whole world should stop when he steps through the front door. To add to her oppression, in his minimalist and dust-free flat, she has nowhere private to keep her stuff. No room to hide even her sprawling, innermost thoughts.

The copy-writing work that keeps her going, not to mention her novel that she periodically returns to, falter in this environment. Their stable relationship seems to pare down her creativity to dumb shampoo slogans. Having to say 'I love you' too many times a week is robbing her of word power, weakening her somehow.

Sometimes she wishes she had a private flat that she could keep as a secret location known only to her. No phone. No visitors. No unannounced guests. She would keep it as dark and inviting as a foxhole, all her mess unchecked. She could imagine retreating to it, holing up on junk food takeaways and chocolate in between failed romantic forays. It would be great. As she lay, nursing her broken heart, on a heap of cast-off clothes, she could smoke and read trashy magazines. Watch the weird Japanese action videos no one else wanted to see. No one would ever ask her to clear anything away. She could dump the remains of her old life and then emerge, like a rare butterfly escaping from her maggot existence.

But Gary pays the rent, adores her and, as her friends constantly remind her, this is a nice place. They think the neo-Californian style, all white with wooden floors and no clutter, is cool. The feeling's not mutual; he can't cope with their cheerful two week-old dust and bit-choked rugs. He claims he has allergies, but she's never even seen him sneeze.

Ester seems to spend all day doing nothing only to feel guilty about not clearing up before His Return. Even the bright sunshine stealing through the velvet curtains looks sour to her this morning. God, once upon a time she could only have dreamed of living in a place like this. Her life had been such a ragbag of existence before. It irks her that she can't move over the sumptuous carpet without it reminding her of how shabby the one in her last place was. That even as her eye notes how everything is in its place, she is longing to see her usual inevitable mess spiralling out of control, her signature that had plagued every hotel room and cheap bed-sit she ever stayed in. It showed she was still alive.

The closest she'd ever had to a home was in a rat trap in downtown Loughborough, right in the thick of the East Midlands 'Ey up, me duck' lilt. She'd had a boyfriend then, but not, as far as she was concerned, an exclusive one. He was a dumb blond who'd spent far too much time revising for his exams.

The terraced house was dark and dusty; too many students were trying to exist there. The party wall meant the stairs veered to the left. She remembers it as a rat remembers a well-trodden run. The twists of the walls and corridors came to have their own meaning after so many mornings and late nights beating the same route.

The entire house was carpeted in a sagging brown slash beige, which rather than not showing the dirt, embraced it. The other tenants had turned the living rooms into bedrooms, and so her world opened up after the steep stairs into a maze of rooms to the right. The ugly fire door, which they hated, kept locking itself shut when she saw out her various lovers.

So then she'd had to climb through her flat mate's window onto the porch in her nighty, trying to scramble back into her bedroom without showing the world her just-fucked vulva.

Her room had been a strange shape with a little corridor inside that led to a built-in wardrobe. There was a small sink that she sometimes peed in, if she had to. Her bed was home-made by the landlord, who'd fancied himself as a handyman. He'd tacked plastic sheeting over wood and stuck an old mattress on top. It was hell to sleep on. For most of her time there, the only luxury that Ester had wanted was a decent bed. And, possibly, real curtains that were not orange relics from the seventies.

In that room, she'd slept with young-looking locals, who said they were eighteen but were probably still at school. They were pink and enthusiastic, less prone to bad breath. But the place had got to her, she'd had no money and, after a long spell unemployed, the only thing she'd wanted to do was escape.

Now she feels perhaps there was something wistful about the creaking student-filled house, where the residents could smoke joints with their morning coffee and never be asked questions. She'd liked the way the rain drizzled the grey-slated roof and made it shine, how the streets felt fresher afterwards. The way lovers only felt sincere when they were leaving with promises she knew they wouldn't keep.

But here she is, right in the heartlands of London celebrity territory, rubbing shoulders with Jude Law and

Johnny Lee Miller, worrying about whether she should dust again before she showers. She thought that she'd left without looking back, and yet sometimes things here feel like they're in the wrong place, even the furniture seems to face the wrong direction.

After all her struggles, this is madness. Oh God, the time in Germany. And the pictures! Gary must never, ever find out about her past.

It is shaping up to be a hotter day than expected. Gary wonders how his German colleagues manage to keep their long-sleeved shirts so crisp, how they can bear to keep their ties clenched in the unconditioned office. Some of them are still wearing full suit jackets while he sweats in short sleeves. The hot July day beats mercilessly down on the glass windows of their Upper Street office. Gary pictures Ester sunbathing delicately on their subtle square of neatly fenced grass, her body encased by her tight bikini. With all the posh money guys hanging around, flexi-time executives and in-between actors, he hopes that she won't get too interested in someone else. It will be hard enough to hang onto her if the photos keep coming. Perhaps he should phone her and check what she's up to. His stomach is still tense and he feels like he is going to have one of his headaches.

In the office today he had a board meeting with five colleagues from the Frankfurt office. They betrayed none of the discomfort he was feeling, in fact their skin was totally resistant to the heat. Their faces seemed a uniform pink that never shined. And Gary wonders again how they really felt on the inside, working on a short-term contract in a foreign language. Living in a city they don't know, asking for the simplest of things that they can't buy like *mett*, the raw pork mince they eat at home on *brötchen*, hard rolls, which not even cosmopolitan London can provide. And yet, though they slipped up occasionally, they never failed to pronounce the silent 'e' in cloth*e*s for instance, for all this they seemed normal. Unlike him.

They never mentioned their girlfriends or wives although he'd met them, of course. They were all trim and uniform, their dyed red hair a fashion statement rather than an unfulfilled promise (Germans these days were bottle redheads rather than Aryan blondes). His old boss had told him that they liked to keep their private lives separate. Private lives meant sex of course, crude desire. It was OK in Frankfurt to go naked in the park at the weekend, as long as you dressed in a suit weekdays and got up early. In London real sex is a foregone conclusion that becomes an anticlimax once you actually have it on tap. That's why the escort industry is booming, why there is telephone sex, internet sex, encounters in every shade and form. But the problem is, when you have a need, it's exploited. He should never have answered the agency in the first place.

Ester is hot; in fact the flat feels unbearably stifling. After stumbling into the fridge for the umpteenth time and picking at an over-ambitious breakfast (she really must keep her weight down somehow) she has decided to go to the park to work on the new Whiskers cat food ad she had to finish by 4 p.m. With a fully charged-up laptop, towel and sunscreen she is free to go and work out of doors. As long as she can be bothered to get on with it once she gets there.

She stuffs her bag with notes, folders and even a few hidden cigarettes in case she gets just too frustrated. An old habit, she's a non-smoker now.

Ten minutes walk and she is there. The park is the

raison d'etre for the popularity of the three-times-standard expense of Primrose Hill. As usual, even on a workday, demi-celebs and professionals throng in twos and threes, walking their dogs and talking loudly. Such leisure here is only a display of extreme wealth.

Ester positions her towel and lays out her 'office'. The air is so still there is no need for makeshift paperweights. All she has to do is make sure the screen is positioned to avoid a glare and try to work out why this particular version of Whiskers should be more enticing than the rest. She is up against it because this one is rabbit flavour, and really even though the customers don't eat it themselves people don't like to think of giving other pets to their cats. For the hundredth time Ester wishes she could work in the production of consumables rather than trying to sort out the nonsense at the other end and make people desire what was best left alone anyway.

She can't seem to concentrate here either. The sun's too hot. After five minutes she eases down the straps of her stripy blue top to get a more even tan. After all, she might as well get a little colour. Using the same rationale, she rolls up her skirt and bares her belly button. Once she's run out of areas she can reasonably expose (thank God she isn't famous) she gets into the flow. She's found the invisible hook she can fasten her angle on to. Finally in control, her fingers start typing faster and the background buzz seems to have been drowned out, as if someone has taken a remote control and turned it off.

Click.

But there is something. A hard, metallic sound. The first one she hears could have been the hundredth. She comes to the end of her sentence and looks up.

A tanned shaven-headed man is standing a couple of yards in front of her, his large camera pointing in her direction. He is lithe but wiry, there is something pleasing about the way his muscles are a touch too visible through his tight white T-shirt. He smiles apologetically. His brown eyes seem pleasant enough. Ester is startled by the attraction she feels. He lets his camera dangle on the string around his neck as he approaches her.

'Do you mind?'

His voice is softer than she expects. She can't place his accent. The camera looks broadcast quality standard, making her more suspicious than flattered.

'Er, depends on what you are doing.' She says, trying not to sound too wary.

The man squats down in front of her. His designer jeans crinkle in all the right places.

'Artistic therapy. Usually all the pictures I take are posed to death.'

'So, you'll lose interest now I'm in the know, will you?'

He isn't put off.

'It just changes things.' He digs into his back pocket and pulls out a business card. It's gun-coloured, rather than white. 'I could do with a model. Somebody who doesn't snort coke for breakfast.'

'I bet you could.' Ester tries to look interested in her laptop. 'I'm a bit busy right now, I'll let you know once I've finished doing my day job.'

The man's expression doesn't fade. He stands, looking clean and tanned, as if he's ordered the sunshine personally.

'Phone us sometime, then.'

He winks then walks away. She watches him go. No more photos. He just goes out of the gate.

Twenty minutes later and she is finished. She lies back to enjoy the sun. After a while the sky clouds over and

Ester packs up, leaving the man's card on the grass for some other model to find.

Because Ester has met her mid-afternoon deadline, and Gary's meeting has gone on longer than expected, supper (in the shape of heated up Marks and Spencer components) is warming up nicely. Expensive Hermes aromatherapy candles flicker over spotless white linen. Ester feels relaxed, looking around the bright white room; this is how it is supposed to be. Is that the timer going off? Oh, just her Dior bag beeping. Gary probably. To say when.

'Hallo,' she makes her voice as seductive as possible. She is sitting alone in high-heeled boots, which normal people don't do unless they are trying to create a certain impression. She is still at the stage of blotting her face with Clinique powder and applying lipstick whenever she can before Gary gets home.

At first she doesn't recognise the voice. Why should she? Then his heavy Berlin accent stabs a frisson of recognition through her, the years peeling back.

'Werner? How did you get my number? In town? No, it's a bit tricky right now. I'm like working. You don't get much free time living in the big city. Give me a ring next time, though, yeah?'

Yeah right. Fuck off. Fuck you. He'd had a slim smooth body with surprisingly thick legs and a wide cock that jutted out apologetically. They'd shacked up together for a week before she found him fucking their landlady in the bathroom. A world she's run away from.

Someone is at the door. Thank fuck Werner is off the phone. She quickly erases his number from her phone register. But whoever it is isn't coming in. *Flup*. A brown envelope, obviously hand-delivered, funny paper, and

235

oddly enough, her name written on it in slanting ink. Ester goes over to the window and sees the back of a grey-haired man striding purposefully away.

She starts to tear the envelope, hoping that the contents will allay her fears.

The door goes again, but this time it's the sound of a key in the lock. There's no time to hide. And Gary just stares at her, as if he knows everything.

He's had one hell of a day. Andreas has given him a hard time about the expenses on his last sales trip to Kansas. Fucking Germans. It was OK to fly business class and check-in to the Princess Marriott, but God help you if you wanted more than a simple supper. And Andreas hated not being called Herr Schulz, as he was titled in the fatherland. Formality was everything over there, but they thought that they were doing the right thing here using first names with clenched faces. In the end, Gary tried to avoid using their names altogether. Which was a pain. And if he didn't get his bonus, he might not be able to make the rent for September, even with his overdraft extension.

But Ester, lovely Ester is there waiting for him. He has pushed this morning's shock to the back of his mind. He'll find the money, somehow. But even as he sniffs the *lamb au creole* opening the door, Ester is standing there …

'What the hell are you doing with my mail?'

'What makes you think it's yours?' Ester steps away, holding the envelope to her chest.

'Oh, I'm sorry darling.' He's thinking on his feet now. 'You see, I never told you. I had this thing with this Russian girl and she took it rather badly when things didn't work out. She sends things. Horrible things, always in brown envelopes.'

'Well, this is addressed to me. Do you think you could sit down to dinner now?'

'Sweets, I think you should show it to me. Someone's just trying to get at you, that's all. There's a love.'

Whilst they're trying to be polite, their a la carte dinner burns in the oven.

They open the envelope together.

Photos. Hundreds of them. Gary loses count of the numerous shots of female genitalia, some he recognises, a tattoo, a reddish tint, the curve of the bikini line. Most of them are a blur. Some of them are the outer limits of breasts, or buttonholes. With time maybe you could pierce them all together. Gary knows he's fucked them all. They are shot impersonally, almost abstractly. Once he's looked at one, he can't stop until he is surrounded by images that look like a mortician's project for a gynaecologist. They were pussy whores, all of them. And he'd paid, good and hard for the pleasure of sucking and rubbing and looking at them. The agency enticed him with pictures, tempted him to specify red pubic hair, and now they keep on coming, regardless. Even though he's not used them for months.

Ester is quiet, like a small stunned child. He can't look at her, so just stares down at his life before her.

Gary has freaked out since he's seen her with the post. He didn't say anything as they opened the envelope or as he flipped the photos one by one to the floor. She can't stop thinking that some might be of her. A flash of furry brown foreground, something that might be a door handle; the backgrounds have some kind of peculiar resonance. They remind her of clubs she's been in, rooms she's fucked in.

Of the feeling of being trapped when the only thing that was free was her breath to suck in or exhale as she pleased. They are the sum of all the places she's had to put up with to get to where she is now. And the nightmare that Germany became. Two years ago she'd gone there to a New Year's Eve party and stayed there, almost living in the nocturnal fetish clubs of Berlin. What with the ecstasy tabs and the rubber masks, three months had gone past in a blur. But in the end, she'd had to get out. Before they caught up with her.

Gary sits tight-lipped, muscles clenched, drinking whisky in front of Nintendo. He's so concentrated he looks like an ad for Game Boy. She's got him a drink, with ice and a slice, the only thing he might touch. She tripped on the kitchen lino bringing it in, almost spilling it on him. He says nothing. The candles burn down to nothing as the forgotten dinner singes through its cardboard in the oven.

Ester gets tired of staring at him when he's like this. If she does it too long she might discover that perhaps there's some aspect about him she doesn't like, and then the rot will set in. She won't be able to look at him without thinking about it. And once it starts it will come on more and more.

And his reaction to the photos, was, well downright weird. Does he relate them to her? She feels like a crack whore with chipped nail polish on the verge of vomiting. Already her body heat is at melting point under the dry-clean-only Whistles dress. Why are sheer nylons so god damn swampy? Her nose is no doubt shining. Worse, she can smell the waft of sweat oozing from her pubic hair and the smell of herself makes her even more paranoid that the photos are some kind of threat to set her closeted skeletons free. What's this ex-girlfriend thing about? What does she know?

She has to do something to stop herself succumbing to this icky feeling all over. His face feels curiously calm and dry when she strokes it, like the face of a doll. *Puppe,* they call it in German, but he doesn't know she knows that; he only knows the carefully constructed confectionery version of her life. Still he's a catch, steady, sorted, fanatically obsessed with her. Sometimes, too much so.

She's startled when he pushes himself into her lap and hugs her legs. For a minute he is praying to her pussy, and she forces a smile. She can hear him breathing heavily. Maybe crying. She eases him upwards and returns his hug. She kisses his mouth, licking the whisky tang out of his mouth. He sticks his tongue into her mouth and slides his hand between her legs.

She can feel him stiffen. She pulls him tighter for a few moments then releases and slides her hand into his free one. They undress each other clumsily; one breast spills out of Ester's bra even before it's removed. As she kneels down and pulls at Gary's boxers his cock flicks up and catches her under the chin. It's bold, surprisingly nubile pink, he has a sweet teenage cock although he's already thirty-two. She grabs hold, licks then sucks, but stops at the first gasp. She teases him until trickles of pre cum squeeze onto his head. They are both groaning, her pussy twitching. She laps up his juices with her tongue and kisses it into his mouth, then pushes him towards the bathroom.

Gary isn't thinking about it any more. He's lying in the dry bath, naked and expectant. The chill of the bath's surface is uncomfortable, but he lies back in expectation, his hard-on rampant. This is his moment. Ester always does it like he tells her. She has to tiptoe on the edges of the bath with her crotch straddled in a pyramid form over his face. It's better when she's aroused herself first so that he gets his first sight of her pussy already open and pink, rosy he calls it, surrounded by the glorious red pubes. Real red hair is actually the least common of all hair types. He read in some science boffin article that it can only be passed on if both parents have the gene. In fact, they say in fifty years it will be extinct. But what he knows from hard experience is that in all of the thousands of borrowed and bought porno magazines he has consumed, and websites he has clicked on, the combo of red and pink is the least common colour for hot chicks. His favourite is actually strawberry blonde; a fetish torn from a porno book he found deep in the woods when he was six. He never got to see the model's face, rain and wear took care of that, but the memory of splayed legs revealing their shock of strange flesh and bright hair remained. The magazine was dirty and old and when he took it home he found that it also contained a live slug, but this mystery woman was the first and the last. What a terror and a mystery it is for him still, the shock of splayed strawberry-coloured pussy.

Ester straddles his face with just the right distance so that he can see everything. And, oh it's good, *gut*! He inhales the aroma of her sex, nudging his nose in at the tight angle. Everything hangs out for him to ogle at. Her pussy is nothing like the tidy waxed-shut slits that decorate the pages of *Playboy*. The women there are so airbrushed they are little more than dolls. Ester is more than pretty for his mates to look at, but her real treasure is the stark redness of her sex. The hair, at times fluffy or slicked-up with cum or juices, sweating and palpitating with a life of its own. She is so, well *real*. Just the sight of her engorged lips, alive, moving, makes him almost lose control then and there. And she'll let him lick it and look at it again and again. But no, he must pretend to be normal and fuck her with his cock, even though this is relatively such a dulled sensory experience for him compared to the all-consuming pleasure of what he can see with his eyes, actually shafting the goddess hole is like a second-hand experience. But, fuck it, tonight he doesn't give a shit. He can finger her to orgasm if she wants it. The world opens up for him with his eyes seeing the hood engorged, sensitive. His cock explodes in slow motion. He can feel every part of his cum's journey ripping into freedom.

Ester looks down at him, pleased that he's come, anything to take his mind off the photos. He looks somewhat ridiculous lying in his own spunk. And he's forgotten that she needs to get off too. No, his finger is there and he's eyeing up her vagina again. She feels a moment of pleasure slide through her and build up. Now he's a fuck slave, doing as she ordains. She looks down to watch him more intently and catches sight of her bush. Shit! Too much blonde. Her roots need doing. She prays that he's too enraptured to notice.

It was the sort of thing you do when drunk. Her old friend Nina had suggested it as an act of nostalgia, and henna dye more commonly used for Nina's head found its way much further south. It was a German thing; over 50% of all women there from *mädchen* to grandmothers sported infinite shades of red hair. It was the new blonde. Inevitably, the girls working the clubs had caught onto the latest trend before anyone else.

241

Nina had done Ester's first pube job. They had giggled and swigged back the vodka and, with slurred mock admiration, paid tribute to each other's results. Nina had slipped a finger in too and dildo fucked her while she was at it, but that was another story. If it hadn't been for Gary, this return to things past would have been a one-off. Now it's a secret. Another discoloured subject not for sharing. The sight of her handiwork had transformed their first night from polite gentle exploration to full-on frenzy. It turned out to be his greatest sexual fantasy to see a real red-head's piece. He was so obsessed he crawled on the floor for her in slave worship. He was so enrapt if she'd weed on him he would've licked it up. And the new-found power was a buzz, more erotic than penetration pranks and the whole suitcase under the bed full-a-toys routine that most guys were into. Her fake pubes are part of what holds them together. And the power of his submission is thrillingly alluring; it takes her back to the doctor and nurse games she played at school when she was in control. Forcing the boys to shut up and watch. It sounds pathetic when she tries to explain the problem to her friends. She is an all-over natural blonde but Gary doesn't know, not yet. She has to keep the henna powder hidden in an empty Tampax carton along with her film roll. She even uses colour mousse to refresh the shade if she's desperate. But it's an extra effort, stretched beyond comfortable management now that they're living together.

Gary falls into a deep sleep. A little voice, the one that criticises everything, reminds him of the weight of his problems, and how it feels to keep a secret that threatens to burst his heart. But tonight, the bitch goddess Ester has soothed him, her body has whispered the secrets of the race of men. He imagines her standing over him once more, her pussy hair scarlet like strands of love, spun fiery gold, as essential an element as water. Now her sex is getting bigger, she's standing taller until the outline of her cleft looms as massive as the bulky face of a cliff, unknowable and timeless. He tries to breathe and her pussy juices suck out all the oxygen, he floats in that web betwixt paradise and dread that even in his dream he recognises as his primal instinct. It gives him an uncomfortable pull that he kicks against. His memory takes him back a step but he doesn't allow himself to follow that path. He sees a cave with nine passages, all of them stretching out into the distance, and turns and takes the easiest one that leads him to a room where he guesses it must be a birthday party. His party. The room is bright and sparkling and a table bedecked with dozens of platters of food looms in front of his vision. The table is groaning with the weight of the delicacies; it's all food, but stuff he's never seen before. Dish after dish is piled high with juicy, ripe, exotic fruits and what looks like jelly. And everything from the table cloth to the glistening, enticing food is red, the colour of a fresh strawberry when stepped upon with a bare foot.

It's 11.36 a.m. and Ester is struggling with a slippery piece of treacherous copy she is attempting to fix on her laptop. Too late for breakfast, but not early enough for lunch, she's been sucked into one of those pockets of time that lull you into a false sense of security and then pull you way out past your deadline. It's shit-miserable sitting here on her own at her breakfast table. And something is wrong with the designer kitchen. Under the lino somewhere maybe, but something stinks. Gary left ages ago. He's still said nothing all night to her that made any sense. Perhaps she should send him an email, maybe one

243

of her X-rated jokes just to nudge him into acknowledging her, while also proving to him she's up and is working on her laptop. She does it and feels a tinge of apprehension after the image leaves her outbox. Oh well, too late now, it's gone.

In what seems like seconds, he replies with 'Important Date Tonight' in the subject heading. It crosses her mind that maybe he wants to dump her, to tell her he knows everything and that it's over. But no, quite the opposite, the strangely formal message reads, 'I want you to meet my father tonight. Please meet me at the Café Larumba. 8 p.m. Wear something smart.'

It's the first time in ages that Gary has set out to meet his father. This time, with Ester in tow, the reality of his exclusive postcode and the German investment bank job in his pocket, he hopes things will be different. He has changed, so at last his father can be proud of him, happy to see him. The restaurant is already buzzing; the clientele look relaxed and sleek, the practiced detachment of the easy rich. Gary hesitates for just a second outside the restaurant window; he has only to go in and it will be perfect, just for once.

Then he spots a lone figure seated stiff-backed and anxious at the cramped table in the corner. Back to reality. It's him. He sighs and feels his light mood bounce away from him. His father looks anything but relaxed.

The expensive black cab is going as fast as it can, but still she will be late. A hurried trip to the hairdressers, and the purchase of the new black dress that she had to iron anyway when she got home, has exhausted the best part of the day. She wants to look elegant smart, intelligent, anything other than a fluffy agreeable blonde.

The fancy lights of Larumba dazzle her as she makes her escape from the cab. She dives inside, slows down, then makes her way to table thirteen, just as Gary had texted her to earlier. The man sitting opposite Gary is fine-boned, grey-haired and bristling with energy, though it is of the anxious kind that pecks at her optimism. And the eyes that sidle into hers when she stops at the table look shocked, panicked. His father looks as if he's seen a ghost.

What the fuck is going on?

But it's Gary's expression, when he sees her titian-dyed locks, that frightens her. He drops the glass of red wine he is holding and droplets of incriminating scarlet freckle his face.

'Ester?' it's like he doesn't even recognise her. Waiters appear out of nowhere and rip off the tablecloth, swab down trousers and coats. Ester can feel her heart beating faster; in a minute she'll probably be able to spit it out on the table for them. They know!

His father stands up and gazes at her calmly. He offers out his hand.

'Hello, I'm Steve Maddock, Gary's father.' His grip is firm. Then she notices the light leather case swinging at his arm.

'Yes,' he says, sheepishly glancing down, 'I expect Gary's already told you I'm a photographer. Human interest. You know, dogs, accidents, that sort of thing.'

They all sit down, Gary's face is flushed; he looks drunk already.

'What did you do to your hair?' his voice is suddenly razor sharp.

'I thought you liked this colour,' Ester says, pointedly.

Suddenly his father sits even more upright in his chair, he must be on strings, he'll be levitating next. Just for a second Ester wonders if he shares his son's carnal preferences.

'I do, it's just the first time I've seen you. First time …' he's slurring now. 'I've seen …' He reaches over to stroke her hair with a faraway look in his eyes. Ester recoils shocked, and excuses herself to go to the bathroom. She can't do this any more; she's left it too late to tell him, even though it wasn't her fault. Not really.

Even in the middle of the busy restaurant, Gary feels alone sitting opposite his father. He shivers. Those eyes, once the centre of his universe, have become older, in a way that's shocking to see. As a kid you think the eyes of a parent, and the authority they command, are eternal, unbreakable.

'Is this what you wanted? To show me this? Sense of déjà vu was it?' There's no love in father's voice, there never has been.

'Dad, I want you to like Ester. She's so special, please try for me.'

'Have you still not remembered? What it cost for your new bike, and the toys, and the holidays.' He gestures towards the toilets. 'She looks like Gina alright. You remember her? Don't tell Mummy. Our little secret. Still-posing in the studio when you were back from school. You wouldn't leave us alone.' His father's voice is becoming more sarcastic. The picture that his erotic inner life revolves around is swelling and bursting into three dimensions. It wasn't a magazine.

'Yeah, your mum was special. Gina was special too. But you ruined it for me. Didn't you, you little prick?'

'Dad?' Gary feels like the lights have been turned out in his head and the restaurant is winding down. Time is playing tricks with him; his emotions are running in slow

246

motion backwards.

'… Tied up and wearing a mask and I stepped out to get another roll of film. When I came back, your mother was there, home early, watching you. Barely seven years old and you had your head stuffed between Gina's legs. And she was writhing, thought it was me.'

Gary is not able to speak. Now he's on a ride at a fair that's spinning too fast. If it doesn't stop he's going to be sick and he wants to get off. But he cannot. He's frozen.

'Bye, bye Mummy!' his father spits out at him.

He wants to say, no it was a photograph in a magazine, and I just found it. That all he wants, all he's ever wanted is just to look. From the corner of his eye he can see Ester with her flaming red hair approaching from the left. And something clicks in his mind. He doesn't want the memory to come back to him. They have to get out of here. He staggers to his feet and flees towards her.

Ester says nothing as they sit side by side in the speeding taxi. Their legs do not touch. Nobody dares to say anything. Gary's mind is whirling so fast he can't tell her anything just yet. It's like his father has just stripped him of his outer skin and revealed the reason for his private, most innermost thoughts. An escort agency has an ad in the back of the taxi which strikes him as odd. God, they are everywhere.

From the corner of his eye he can see Ester's shining hair curled at the ends; it gently bounces when she moves her head. Secretly, he scrutinises the new shade. Does he really like it or is it just a memory surfacing? Does Ester only remind him of someone he doesn't remember? Meat without a face? Is that why he likes to look at their cunts rather than kissing their faces?

Ester is gearing herself up to say something. She's

making that cough she does before speaking directly. Perhaps she wants to get out of the cab, leave him. When she speaks, her voice is strange, more nasal than he's ever heard it: 'Do you know, Gary? About me?'

What the fuck's she saying?

'I know about me,' he mutters, and more to himself than to her.

This time they don't bother to turn the lights on when they get back to the flat. After not touching in the cab, their bodies sidle together after he has fought with the key and they slide through the door. In the darkness they spring upon each other. This time he doesn't need to see. There is only skin; a warm mass of beating pleasure. She takes off her clothes quickly; he can hear the sound of her zip unfastening. And the sound of her panting excitement. The smell of her skin gets his cock hard. He rips off his trousers and feels the tip of his cock pulsating, secreting the first slither of sex. There's no light to see her with, but he's already feeling her, the curves and plump breasts. He has to touch her. He wants to feel her all over, to rub his skin against her.

A small sound, perhaps a gasp, escapes from her lips. He kisses her, pressing his tongue hard into her open mouth while his cock rubs against her leg. She humps it like a hot bitch. She's aroused, mindless, as ever. He smears his saliva all over her. Her tongue is molten, each lick lifts his penis in waves of excitement. His hands reach down to feel her tits. Unseen, her breasts feel enormous. Gary tongues each one diligently, his attentions fevered, rapt.

She's moaning now, and he can smell her heat; she's rocking her crotch over and over his cock, which is straining to burst. She smells good. With his hands he reaches for her pussy. She opens her legs and he pushes his fingers inside. He jabs: one, two, three times. She shudders with pleasure. He wants to come, to pump it out into the darkness, but instead he pushes her down to the carpet and slips his cock all the way in.

Both of them are shouting, pushing, clawing. Her breasts are smacking against him. He can just about make out her face in the darkness, when his cock lets go and he shoots deep. Deep inside her.

They lie together in bed looking at each other by the light of a single candle.

'Ester.' His voice falters and his eyes fill with tears. 'I know you must feel like I'm some kind of fucking pervert. But I was so young. I didn't know what I was doing.'

She looks intently into his soft brown eyes, takes his hand and places it on her lush pubic hair. 'Gary, would you forgive me no matter what I've done in the past?'

He looks at her, surprise in his eyes, but smiles a yes, and his kiss touches the end of her nose.

'I'm not real down there. I'm a natural blonde all over.'

She feels his hand tremble, but it doesn't pull away.

'I lived in Berlin for three months and worked for a … dominatrix I guess you'd call it a fetish club. I really needed the money. There was no sex involved. Just tying people up. A bit of slapping and pinching. But we worked bottomless and colourful pussies was the theme of the club. A lot of important people got off that way.'

Gary wants to stroke Ester's face, to encourage her. But he can't let go of the warmth between her legs, and his other arm is propping him up so he can look at her. He settles for what he hopes is a reassuring expression.

'Most of the time we were stoned and it was no big deal. Then this old guy, some local bigwig, got a bit overexcited when he was restrained. It was busy that night so once he was hanging, the two of us were left alone. Whilst I was beating him he got a hard on, and must have had a heart attack or something. With me being wasted and with him in his face mask I just didn't notice. Just kept hitting him. God knows how long it was before I realised that he wasn't breathing. When I finally did, I just got dressed and ran. I'd already left Berlin before the police started asking questions.' She stops, her heat beating as if she's only just stopped running.

'It was a big thing in Germany. They didn't connect me directly, but there were pictures of me and the other girls in the club. Nina brought the papers over when she moved here. When the atmosphere with your Dad was so strange, I thought he must have known about the case.'

Gary finally moves his hand and strokes her face. She can smell herself on him. His expression is unreadable. He says, simply, 'But it's all over now, you're safe here with me.'

They curl up with each other and just rock themselves to sleep. Gary wakes to find Ester sitting on the edge of the bed. 'What you doing?' he asks fuzzily.

She shows him a roll of film cupped in her hand.

'There was an automatic camera in the room. Once they were masked, the customers liked it to be on, as an extra risk, or buzz or something. It was going that night. And I stole the film when I left. Never developed it.' She holds it out to him. 'I want you to have it. My life in your hands. See who I really was. So you can understand the real me.'

Her blue Persian cat-shaped eyes are as innocent as ever. Gary takes the film roll and holds it tightly as if it's

250

the key to his future.

The rest of the night he sleeps badly. Images of the red woman try to push their way into his dreams. I'm sick, he reminds himself. When morning comes and he wakes fully, he turns towards Ester's side for some creature comfort. But the bed is cold and empty. His sleeping princess is gone. He jumps out of bed and runs around the flat, calling and hoping she's just making coffee. But although her things are still are in place, Ester has disappeared.

'Fuck!' This is his dirty old man's fault. *Fucking pervert. Like father, like son.* But she can't have left him yet. No, she's left her precious roll of film. Which must mean, she's coming back. God almighty, both of them now have pictures haunting them. What a pair. Perhaps he should develop it, release the ghosts, before she changed her mind.

Ester walks through the quiet of early morning, trying to decide what to do. She's worried about Gary. She needs to talk to his father, to try and get them to sort things out. She rings the home number she has taken down but there's no reply. She tries his mobile. Nothing.

Gary decides to use his father's darkroom. After all, the miserable old sod has to be of some use.

He lets himself in through the front door and enters the cold emptiness of the imposing Victorian town house. He can see his own obsessive neatness in his father's meticulous place. He'd rung ahead to make sure his father's not there. If he comes back, Gary will just say he's doing something for a friend, which in a way, is right. He busies himself getting the chemical process ready. And then comes the exciting part, when the white paper begins to ghost into faint images. Perhaps if they look too graphic he'll kill them before they focus into clarity. He waits for it; this moment he has always loved.

But the chemicals perform no magic this time. The paper remains resolutely blank and his emotions shrink back in shock. She gave him a blank film. Is this what she means by develop this and you'll understand the real me?

Ester has been roaming the streets trying to sort out her head. It's weird Gary hasn't rung her, but it gives her a breathing place to sort something out. She can't stop thinking that the man she saw delivering all those photos might be Gary's dad. Shit, what kind of fucked-up situation was this?

It's past lunchtime when Gary's dad finally answers his mobile. He sounds out of breath. As if he's been jogging, his breath rasps in little jerks.

'Yeah?'

'Hi, it's Ester, Gary's girlfriend.' This is answered with a grunt. 'I'm worried about him. I need to talk to you.' Silence.

'There's a quiet pub where it's possible to talk.'

It's an old boozer. No music. Hardly any punters. Carpet scuffed and sticky, seats dark from stains. Gary's dad waves her over. She tries to look confident. Probably fails. Once the pleasantries are over and drinks are purchased, Ester tells him how worried she is.

'You're worried!' His scorn is intimidating. 'I've been mopping up for that little fuck for years.' He leans as far forward as he can. Ester wavers but doesn't retreat back.

'In his college room, the cleaner found pictures, all stuck together like the old dirty joke. I had to sort that out. Make excuses. He's gone out with girls who I knew, the daughters of friends, and I've heard back how they giggled and mocked him. Or were just scared and sickened.' He eases back in his chair and smiles. Ester finds this even more threatening.

'I don't suppose he's told you about the agency?'

She is cautious but needs to be honest. She shakes her head.

'I got them to contact him. Set him up with girls who didn't give a shit. Red all month around, as he likes them. They'd pose for a little souvenir afterwards. So we could keep him happy between times. Then you turned up and he didn't go any more.'

Ester is relieved and must be showing it.

'No one pays when they can fuck it for free!' His voice is a snarl now.

'You're just another opportunity for him to fuck up. I bet he sniffs you like he's still a kid.'

Ester's had enough. 'No wonder he's messed up with a shit like you for a father!'

Gary's dad just shrugs. 'I've kept the pictures coming you know. They're all in the little shrine we share. I've been there today while you were out. All nicely embalmed. Get him to show you that.'

Ester stands, unable to bear his company any longer. 'No wonder you chose this pub. It's as filthy as you are.'

She strides away, ignoring the laughter behind.

As Ester enters their flat she hears muffled sobs. Following the sounds she goes through to the kitchen.

'Jesus!'

The linoleum has been rolled up, the fridge pushed back and a panel removed revealing a stairwell leading down into darkness. There is a fishy smelling stink in the room. Cautiously Ester steps down. Probably this was some kind of an air-raid shelter in the Blitz. It's a weird space, bigger than a crawlspace, but not big enough to stand up in completely. She didn't even know it existed.

As her eyes adjust to the gloom she sees Gary crying, head in hands, sitting on a grubby old sofa. She almost slips on something glossy underfoot as she goes towards him.

'Darling!'

He looks up, pathetically grateful.

'You're back!' His expression turns to embarrassment. Ester's stomach clenches.

'Did you develop the film?' she asks in a timid voice.

He shows her the blank paper. 'What, you mean there was nothing?' Something inside her is disappointed not to see her old Berlin club days revealed in all their glory. And she was so stoned ... Do the photos still exist somewhere else? There's no point in worrying now. Gary needs her.

'Gary, I went to see your father today. To confront him. He told me that you have some kind of a private collection together. Do you know what he means?'

Gary sighs and flicks on a lamp by his side. 'Ester, these are my photographs,' he says simply.

Clear plastic wrapped objects are scattered on the floor, and on shelves and tables. Ester reaches down and picks one up. Although they're wrapped in plastic, the smell reminds her of what an old used condom is like if she leaves it in the bedside bin too long. She looks around then studies her selection. This photo is like the others, but seems older. The pubic hair is natural, no bikini line. She guesses that it's a photo taken in the seventies. Gary pulls out more from a cupboard. The pictures are wrapped carefully in cellophane and another substance, dry, yellowy-looking, lies neatly above them, encased between tightly sealed cellophane sachets. As the photos are moved the smell becomes overpowering and she wants to gag. Is it? It can't be. Gary's face is expressionless. 'Yes, it's cum,' his words ring out in the confined space. Ester rifles through the images until she finds the one that is the most preserved, the biggest. It's in long shot, and shows a model all tied up with no visible face. She is pale and muted, but reveals a fiery-red bush between her splayed-out legs.

As gently as she can Ester gathers the photographs in her arms and puts them to one side.

'We'll throw them all away darling,' she says, stroking his hand.

Now that the shroud of secrecy and guilt has melted away, Gary feels like he is here for the first time. What did his dad mean about having this together?

Towards the corner of the room there are more photos than he remembers. Surely he didn't have that many? He goes to examine them. They are photos of him and Ester leaving the restaurant, that night with Dad. Ester's face looks anxious under her red curls. But her upper body is peppered with drops of what looks like fresh cum. They gaze at each other stunned.

'I haven't seen this before,' he protests.

'It's him. He said he visited your *place* today. Here.'

Dimly, he remembers giving his father a key when he first moved in, just in case he got locked out or for emergencies. And Dad had found this place for him, told him about the cellar. Almost as if he was planting a seed in Gary's mind. His hands wildly look through the photos again. His father must have been planting them, maybe jerking off as well. He suddenly needs fresh air.

Gary runs back up the stairs into the stark-lighted calm of the kitchen. Ester collects bin bags from under the sink and starts gathering the photos into them. She's determined, just as she always is. It's easier to get rid of these than a dead body.

'Gary, we can get over this. Put these things to rest.' Ester drags the bags outside, not caring if she wakes up the neighbours. She returns and walks purposefully to the bathroom. Her boots are strident, tap-tapping on the bare floor.

He can see how well the role of dominatrix would suit her. But no latex gear today. She strips and stands facing him, her red fur glinting in the reflected glow. She takes a towel, wets it and sponges over her pubic hair before squeezing a mountain of shaving foam over it. But it's in Gary's hand that she puts the razor.

'Shave me clean, darling. Shave me of all our sins.'

STRAWBERRY PINK WAS OUR first writing collaboration. From the early nineties, Kevin and I would bump into each other at various horror writers' events. I was a journalist who talked about writing stories and sometimes wrote fragments which were never finished. Kevin had already published a handful of horror short stories, although he didn't write as much as he wanted to. A couple of years after I moved to Germany, we met again and I'd finally written one of the stories, *The Scarless*, that I'd been talking about for years. We decided to write something together.

The story was originally called *Snap!* Kevin came up with a synopsis in response to an anthology call for an erotic story involving photographs. The first concept was much darker and involved child pornography, but we felt that concentrating on Gary's fetish for strawberry-coloured pubic hair would give us the chance to delve into the psychological creation of his fetish without alienating readers. Kevin (as you might expect from a man) was interested primarily in the provocative role of the photographs, but I was fascinated by the idea that in this posh flat something was wrong. Many people live in terraced houses, and if you get used to living on the right hand side of the divide, it would perhaps feel weird if your next place was set out on the left side. We didn't have the ending in mind when we began writing, but the feeling of disenchantment with this very expensive flat was there from the start.

The story is set in Primrose Hill, where I'd spent considerable time in the late 90's. First of all I had a boyfriend who worked in the film industry who lived there (no resemblance at all to Gary) and then a wonderful female friend written about in the story *The Girl Who Was Sleek*. For me, a working-class girl from the other side of the sticks in Walthamstow, Primrose Hill seemed to represent everything that could be good about London, as well as everything I was not.

The nicest thing about the collaboration was the lengthy telephone calls Kevin and I had discussing every minutiae of the characters' actions. The story went through at least twelve drafts. Kevin is good at shaping the plot with minimalist strokes, I am a sucker for detail, so together we write quite differently. Our second collaboration was the horror/erotic story *Underneath* set in the London Underground.

Author Biographies

Matt Thorne was born in Bristol in 1974 and educated at Cambridge and the University of St. Andrews. He is the author of six novels, *Tourist* (1998), *Eight Minutes Idle* (winner of an Encore Award, 1999), *Dreaming of Strangers* (2000), *Pictures of You* (2001), *Child Star* (2003) and *Cherry* (long-listed for the Man Booker Prize, 2004), as well as a sequence of novels for young adults, *39 Castles* (2004-05). He also co-edited the anthologies *All Hail The New Puritans* (2000) and *Croatian Nights* (2005). His short fiction has appeared in a number of anthologies including *Piece of Flesh*, edited by Zadie Smith (2000); *New Writing Vol. 6* (1997), edited by A.S. Byatt and Vol. 13 (2003), edited by Toby Litt and Ali Smith), and *The Mammoth Book of Best New Erotica Volumes 1, 2 & 7*. He has also published stories in *The Times* and the *Independent on Sunday*. He also contributed to Maxim Jakubowski's jointly-written novel, *American Casanova* (2006). He is a regular reviewer for several major newspapers and appears as a critic on radio and television and is currently working on a critical study of the pop star Prince to be published by Faber in 2011.

Justine Elyot has been active on the erotica scene for a little over a year, but in that short time has managed to cram herself into more than ten anthologies and produce her own short story collection, *On Demand*, published by Black Lace. She can be found in books from Cleis Press, Xcite and Black Lace and delights in writing material that pushes boundaries and expectations.

An erotica fan from an impressionable age, after finding *Fanny Hill* lurking unexpectedly between John Bunyan and Wilkie Collins on her parents' bookshelves, Justine has an active and insatiable curiosity about most forms and expressions of human sexuality, and is happiest writing about the dynamics involved in domination and submission.

Her second full-length work, *The Business of Pleasure*, will be published by Xcite in autumn 2010.

Francis Ann Kerr is the childhood pseudonym for a writer who needs to keep her identity under wraps. She believes that writing about bad sexual experiences is just as essential as detailing life-affirming ones and hopes to see an end to orgasm plot-driven erotica sometime soon.

Valerie Grey has published a few novels: *Rocket Girl* (Blue Moon), *Aimee and Chloe* and *How She Lost Her Cherry* (Olympia Press) and *Bad Wife* (Ophelia Press). She has two novels forthcoming from Kensington. She has published stories in the anthologies *The Mammoth Book of Women's Fantasies, Short and Sweet,* and the journal *Fiction International.* She lives in Sedona, Arizona, where she works as a psychic reader and a bartender.

NJ Streitberger is the pseudonym of critic and journalist Neil Norman. He began writing erotic fiction with a twist just over a year ago when he fell into bad company and is now a regular contributor to *The Erotic Review*. For seventeen years he was employed by the *Evening Standard* as a film critic and feature writer and returned to the freelance life just before the Russian take-over. One of his wilder ambitions is to become the Edgar Allan Poe of erotic fiction. In addition to stories and journalism he has written five plays, three screenplays, two novels, several film books and biographies and made a short movie. He used to write poetry but has refused to show it to anyone even under torture. He is currently the Dance Critic of the *Daily Express* and occasionally contributes to the *Observer Food Monthly* as it guarantees a free lunch. He is also a regular contributor to the Press TV programme *Cinepolitics* which discusses political movies and documentaries of every hue, religion and creed. His literary heroes are Poe, MR James, Wilkie Collins and Joseph Conrad. He is a Londoner by birth and metropolitan by the Grace of God.

Kristina Lloyd is the author of three erotic novels, *Darker Than Love*, *Asking for Trouble* and *Split*, all published by Black Lace. Her short stories have appeared in numerous anthologies and magazines both in the UK and US, and her novels have been translated into German, Dutch and Japanese. She is one of the co-founders of *Erotica Cover Watch*, a campaign to challenge the sexism in erotica publishing, and is a contributor to the *Guardian Online*, writing on feminism, porn and sexuality. She's lived in London, Istanbul and Barcelona and has had travel pieces published in *The Sunday Times*.

Kristina has a master's distinction in Twentieth Century Literature, and has been described as 'a fresh literary talent' who 'writes sex with a formidable force'. She lives in Brighton on the south coast of England. For more, visit http://kristinalloyd.wordpress.com

Lily Harlem lives in beautiful rural Wales, juggling two musical teenagers, a workaholic husband and an ever-increasing menagerie of rescued pets ranging in size from fish to horses. Before starting her writing career two years ago Lily studied at Oxford University and then went on to become an Accident and Emergency nurse working just outside London.

She now lives a much quieter life with a desk overlooking rolling hills and farmland and has shaken the dreaded manacles of shift work. Without a hospital gown in sight, except in a few naughty stories, her over-active imagination has been allowed to run wild and free and has literally burst from the seams.

This year Lily received first place in the long story section of the *LoveHoney* Vulgari Award for Erotic Fiction with an American inspired tale entitled 'Madam President' – think seriously hot politicians up to high jinks in the Oval Office. She also has a spankingly naughty tale called 'Stable Manners' in *Best Women's Erotica 2010*. On a daily basis Lily finds that writing for Xcite and for Total E-Bound keeps her fingertips out of trouble – most of the time.

When looking for inspiration Lily often calls on the many characters she met in her past life as a nurse which means her stories are made up of a mixed bag of people with real bodies, flaws and insecurities. Plots travel on everyone's favourite journey, falling in love and on route her characters explore their sexuality and sensuality in a safe, consensual way. With the bedroom door left wide open the reader can hang on for the ride and Lily hopes that by reading sensual romance people will be brave enough to try something new for themselves- after all life is too short to be anything other than fully satisfied.

Maxim Jakubowski is a twice award-winning British writer, editor, critic, lecturer, ex-publisher and ex-bookshop owner. He shares his time between the wonderfully dubious shores of erotica and the perilous beaches of crime and mystery fiction. He is responsible for the *Mammoth Book of Erotica* series and the *Mammoth Book of Best British Crime* series, is editor of over 75 anthologies and counting, as well as being the author of two handfuls of novels and short story collections. He was crime reviewer for *Time Out London* and then the *Guardian* for nearly twenty years, and also makes regular appearances on radio and television. He also co-directs Crime Scene, London's annual crime and mystery film and literature festival, and runs the MaXcrime imprint. *I Was Waiting For You* is his latest novel.

Though based in London, he has been known to travel and frequent hotel rooms with depressing regularity, which no doubt inspired his *London Noir*, *Paris Noir* and *Rome Noir* collections, as well as the *Sex in the City* series. He has lived in, or regularly visited, every city featured in the *Sex in the City* titles published so far. When not writing or sighing at the sight of women, he collects books, CDs and DVDs with alarming haste.

Originally from Rotherham, South Yorkshire, **Elizabeth Coldwell** has lived and worked in London for over twenty years. For much of that time, she was editor of *Forum* magazine, where she helped launch the careers of a number of well-known authors and was one of the co-founders of the Guild of Erotic Writers. She also wrote two novels for the long-defunct Headline Liaison imprint. She still contributes to Forum on a regular basis, while also concentrating on her own fiction, which has long been featured in anthologies published by Black Lace, Cleis Press, Circlet Press, Xcite Books and Ravenous Romance, as well as the *Mammoth Best New Erotica* series.

Her other great passion apart from writing is Rotherham United and the men who play for the team. If you see the 'London Millers' flag at one of their games, you know she won't be very far away ...

Clarice Clique lives in a small terraced house in England dreaming of all the lives she is not living. Some of these dreams make it into stories and some of these stories make it into print. In 2009 she had her first novel published, a BDSM, sub/dom story called *Hot Summer Days*, by Pink Flamingo Publications. She is currently working on her next three novels, simultaneously hoping that somehow she will finish one of them in the next few years. However, she is too easily distracted from her work by an internet addiction which means her brain is brimming over with 'facts' about obscure television stars gleaned from Wikipedia. She owns many different shades of thigh-high boots ordered from a surprising variety of internet shops; she can count to ten in ten different languages; she has a secret life as a tall blue woman complete with tail, hooves and horns in a certain online game, and she is having several simultaneous internet affairs, wondering if cybersex and a nice vibrator might not actually in fact be better than the real thing.

Carrie Williams is the author of three novels for Black Lace – *The Blue Guide*, *Chilli Heat*, and *The Apprentice*, as well as countless short stories in Black Lace anthologies, some of them under the pseudonym Candy Wong. Her erotic fiction has also graced the pages of

Scarlet magazine and *The Mammoth Book of Best New Erotica*.

As an established travel journalist, Carrie visits and reviews some of the finest hotels, restaurants and shops around the world. Her adventures abroad inspire and inform her fiction, from street markets and temples in India to spas in the South of France, as do the many fascinating characters she meets on her travels.

Carrie began writing erotica after becoming immersed in the work of Sigmund Freud, Georges Bataille and the Surrealists while studying French literature at Oxford. She wrote her dissertation on the work of the female Surrealists, most notably the Argentine painter Léonor Fini, best known for her graphic illustrations for the *Story of O*.

Carrie is usually on the road but can often be found in London, Manchester or Paris. When not writing fiction, she enjoys gardening, the theatre and cinema, vintage clothes shopping and spending time with her Russian blues.

Marcelle Perks originally comes from Stourbridge, West Midlands. She spent her twenties in London and has lived in Hanover, North Germany since 2001. She is the author of the non-fiction books *Incredible Orgasms* (2005), *A User's Guide to the Rabbit* (2006) and *Secrets of Porn Star Sex* (2007). Her erotic fiction has appeared in *Sex Macabre, Three-Way, The A-Z of Naughty Spanking Stories*, *Dying for It*, *Ultimate Burlesque*, *Ultimate Decadence* and *The Mammoth Book of Best Erotica*.

An avid film fan, she has written for a range of publications, including *Alternative Europe: Eurotrash and British Exploitation Cinema*, *The Goth Bible*, *The BFI Companion to Horror*, *British Horror Cinema*,

Cinema Macabre and the magazines *Gay Times, Nerve, Fangoria, The Dark Side, Videoworld, Shivers, Flesh and Blood* and *Kamera*.

She appeared as a dominatrix in the film *Molotov Samba* (2005) and as a mud-smeared Satanist in *Faust – Love of the Damned* (2000). She did dialogue work on the award-winning Danish erotic film, *All About Anna* (2005).

Although she has known Kevin Mullins for years, they only began to collaborate on writing projects after she moved to Germany.

Kevin Mullins lives and works in the wastes of Slough. In the 90s he became associated with the miserabalist group of 90s horror fiction writers and had stories published in *Darklands, Darklands 2, The Tiger Garden, Peeping Tom* and *Squane's Journal*. It's fair to say that all of his fiction is edgy and he also wrote about the film *Don't Look Now* for *Cinema Macabre*, a book of horror writers discussing their favourite horror films.

Mullins is a bit of a connoisseur of girls like Ester. He regularly attends erotic events and clubs and knows London like the back of his hand. Although he has red hair himself, he doesn't share Gary's obsession.

More titles in the Sex in the City Range

Sex in the City – New York
ISBN 9781907106240 £7.99

Sex in the City – Paris
ISBN 9781907106257 £7.99

Sex in the City – Dublin
ISBN 9781907106233 £7.99

www.xcitebooks.com